Meet Paul Armstrong, a late-twenties computer "consultant," as he and his fellow TeraMemory engineers lament their mostly hypothetical love lives.

"She was into Rolfing and macrobiotic food and past lives and other random stuff. But when I ordered carpaccio, she looked at me like I'd killed somebody."

Watch him select a latte from the office coffee cart and poke at his Chinese lunch special while his longtime pal Steve Hall, hacker extraordinaire, foretells the Valley's demise.

"These days, the whole scene is growing less unique by the nanosecond. True hackers are nearly extinct—run off the landscape by cyber-capitalists."

Meet The Man: Barry Dominic, the flamboyant, lecherous, millionaire founder of TeraMemory. He insists they're poised to revolutionize networking with the Next Big Thing, appropriately called WHIP.

"Nobody fucks with Barry Dominic."

That's where Liz Toulouse comes in. A Stanford English Lit grad and TeraMemory marketing associate, she accidentally cc's the entire company on a snide e-mail about The Man's bad grammar on her very first day. . . .

"If only I'd had any idea. I'd have stayed in school. I'd have changed majors. Gotten a master's. Anything."

SILICON FOLLIES

a dot.comedy

THOMAS SCOVILLE

WASHINGTON SQUARE PRESS
PUBLISHED BY POCKET BOOKS

New York   London   Toronto   Sydney   Singapore

WSP

A Washington Square Press Publication of
POCKET BOOKS, a division of Simon & Schuster, Inc.
1230 Avenue of the Americas, New York, NY 10020

Copyright © 2001 by Thomas Scoville

Originally published in hardcover in 2001 by Pocket Books

ISBN: 0-7434-1121-8

First Washington Square Press trade paperback printing March 2002

10 9 8 7 6 5 4 3 2 1

WASHINGTON SQUARE PRESS and colophon are registered trademarks of Simon & Schuster, Inc.

For information regarding special discounts for bulk purchases, please contact Simon & Schuster Special Sales at 1-800-456-6798 or business@simonandschuster.com

Cover illustration by Mark Fredrickson

Printed in the U.S.A.

for Beezus, who led me out

ACKNOWLEDGMENTS

The author would like to heap laurels upon . . .

Scott Rosenberg at Salon.com, for his gentle editing and strong sense of fun.

Hughes Hall, for his mojo.

Deanna Hodgin, for her keenly observed notes from the field.

Adam Long, who taught me a thing or two about comedy.

Richard Morgan, who gave me the day off.

Kate Meredith and Amit Uttamchandani—web provocateurs deluxe.

Ken Thompson, Dennis Ritchie, Brian Kernighan, Douglas Englebart, Ted Nelson, Larry Wall and Richard Stallman, for creating the playground.

The crew at Xs.com.

And the readers of Salon.com for their encouragement and support.

SILICON FOLLIES

ADRIFT AMONG THE CUBICLES

IT WAS A sea of cubicles. Every twenty yards an oversized potted palm rose up like a desert island, a cluster of upholstered chairs marooned and huddling at the base. High overhead, box-girders braced up a brooding sheet-metal sky. Banks of lighting hovered at regular intervals, regiments of incandescent clouds. All natural light had been banished.

Once it had been a manufacturing plant, but the waning of the aerospace business had pressed it into other uses. Now it was a thought factory. The industrial designers' attempts to humanize the anonymous, cavernous space had only made it more surreal.

Aesthetics weren't the only problem. The leviathan imposed a number of logistical challenges, foremost of which was the Question of Caffeine: what happened when one hundred thousand square feet of personnel simultaneously converged on a common area for coffee? What would such a concentration of volatile, under-socialized engineers, passive-aggressive managers and other assorted hard-charging corporate over-achievers yield?

Management decided such a critical mass wouldn't be in its best interests. It didn't like the sound of all those lost man-hours spent walking back and forth, either. But this was the Silicon Valley: coffee wasn't just the ordinary cup of joe; this was vente-double-macchiato-with-an-almond-shot country. Labor-intensive, gourmet coffee beverages, in every conceivable roasted mutation and international variation, were standard corporate perks. You could lose engineering talent without viable coffee options; they'd wander off-site to Starbuck's for a jolt. Sometimes they wouldn't come back, recruited away by a company that gave caffeine its proper consideration.

So management declared the coffee must come to them; rolling espresso carts, masts flying café-style awnings, piloted by captain coffee-jerks, navigated the cubicle sea like Chinese junks.

It was with this gravity of purpose that the coffee man jibed down aisle 4N. As he approached his usual stop, the electronic chime announced his arrival.

Rumpled-looking young men emerged blinking from their cubicles like rodents flushed from their burrows.

"What'll it be?" barked the coffee man.

"Double latte," one engineer called back. "Single mocha, vanilla shot," ordered another. The hissing of the espresso machine commenced.

Paul Armstrong did not emerge from his cubicle, though the fragrance of brewing beans called out to him. He furrowed his brow, peering into his terminal at a lump of code in curly brackets.

He was looking for a leak. Somewhere in this tangle of a strange and foreign alphabet, bits were leaking out. Deep within the guts of this binary beast, something wasn't sealed tightly enough—logically speaking—and tiny atoms of information flew off unpredictably into the digital ether.

Of course, this minute and trivial defect meant that the whole system would melt itself into a pool of logical slag at totally random intervals. Not only was this generally bad for morale, it was making his project manager inconsolably cranky.

He sat motionless for several minutes, just staring, then gingerly added a few keystrokes he feebly hoped might plug the hole. More staring. His hands flashed across the keyboard, initiating yet another iteration of the compile cycle, this time with the addition of some obscure "flags" and "arguments"— desperate twists and variations on the same old compiler operation. He didn't really expect it to work, but the time it took to execute would buy him a moment before the coffee rolled away and his debugging resumed in earnest.

Not a moment too soon; coffeeman was preparing to set

sail for other ports. As Paul waited for his own double latte, he was drawn into a chat with one of his project members. He listened as his colleagues speculated on the project's short-comings.

"I'm telling you, man, it's down in the presentation layer," one particularly earnest programmer geeked. "This is asynch, baby, and you know we don't do asynch worth a damn yet. X.25 is *not* TCP/IP, and it sure as hell isn't SNA, either." He turned to Paul. "You know that as well as I do, Arm-strong—you wanna back me up here?"

Paul tried to conjure up some useful response, and failed. He gamely contorted his face into a suitably thoughtful shape, and groped to say something that would have suggested he'd even been paying attention. But he felt . . . distracted—by a persistent notion, the same moldering misgiving which of late had become the backdrop of his career:

This wasn't what he had expected to be doing with this life.

Five years had passed since Paul graduated with a degree in journalism. And here he was—slumped in front of a ter-minal, debugging an error-handling routine using a debugger that itself was full of bugs, on a product that would probably never see a customer.

His title was consultant.

How had this happened? How, after preparing for a career in letters and culture (and secretly dreaming of writing the

Great American Novel), had he ended up as an engineer, enmeshed in an endless dialog with the cold complexity of idiot-savant machine logic?

He retraced the steps derailing his literary career: a boyhood friendship with Steve—a socially backward, withdrawn, gangly delinquent with a destructive curiosity and a talent for re-engineering the telephone system. Paul and his adolescent pal had electronically journeyed—with a little help from the parts department at Radio Shack—from the rotary-dialed telephone on his mother's kitchen wall to the central switch for their Northern California suburb.

Then there was his natural quantitative inclinations, unbidden but insistent. After Paul demonstrated a knack for geometric proofs, a high school math teacher insisted he join the school's computer club. A class in formal logic fulfilled a dreaded science requirement at his university.

Then, in his first real job as a research assistant at a Santa Clara County newspaper, he salvaged an editor's work—presumed lost forever—from the minicomputers linking the paper to the wire services. It was simple for Paul, having cultivated an understanding of the literal-mindedness of digital machinery.

But it had impressed his boss, and led to an immediate promotion. His shiny new title—senior systems analyst—and the twofold increase in pay had deferred his attention from the fact that his career had taken an irrevocable turn from the life in the humanities toward the life of machines.

That was 1990. Just the beginning of the explosion. The Silicon Valley was already well established as a hotbed of electronic enterprise, but sometime in the late 80s, things had gotten way out of hand. Overnight, it seemed, computers had emerged from the hermetic world of scientists, defense contractors, Ma Bell, and geek hobbyists, and suddenly became everyone else's business, too.

Technical talent was suddenly in vogue. If you could even spell COBOL, Pascal, or—especially—C, you became the object of relentless attention by technical recruiters. They would track you down, buy you a series of expensive lunches, and pledge to triple your paycheck.

After a few months in his new position, the recruiters had zeroed in on Paul, too. He was happy to give in; after all, how was pushing bits for a newspaper any different from pushing bits for a software or semiconductor outfit? Besides, technology companies were much more flush-and-plush than publishers—way better perks, rapidly escalating pay.

But what had really set the stage for his incipient malaise was the day he became a Believer: the day, convinced that XYZ Corp's newest "insanely great" technology would change the world (he could barely remember what it was now, and neither could the world), he signed up with the fledgling startup—in exchange for stock options.

Paul had toiled there for three years of eighty-hour weeks. Then, on the eve of the IPO, management accepted a takeover offer, leaving employee options high and dry.

That had wrecked him. Not financially, of course; he had been paid reasonably even without stock options. But he'd never Believe again. After that he insisted on the money up-front, at an hourly rate, as a private consultant. A black hat. A mercenary.

Which is how he found himself here, in this cubicle, with his hands over his eyes, shaking his head: tired, well off, twenty-eight years old, adrift.

THE DISINHIBITION OF
MARKET LEADERS

BARRY DOMINIC LOOKED out across the bay from his office on the twenty-first floor of TeraMemory headquarters. He frowned. From the eastern shore, Fremont frowned back. Reclining his leather throne, he slung his feet up on a desk of exotic hardwoods big enough for a tennis match.

He continued scolding a sleek speakerphone module perched at midcourt.

"You tell those guys at MicroMillennium that if they don't like the deal they can go out and find their own VARs. They don't like our terms, then we don't have to hook 'em up with our market."

And if they try, he added to himself, we'll just tighten our margins for a few months—just long enough to pull the rug out and send 'em packing back down El Camino Real.

Without a good-bye he mashed the orange button on the module, hanging up.

"Nobody fucks with Barry Dominic," he muttered to himself.

He swung his chair back around to his workstation console, where he had been drafting a company-wide email flogging the troops.

> . . . establishing TeraForms as the premier product line for medium- to high-end RDBMS proprietary solutions. It's impearitive to aquire foreign market's and establish a dominent position in Asia as well in advance of what the competition is. When the other guys arrive in the Asian marketplace, there going to see a sign saying 'Property of TeraMemory—keep out.'

> For that reason, it was decided to accelerate the WHIP initiative by three months. I know this means some extended hours and indeed a few all-nighters during the holidays, but for all intensive purposes it will all most certainly be riflected in employee equity partici-pation—your's and mine.

> This is a criticle time in the development of our business flow, and I know your all going to pull together to get Tera to where we need to get to.

He forwarded the message to his assistant. She'd polish it up.

"When there is no food, an army must march on hope," he grunted, quoting an aphorism he was sure was from Sun Tzu's *The Art of War*. And if it wasn't, well, it should be.

The module spoke again, this time with the receptionist's voice.

"Line one, Mr. Dominic."

"Busy," he snapped.

"It's Mr. Lowell."

Miles Lowell—of Lowell, Kraft & Khougat—was the lead attorney handling the divorce with his wife, Kiki.

"Go ahead," Barry conceded. "Miles, what's the good news?"

"No go on our last settlement package, Barry. She still wants the house in Woodside, plus twenty K a month. She says that was your deal all along."

"Tell that bitch vampire she'll have to kill me herself if she wants another drop of blood. I'm through playing games, Miles. I can tie this thing up in court forever if I have to. I'll make you and LKK as rich as me before I cough another dime."

"It's your call, Barry."

"I want the estate and I want her gone. As in Idaho. Make that Siberia. Make it happen. Hardball. Execute, buddy." He pummeled the orange button.

Damn that woman, he thought. He should never have married so young. If only he could have seen his future, he would have moved forward as a free agent. Here he was, the most desirable guy on the market, and she was holding a first lien on his second bachelorhood.

Marriage, he scoffed to himself. Totally obsolete institution. This was the goddamn twenty-first century, almost; relationships should be run like businesses—everything else was, for Christ's sake. If only he hadn't been such a goddamned naïve, romantic gypsy dipshit back in his twenties.

He scanned a framed cover of a recent *San José Magazine* mounted on the wall behind his desk. MOST ELIGIBLE BACHELOR IN CYBERSPACE read the headline over his picture. The teaser copy underneath: "He made a billion dollars. He commutes in a MiG-21. Who will he take to the company BBQ?"

He'd sent the editor to Maui for overlooking his status as a technically married man. And why not? The divorce was supposed to be a done deal by now. How was he supposed to know, when he was twenty-two years old building circuit boards in Redondo Beach, that it'd turn out this way?

And now Kiki was raining on his parade. *His* parade. How was he going to get any real action while Kiki was spreading those stories to every XX chromosome in the Valley about his "maturity issues with partnering"?

The console signaled incoming email.

From: csawyer@teramemory.com
To: barry@teramemory.com
Subject: Staffing requirements

Candy Sawyer. Now there was a woman he could respect. Five foot eleven, twenty-eight years old, blonde, great shape, college volleyball captain at Pepperdine. Hardbody. Killer market instinct. "From volleyball to valley-ball," she had joked during a marketing strategy meeting. He could bet she didn't have any problems with "partnering issues." He continued reading:

> Barry,
> I've been hoping for some additional manpower to help with penetration of my prime territory. Staffing off the org chart, of course. Is there a space in your busy schedule for me?

He could feel his interest in human resources rising. He clicked the REPLY TO button:

> From: barry@teramemory.com
> To: csawyer@teramemory.com
> Subject: Re: Staffing requirements
>
> I'm well aware of your staffing needs. You have my attention. Let's schedule a meeting. How about Farallon at eight?
>
> I'll send a car.

Barry observed with satisfaction that he didn't pick up women anymore.

He hired them.

HACKED IN SEATTLE

THE MAN'S CLUELESSNESS never ceased to amaze him.

Steve Hall worked the keyboard in the near-darkness of his studio apartment. Screenfuls of file listings scrolled past his eyes. Blue Power Ranger, feet glued to the top of the monitor, pumped his plastic action-figure fist up into the gloom.

A scant fifty yards away, the last Caltrain of the evening bumped and rumbled through the darkness, wailing mournfully.

He was probing the filesystems of Seattle Federated Bank's data cores. He was not liking what he had found. His thoughts were a cocktail of contempt, defiance, and hurt feelings.

He muttered to himself in dark tones. "Is that the best

you can do? Is that what you call security? After all I've done for you? What? You don't like little Stevie anymore?"

Weeks ago he had hooked up with a SeaFed systems administrator on Usenet and helped him to performance-tune the OS in the bank's dataserver. In exchange, the admin had provided Steve with a guest account on the bank's beefy server cluster. Fair was fair, but now the admin had apparently experienced a change of heart. It appeared he had pulled Steve's account and tried to lock him out with a gauntlet of security patches and trip wires.

That's what had hurt Steve's feelings. And for all his hostility, aggression, and problems with authority, Steve had tender feelings. He would make his displeasure known.

The phone rang. Steve answered on the headset looped over his ear.

"Steve's hack shack. Would you like to be compromised?"

"Uhhh, my computer's, like, stuck or something," came the voice on the other end, a Beavis-and-Butthead facsimile.

"Young Paul Armstrong, all-American boy," Steve pitched in his best Golden Age of Radio voice. Then, shifting to his best angry third-world radical, "You still working for The Man, or have you come to beg for *ab-so-loo-shun*?"

"I've come to beg, but strictly out of self-interest. We're on a big bug hunt over at Clueless/Packrat. I need your brain for a few cycles."

"Oh, man, and here I was thinking you loved me."

Paul could always rely on his oldest friend. "Bitch. Now, get to steppin'."

Paul characterized the problem at work as he listened to Steve tap away in the darkness. He began to recite a login and password for his client's host, but Steve waved it off.

"Never mind, pink boy. I'm in. Now, tell it all to papa."

Sixty-eight minutes later, the bug hunt was over. Steve had traced it back to a vestigial feature in the OS stuck way back in a place neither Paul nor anyone on his project team would have ever looked. Paul tried to stroke him, but Steve shrugged it off, as if it were praise for his excellence at cleaning toilets.

"This stuff ain't rocket science. You just gotta pay *attention*. There's this crusty old module way down in the kernel, left over from the dark ages of Sys3, and every time they port this stuff to a new machine, it comes back to bite 'em on the ass. Happens every time. Now go and whack your client upside the head with a clue-by-four. And do yourself a couple of times while you're at it. I swear, sometimes I don't know why I hang out with you."

"It's for all the perks. Remember?"

"Well, you owe me big-time for this one. I'm talking Chez TJ and a bottle of Chateau Margaux. And then I get to kick your ass in the simulator at Fighter Town. If I can still stand up."

"You know, young son, you could pull down some serious green if you got out of that hellhole studio and signed up for some contracting work. You wouldn't have to wear a tie. Or shoes, even. I could hook you up with the right bodyshop. You could quit whenever you're full."

"And give up this life of beautiful women and high adventure? What are you, nuts?"

"Well, at least you wouldn't have to spend your life hand-holding slime like me just for a dinner at TJ's. When was the last time you got out of town for the weekend, anyway?"

"Well, I happen to be romancing a little number in Seattle even as we speak."

"Telnet doesn't count, you moron."

They penciled in a date for TJ's. Paul made one last attempt to sing the glory of Steve's talent, but in the end all he could do was say thanks and hang up.

Steve returned to his little project in Seattle.

His worst fears were confirmed. The little worm had tried to lock him out. No explanation, no good-bye, not even a peck on the cheek.

He set to work on the dataserver. Forty minutes later, he had recompiled the kernels on every machine in the bank's cluster. He savored the moment, leaning back in his patio chair, stretching his arms over his head and cracking his knuckles. A maniacal grin eclipsed his face. Extending his right index finger, he made a sweeping, histrionic arm gesture, a devil-windmill arc delivering a single poke of that finger squarely in the center of the ENTER key.

Somewhere in an office building in Seattle, a junior systems administrator on night shift noticed some unusual activity on the central dataserver's console. Rolling his chair across the raised floor, he took a closer look. His mouth opened slowly, steadily into a perfect O.

```
    YOU'LL NEVER CATCH ME. I'M TOO POWERFUL.
    ... AND NOW, YOUR DATA DISAPPEARS
    [POOF]

    Segmentation Violation [core dumped]#
    panic
```

THE CLAW AND THE CLASSIFIEDS

LIZ SAT WITH her knees tucked up under her chin. Laurel brooded over her mocha, lanks of hair exaggerating the dejected set of her swimming-pool blue eyes. The sun eased into the foothills, energizing a riot of clouds with pink light.

"If only I'd had any idea," Liz lamented, "I'd have stayed in school. I'd have changed majors. Gotten a master's. Anything."

A brand new Porsche convertible, too young to have its own license plates, rounded the corner at Printer's Inc. It oozed lewdly down the street fronting the bookstore's outdoor café. The improbably self-satisfied young turk at the wheel twisted slightly and angled his smirk at the women as he drove by.

"Oh, I'm in love," said Laurel with a sarcastic curl of her lip, then her face dissolved into pleading: "I wish it was two years ago, and it was exam time, and that I hadn't studied for anything, and we were sitting in the sun by the claw."

"The claw" was the nickname of an unfortunately styled fountain in the quadrangle by Stanford's main bookstore. Aesthetically it was hideous, but it served a number of critically important functions in Stanford University life.

It was a great source of school unity; no matter what other academic debates divided the student body, everyone could agree the claw was hideous. This status as a sculptural misdemeanor made it the default point of reference; its nickname was instantly recognizable, because it was so apropos. Tell someone "meet me at the claw," and they'd understand, even with the frosh orientation still fresh in their ears.

Most importantly, it was the first and most accessible opportunity to express a mild and benign disrespect for the parent institution, so essential to student morale at any expensive, elite liberal arts university.

So the claw was all of these: landmark, catalyst for idle student rebelliousness, and backstop for aesthetic critique. What more could the sculptor have hoped for?

Liz Toulouse and Laurel Waites had benignly disrespected with the best of them. First year roommates at Stanford, they had shared their living situation through most of their undergraduate tenure—sometimes along with others, sometimes just the two of them, as they lived now, huddled for warmth.

Graduation had emboldened them with hope and high prospects, but that euphoria had been short-lived. Two years later, both women felt like they had no place in the world. Or the Silicon Valley, anyway.

Liz, who had majored in English literature, and Laurel, with her degree in art history, had been roundly rebuffed by the job market of the mid '90s. There wasn't much demand for editors and art historians, not even with freshly minted Stanford degrees. The interviews were discouragingly competitive, the rejections relentless.

Regular expeditions to Stanford's office of Career Planning and Placement confirmed what they were already beginning to fear: their most promising options were as second-string investment banking recruits or over-educated marketing droids for high-tech firms.

They had held out, contemplating the inevitable while supporting themselves as typists and waitresses and teachers of English to Japanese technology executives.

Throughout all of this they endured the spectacle of cocky young engineers tooling around town in expensive, late-model roadsters. They were the darlings of the job market, these socially deficient, overwhelmingly male, tech-savvy careerists, who had graduated from college unable to distinguish McDonald's from Modigliani, DOS from Dostoyevsky. Yet they were coveted and prized like champion Airedales.

Liz, being the more ambitious and tightly wound of the two, found this particularly egregious. It was not her nature to sit patiently by, gnawing a crust of stale bread while hordes of undeserving technocrats feasted at the richest vocational banquet of the century.

But the world of technology repelled her. To Liz it was a colorless place where throngs of badly dressed, under-socialized men with unfortunate haircuts talked for hours in frantic, desperate tones about absolutely nothing important, a blizzard of acronyms and jargon in a vacuum of time-delayed adolescence. Liz had successfully negotiated a working partnership with her own computer, but could see no point in making a career of it.

But then, there was the rent. No small consideration in the most cutthroat housing market since the California Gold Rush.

"I'm actually thinking about it," Liz said. "I'm actually thinking about submitting a resume to one of those ads in the Sunday *Mercury*."

"What ads?" Laurel queried weakly, knowing full well the horror on which Liz deliberated.

"One of those 'seeking dynamic individuals to be a part of our world-class team of marketing associates.' Places like Sun, Oracle, TeraMemory. Those engineers can't write to save their lives. They dance a jig if it passes the spell-checker."

"Oh, honey, has it really come to that? Think about it first. You've got so much to live for."

They sat for a while longer, glumly staring into their saucers like a pair of dejected cats, while the sky lit up like a bonfire.

ADDRESSED FOR SUCCESS

ONCE LIZ DECIDED to compromise her principles and join the infotech juggernaut, it wasn't long before she was working.

Flashy, hyperbole-packed high-tech recruitment ads devoured page upon page of the Sunday *Mercury*. She faxed résumés to a dozen of them.

Only days later, the interviews began in earnest.

Liz wore her designated power suit. It was an Armani number her mother had given her for graduation. Sometime thereafter—to Liz's sartorial chagrin—this particular design became the official dress of the Heidi Fleiss Hollywood Madam trial. Now it struck her as ironically appropriate: a liberal arts major interviewing at a slew of high-tech companies might well be construed as an act of pandering, albeit of a more obscure and cerebral sort.

But it felt good to be in demand. Her newly expanded prospects buoyed her spirits visibly. Laurel had begun referring to her as "New Attitude Girl."

Liz's new attitude wilted considerably after the first round of interviews; the harried indifference of Silicon Valley recruiters spoke bluntly between the lines: she was nobody particularly special, aside from being a Stanford graduate, willing to work in technology, attractive, and female, in that order. The gods of high tech needed bodies to stoke the engines of innovation.

With her own qualifications so established, Liz surveyed her potential employers' corporate personality traits. She noticed some peculiar similarities.

First was that they weren't interested in the particulars of her education or experience so much as her willingness to subordinate every aspect of her life to the care and feeding of the corporation's digital agenda.

Next was the ubiquitous, reverential reference to the company "mission." Initially, Liz had found this charming; it had an appealing ring of high-minded earnestness. She soon learned it wasn't high-mindedness, at least not in the "it's our mission to end world hunger" sense. It was more like tunnel vision, as in "it's our mission to establish MegaCyberCo as the premier vendor of PDQ-based thin-client solutions for the nomadic computing user base."

This industry habit of cloaking the business in grandiose, heroic rhetoric was in some ways an encouragement to Liz.

Her background in literature might come in handy crafting these flights of corporate marketing fancy; if there was an Homeric angle to the quest for a faster network interface or cheaper postscript printer, she'd find it.

In the end, she accepted a job as junior marketing associate at TeraMemory. Not because "Tera"—as insiders called it—stood out in any way, but because of the commute. Liz had quickly learned that you could spend the entirety of your non-working life gridlocked on 101 if the drive-time geography was against you.

From then on, time seemed to collapse into nothing. By the end of her first morning, Liz had a health plan, a TeraMemory ID card, and a token stock-option package. By afternoon, she had a cubicle, a phone extension, a computer, and an email address.

By the end of her first week, her coworkers had begun to designate her as "marketing's resident expert on the enterprise server product line." This had made Liz a little nervous; she was reluctant by nature to claim expertise on anything after five short days—never mind TeraMemory's complex technology. But her manager had been insistent: "This is high tech," she had asserted. "Everything happens quickly. Welcome to the fast lane." Liz had decided that her manager was at least partially correct; certainly employees quickly learned to tap-dance furiously around their own knowledge gaps. In a pinch, a rapid-fire, buzzword-studded glibness could always substitute for actual understanding.

Monday morning of her second week found her sitting in a tiny conference room at TeraMemory headquarters, analyzing task requirements with her fellow marketing associate, Barbara.

"You joined at a crazy, crazy time," Barbara explained with a slightly desperate edge in her voice. "Things are really starting to jump around here. There's a rumor that WHIP has been moved up by three months. There's supposed to be a company-wide memo this afternoon."

In Liz's survey of the company's product line, she had never seen the name "WHIP." She decided to risk looking uninformed.

"What's 'WHIP'?"

"Secret," Barbara informed her, sounding a little conspiratorial. "Next generation something-or-other. Really important."

"What does the project mean for us?" Liz asked, trying her best to sound like the team player.

"Mostly more deadlines. We were already way behind on the WHIP marketing push, and now we're way, way, way behind. We'll really be able to use you around here."

"Well, I really don't know anything at all about this WHIP thing. Maybe I should spend some time coming up to speed . . ."

"You'll figure it out. Straight into the fire, babe."

Barbara picked up a thick stack of papers and set them down in front of Liz. "We've got a mountain of techie-speak to fluff up for the trade shows. And you won't believe the communication problems with engineering—from getting a clear statement of priorities all the way down to the grade school grammar."

Later, sitting in her cubicle surrounded by marked-up drafts of white papers and spec sheets, she read an email. It was from the president of TeraMemory, Barry Dominic.

To: corp@teramemory.com
From: barry@teramemory.com
Subject: WHIP initiative

She scanned the memo. It was exactly as Barbara had anticipated. But as she read more closely, Liz's apprehension of the increased workload was eclipsed by her morbid fascination with the structure of the prose.

For that reason, it was decided to accelarate the WHIP initiative by three months. I know this means some extended hours and indeed a few all-nighters during the holidays, but for all intensive purposes it will all most certainly be riflected in employee equity partici- pation—your's and mine.

This is a criticle time in the development of our business flow, and I know your all going to pull together to get Tera to where we need to get to.

Oh, my God, Liz thought as she tried to digest the message. Our CEO writes like a twelve-year-old. A twelve-year-old weaned on Tom Peters instead of Marvel Comics.

Still reeling, Liz composed an email by clicking the REPLY button. She replaced the recipient with Barbara's address.

From: ltoulouse@teramemory.com
To: bschuck@teramemory.com
Subject: Re: WHIP initiative
Cc: corp@teramemory.com

> This is a criticle time in the development of our
> business flow, and I know your all going to pull
> together to get Tera to where we need to get to.

Barb,
You were right. Amid a storm of misspellings and mala-propisms, forced march has been decreed by the King of the Dangling Preposition.

We are driven before the WHIP.

Liz clicked SEND at the very same instant she glanced at the message header and noticed the extra line. She'd cc'ed the entire company.

"Oh, God, this can't be happening," she whispered sharply to herself. Her heart launched itself skyward, she turned as white as a turnip, and the gruesome reality began to sink in. She lingered for a few moments, staring at the screen in a paralysis of fear, adrenaline shooting through her veins.

Then the emails began to arrive from all over head-quarters, RE: RE: WHIP INITIATIVE.

She wanted to disappear.

LARGE NUMBER ELEVEN AT THE TUNG KEE NOODLE HOUSE

TEN MINUTES after one and the lunch rush showed no sign of slowing down; a crowd of young male engineers crushed together at the door, waiting. Tung Kee Noodle House was in full swing—white-shirted waiters lifting trays of steaming bowls, chow mein, and glasses of sunset- and radium-colored tapioca noodle drinks.

The noodles were good, but the efficiency was terrifying. Tung Kee was a model study in time and motion. The busboys never stopped moving; they trolled the restaurant in endless circles, clearing, wiping, and setting tables in seconds. Each dish had a number—no name, no substitutions. Waiters beamed orders to the kitchen with handheld wireless units. The food arrived quickly—so quickly, in fact, that it sometimes arrived before your waiter had made his way back to the kitchen. Paul found this breach of dining cause-and-effect to be obscurely unnerving.

But you could get lunch for three dollars, which ensured that the place was constantly packed. At other times of the day you might see a wider sample of humanity: teenagers, older people, Asian and Latino families. But at lunch, the engineering-aged male ruled.

The waiter had wedged Paul and Steve into a window booth. It was cramped, but the entertainment was a consolation: the congested traffic struggled comically down Castro Street. Hostile, high-strung Silicon Valley hard-chargers leaned on their horns and jockeyed for position against the traffic light, a festival of low-speed road rage.

In the next booth, a tech-support rep yelped into a cellular phone, guiding a customer through a router configuration. Steve gave him a sidelong glance and rolled his eyes.

"Look at this joker. He's going to spend three bucks on lunch and twenty on the phone call. Pager, cell phone, palmtop—he might as well be wearing a leash. And a shirt that says 'Property of The Man.'"

"Hey, I resemble that remark," Paul commented a little self-consciously, fresh from his own client's site. "It's just the nature of the game, isn't it?"

"Nah, just the latest iteration of Decline and Fall."

"Oh, you going on with that cyber-commie shuck-and-jive again? I can never quite figure out what you're talking about."

Steve pushed his tangled hair up on his forehead and

gave his friend a comically weary look. "OK, I'll give it to you one more time," he volunteered. "Look, the original soul of the Valley was forged by hobbyists—the Homebrew folks, the guys with the Altair kits, all the people writing freeware just for the joy of watching the bits jump around.

"Most of those guys were real weirdos—nobody had any idea what they were up to; they were in their own little world, doing it all on their own time, with their own money. And it wasn't like it is now—chip-sets didn't come free in a box of cornflakes. It was a real challenge back then to build digital machinery on a budget.

"But they didn't care—not what people thought about them, or even how they looked." He straightened his hands and held them an inch apart, for emphasis. "We're talking real misfits: fat, pasty, wearing the same jeans and T-shirt every day, no shoes, bad personal hygiene, the full deal.

"Sometime in the recent past, that soul was stolen and enslaved by The Man; now this place is run by The Man and his money. He moved in with his venture capital, and his intellectual property lawyers, and he slapped an NDA and a corporate ball-and-chain on anybody with a clue. Funny thing is, most of them don't seem to have noticed they've become intellectual indentured servants.

"But The Man likes to tell his slaves a little fairy tale about how they're just like those old hackers who started things off—so they get to wear the jeans and the T-shirts and the Birkenstocks in the privacy of their own cubicles. But it's just a pose. They're all wearing suits and ties on the inside. The rest is just jive."

"Wait a minute," Paul debated, bean sprout dangling from the corner of his mouth. "I thought that the free market was suppose to optimize innovation. Doesn't The Man—as you call him—create the conditions for positive change?"

"Oh, that's the standard Adam Smith's invisible hand routine. Problem is, Adam Smith's invisible hand is wedged up his invisible ass; business only cares about business. Truth and beauty never survive the commercial shuffle—haven't you noticed?"

Steve didn't wait for Paul's answer. "Oh yeah, sure, the suits will tell you a different story—they'll say that innovation gets rewarded, the cream rises to the top, blah, blah, but that's bullshit. Greed floats. Treachery gets rewarded. You can steal your core technology from Xerox PARC and everybody thinks you're a genius just because Xerox was too lazy to go after you and take it back. Hell, if innovation was really rewarded, Ted Nelson would be as rich as Bill Gates. Last I heard, Nelson was shilling at some Japanese consumer electronics trade show. Is that pathetic, or what? I mean, the guy invented hypertext, for God's sake."

Steve captured a beef ball from his bowl and slurped it from his spoon. "The large and the nasty reap the rewards," he preached, chewing righteously. "True hackers are nearly extinct—hunted down and run off the landscape by cyber-capitalists.

"But that's cool," he continued optimistically. "The Man is going to get his 'cause he already killed off the golden goose. It's only a matter of time before he runs out of Big New Ideas, because he's murdered the soul of the place. When the money dries up, this place will be just like anywhere else. It was never the *place,* anyway—that's what The Man will never understand. It was the unique approach to problem-solving. These days, the whole scene is growing less unique by the nanosecond. Capital has displaced culture. Innovation has given way to imitation."

Paul eyed his oldest friend with a friendly skepticism. "Right on, comrade," he said sarcastically between slurps. He wasn't going to give up any ground to his trusty but radicalized companion.

But he had to admit, as he rooted through his large number eleven with plastic chopsticks, life in the Valley wasn't nearly as much fun as it used to be.

DEATH BY A THOUSAND EMAILS

LIZ PICKED HER way through the flurry of incoming email, blood rushing to her face. There was a palpable buzz in cubicleville; only fifteen minutes had elapsed since her online faux pas and already everybody at TeraMemory headquarters knew.

Her heart sank with every message on the stack. Each brought her a completely new experience of shame. Who knew it could come in so many, many varieties?

Some were smirking and nerdy:

From: dbrown@teramemory.com
To: ltoulouse@teramemory.com
Subject: Re: Re: WHIP initiative

Hoo, boy! That's a first—professional suicide by SMTP. Couldn't you have just gotten drunk and fallen over at the holiday party instead?

It was nice knowing you. What did you say your name was?

>> This is a criticle time in the development of our
>> business flow, and I know your all going to pull
>> together to get Tera to where we need to get to.

> Barb,
> You were right. Amid a storm of misspellings and
> malapropisms, forced march has been decreed
> by the King of the Dangling Preposition.

Some were congratulatory:

From: rscott@teramemory.com
To: ltoulouse@teramemory.com
Subject: Re: Re: WHIP initiative

> You were right. Amid a storm of misspellings and
>malapropisms, forced march has been decreed
>by the King of the Dangling Preposition.

Hey, that's pretty funny. Those may be your last words, but if it's any consolation, the whole floor is in hysterics.

Some were pedantic:

From: tchun@teramemory.com
To: ltoulouse@teramemory.com
Subject: Re: Re: WHIP initiative

First Commandment: Know Thy Email Client.
Good luck at your next job.

And some were almost admiring:

From: nkishore@teramemory.com
To: ltoulouse@teramemory.com
Subject: Re: Re: WHIP initiative

Either you're completely clueless or you just don't care
anymore. Either way, that was sublime. If you're still
here in three weeks, I'll buy you lunch.

But they all shared one theme in common: Liz was finished at TeraMemory. All except one, from a Candy Sawyer,
which was ominously cryptic:

From: csawyer@teramemory.com
To: ltoulouse@teramemory.com
Subject: Re: Re: WHIP initiative

>You were right. Amid a storm of misspellings and
>malapropisms, forced march has been decreed
>by the King of the Dangling Preposition.

King of the Dangling *Proposition*, you mean.

On the twenty-first floor, Barry Dominic was bursting a
hose. He lurched into the antechamber of the executive suite
to download his fury on the administrative assistant.

"What do you mean you sent out the memo without pol-
ishing it up? What in God's name am I paying you for? I . . .
am . . . *not* a details guy. I'm the goddamn CEO, that's who I
am. I don't have time to pick nits," Barry spat.

His fury arced into a spectacular crescendo. "I'm trying to run a billion-fucking-dollar company. And you have to go and make me look like a goddamn idiot fuckup in front of the whole crew."

He caught his breath while his assistant stared gravely at her manicure. A blood vessel stood up festively on his receding forehead.

"What in God's name did I hire you for?" he snarled as he stalked back into his office. "And you get this Toulouse individual up here first goddamn thing in the morning," he shot back over his shoulder.

Barry slumped in his chair, stuck out his jaw and seethed. He'd always been a little sensitive about the gaps in his nontechnical education. But he'd be damned if he was going to let some new hire poke fun at him over it.

Meanwhile, Liz was already packing up her things in haste. She hadn't been at Tera long enough to personalize her cubicle very much—just an art-nouveau calendar and a picture of her cat, Angus—but her instincts told her to cover her tracks and leave as little trace of her existence as possible.

Her phone rang. It was Mr. Dominic's administrative assistant, every sentence a question.

"Ms. Toulouse? Mr. Dominic would like to see you? Tomorrow morning in his office on twenty-one? At eight-thirty?"

Liz blanched, but somehow her recently acquired corporate compliance reflex caused her to say something that she, in no possible, conceivable way, meant.

"Yes. I'll be there."

She put down the phone and swallowed hard.

An hour later, Barry's tantrum continued unabated. He dialed his receptionist on the speakerphone, though she sat in the next room.

"Did you schedule that insubordinate moron for the morning?"

"Yes, Mr. Dominic."

"Good. Now, you're fired. You can go straight to HR," he snapped, and squashed the speakerphone's orange button beneath his thumb.

PSYCHRIST, THE SEMIOTIC DEMOLITION DERBY AND DEATHMATCH 3000

STEVE AND PSYCHRIST had walked for miles in the foothills of the Valley's western slope. Through lush meadows, past stands of old, eccentric oaks, the surroundings offered an impressive display of fauna: lizards, squirrels, hawks, songbirds, an occasional deer.

The surrounding hills, dotted with grazing cattle, stood much as they had a hundred years earlier. The frenetic pace of urban growth hadn't yet touched this place.

This was all the more amazing, Steve thought, because they were only a mile or so from El Camino Real. It felt much farther, and he was never much at ease out in the middle of nowhere. He turned and walked backward for a few steps, reassuring himself with the view. This was a great place to survey the Valley's geography and larger architectural landmarks. He could see the whole thing laid out before him as if in miniature: San Francisco Bay, Hoover Tower, Dumbarton Bridge, Mission Peak, Moffet Field, Great America, San José.

If there was any bucolic splendor left in the heart of the Silicon Valley, Stanford University seemed to own it. This particular stretch lay just above the campus, and there was no better—or nearer—place to escape the ever-accelerating pace of the Valley floor. The only evidence of human artifice was the university's huge, dish-shaped radio telescope. This day it was cocked in a southwesterly attitude, a pair of hawks perched on its rim.

"Technology is a myth by which to mobilize people," ruminated Psychrist, his own forest of dreadlocks knocking together in the breeze. "It contains most of the elements of magical thinking and omnipotence. It's the proverbial genie in a bottle."

Steve listened attentively, which was completely out of character. With anyone else, he would have riddled the conversation with obscure puns and sardonic aphorisms. But Psychrist was more than an acquaintance. He was one of Steve's heroes. And a hacker needed heroes.

Psychrist described himself as a "cybernetic infiltrator/ provocateur." The Bay Area arts scene—such as it was—had embraced him as a performance artist. Fortunately for him, the ballistic nature of his performances guaranteed a large following among the nerds, techies, and otherwise culturally challenged males who wouldn't be caught dead at a French impressionist retrospective. Imagine an event somewhere between a fireworks display and a monster truck rally, but heavy with symbolic content. Demolition derby as conceived by Umberto Eco.

His relationship to technology began as it did with many adolescent males, forged in the glee of destructive curiosity. As a child he had an earnest enthusiasm for explosives. After pyrotechnically pulping every mailbox in the neighborhood, right around the time his voice was changing, he began to refine his interests: rocketry and electromechanics.

The young Psychrist had shown considerably more passion and dedication than the average destructive juvenile delinquent; by sixteen he had launched a number of increasingly sophisticated miniature ICBMs from his parents' backyard. Somewhere along the way—and much to his mother's horror—he'd lost a finger on his right hand to one of his surprisingly powerful but unstable fuel formulations. Undeterred, he counted the absent digit as the cost of his education and continued to pursue his discipline with the unflinching passion of the true rocket scientist.

But his avocation was brought to a hasty conclusion by the Department of Defense after one of his comparatively modest rocket creations lifted and explosively scattered a hefty payload of aluminum confetti—radar chaff, engineered for maximum reflectivity.

Ordinarily this wouldn't have been a big deal, but the

timing and test range Psychrist had chosen for the project ensured the prompt and vigorous attention of the North American air defense authorities; his experiment generated a shockingly large radar profile in the airspace directly above Mountain View's strategically significant "Blue Cube," right in the middle of the Cold War.

The ensuing state-sponsored supervision encouraged new hobbies. He became an avid reader, moving quickly from pulp science fiction to authors far outside his experience and education: Marx. Veblen. Bourdieu. Spengler. His aesthetic judgment sharpened. His rhetoric attained critical mass. And after the remedial regimen cooled down a bit, he merged the old hobbies with the new ones: he became a culture hacker of sorts, a semiotician with a blowtorch. He lived for the symbolic reevaluation of the cultural frame of reference.

Especially when the symbols tore each other to pieces and burst into flames.

He never announced his performances in advance; if you had the good fortune or connections to bear witness, you were one of a very few elites. Steve had only heard about them or seen the popular video documentaries.

But now Psychrist had come to him. He had sought Steve out, based on his hacker credentials. They were discussing a collaboration on his latest "installation."

"See, the question is not how much technology can do for us, but how much are we going to let it do for us. Let's just assume that soon machines'll do everything we want. We've let the genie out of the bottle and we get our three wishes, no strings attached. What do we want? 'Okay, computer, do all my work for me so I can sleep all day.' 'Okay, computer, I'm bored—entertain me.' 'Raise my children for me.' And this is where it gets really scary—'Computer, dream my dreams for me.'

"Eventually, automation replaces all effort, and humanity succeeds in attaining Ultimate Sloth. Yippee. Total prosperity for everyone.

"But at that point, what have we become, generally speaking? We've forgotten how to make things, be nice to each other, tell stories. We're just these squalling mouths feeding on some senseless digital stimulation. No capacity to dream, which means no self-determination. Not human anymore; just sidecars to the Machine, ready to be sloughed off.

"Marx got it right. As automation advances, people become appendages of the Machine. But don't price it yet: eventually we become more like vestigial organs. Then what happens?

"There was this guy, John Lilly: psychologist, cyberneticist, intellectual outlaw weirdo, and general threat to the status quo. Well, he got into some really twisted stuff: went to Big Sur, loaded up on a cocktail of unspecified, unpronounceable psychedelics, hopped into a sensory isolation tank—a sort of hermetically sealed hot tub for solipsists—and waited."

"Waited for what?"

"Messages. From anywhere. As in, 'here I am, as unencumbered by my sensorium as I'll ever be, and hopped up on goof-balls to boot; my disbelief is completely suspended. If there's anybody on the line, speak now or forever hold your peace.'"

"Jeez. Pretty extreme. What happened?"

"Well, he claims to have received an interplanetary update, sort of a galactic version of headline news. And the message is this: the main event—galactically speaking—is this ongoing war between carbon-based and silicon-based lifeforms. Newsflash: the battle has just been joined on Earth. That workstation on your desk? The one you've been spending all your time with? That's just a primitive, viral-type organism. Just hang around a few hundred years. That's when the real fireworks begin.

"And here's the amazing part: this was all back in the early '70s."

"Whoa. Totally outside."

"Isn't it? That's where I got the idea for my latest installation. 'Deathmatch 3000: C versus Si.' It's a kind of kinetic parable about freedom and self-determination. I'm still working out the details, but I've nailed down a partial grant. I think I can scrape the rest together myself. But I'm going to need a good hacker—I can't do the network programming myself."

Daylight fled as they walked back down, hands in pockets. Freeways and office parks began to shimmer below. Steve gazed out at the derelict dirigible hangars of Moffet Field, twin slugs creeping infinitely slowly across the Valley floor.

"The real question," said Psychrist, rubbing his perfect goatee, "is how to keep the animal rights people off our backs."

LIZ FACES THE WRATH
OF THE NERD KING

LIZ SIPPED HER mocha and absentmindedly turned over the pages of *Le Figaro*. In twelve hours she'd be standing in the personal office of Barry Dominic, the Valley's own Great and Powerful Oz. But there would be no ruby slippers for her; she would be humiliated, terminated, and thrown from the top of TeraMemory headquarters by flying monkeys. Or escorted out by security, at the very least.

Laurel scrutinized the coffeehouse's Belle Epoque-inspired mural and wrinkled her nose. "You could call in sick. Or you could just quit by phone—or email, even. You don't have to go back just to get slapped around by some nerd with a bank account. Even if he is a famous nerd."

"But I said I'd be there," Liz countered.

"So change your mind. It's a woman's prerogative, right?"

"That's not my style. And what's the worst that could

happen, anyway? He's just going to fire me, that's all. I'll say thank you, collect my paycheck, and leave. Then I'll be in the same place I was three weeks ago. It's not the end of the world."

At 8:28 A.M. Liz stood in the main elevator at Tera-Memory headquarters. She pushed the button for the twenty-first floor softly, as if it might explode.

Of course it stopped seventeen times on the way up. A parade of serious-looking Silicon Valley careerists circulated through the elevator at almost every floor. It was excruciating. Liz was positive that every one of them knew who she was and where she was going. Her infamy must surely be visible.

The receptionist in the executive suite was friendly in a perfunctory way. She offered Liz a seat and advised her to wait.

At 9:19 the receptionist cheerily announced, "Mr. Dominic will see you now." She exaggerated her words in a hushed voice, gums a-crackling, as if Liz were an avid lipreader.

Liz entered the inner sanctum of the Nerd King. He sat at an enormous wooden desk in what looked like a BarcaLounger with postmodern pretensions. She approached the throne.

"Don't sit down, Ms. Toulouse," he began curtly, "this shouldn't take long. First, I want you to know that your insubordination has hurt this organization deeply. In a dynamic, cutting-edge operation like Tera, it's critical for all of us to be team players. It's clear you haven't read the *Five Habits of Effective Market Leaders . . .*"

The mounting cadence of Barry's speech put Liz in the grip of a sudden panic. She had been expecting a quick reprimand followed by termination. She could handle that. What she had not anticipated was a slow professional death by trendy management rhetoric. Anything but that. She felt a wave of desperation. She searched her mind for a plan of escape. And, barely believing her own brass, she interrupted.

"Look, Mr. Dominic, I made a mistake. I never intended for you to see that email, and I'm honestly, truly sorry for any disruption it may have caused. I'm not a techie, and I obviously don't belong here. I'd like to do us both a favor here and—respectfully—resign. So if you'll excuse me . . ." Liz turned to walk out.

Barry was not accustomed to back talk from women. Especially not young, attractive women. And nothing prodded his interest more than a preemptive rejection. Especially from a young, attractive woman. He quickly recalculated his agenda.

"You don't understand, Ms. Toulouse. Please come back. I didn't bring you here to fire you."

"You didn't?" Liz asked incredulously from the door.

"Oh, no, not at all," he offered in his best management seminar dynamism. "I value your point of view, even if it did somehow slip out in a way that embarrassed me. Diversity of opinion is more important than ego. And you're right—we do need better communication here at Tera.

"I'd like you to work for me. Up here on twenty-one. As

my administrative assistant. You can make sure that my clunky memos never escape without a coat of polish again."

Liz stood speechless. Something about his offer made her suspicious.

Barry moved to consolidate his gains. "You'll sit in the front office of the executive suite. Be my personal writing coach." Then he twinkled. "The pay's a lot better than the school system."

After a brief skirmish between her corporate compliance reflex and her better judgment, Liz agreed. "I'd be willing to try."

"Good. Starting today. We'll go over a few things after lunch."

Liz returned to her cubicle to prepare for her move to the executive suite. She passed Barbara's cubicle on the way.

"How's it going, spam-queen? Still have a job?"

"Apparently," Liz returned. Barbara looked surprised.

"Really. Well then let's get back to work. I have some more feedback from engineering to fold into the WHIP venture capital pitch."

"Can't," Liz shot over her shoulder, turning to leave. "I've been transferred. I'm working on twenty-one now. For Mr. Dominic."

Barbara raised her eyebrows. "Lambs to the slaughter," she sighed. Then, giggling, "Pearls before swine."

THE WHIP COMES
DOWN ON PAUL

AS THE END of Paul's contract approached, he made the decision not to renew. Life on the Sea of Cubicles—as he called his client's cavernous, institutional office space—had depressed him relentlessly. It was comfortable work, but unchallenging and insidiously bland. He had hoped for a bit more excitement to pull him out of his career ennui. He was ready for a change; the Valley's insatiable hunger for technical talent ensured he found one almost immediately.

Paul's new client was a bona fide Silicon Valley rocket. TeraMemory had roared to the top of the NASDAQ a scant four years after IPO, led by the company's flamboyant, hard-driven founder, Barry Dominic.

"Tera"—as insiders called it—provided high-end databases and "data mining tools" to the Fortune-500s. Successful exploitation of this market had earned the company a ton of money and a secure franchise in the world of "corporate productivity solutions."

But the rumor circulating through the business was that Barry Dominic had bigger fish to fry: the company was moving out of familiar territory and into the "main action"—networking and the Internet—with some sort of cutting-edge, whiz-bang technology. It was all very hush-hush, until Paul signed the standard nondisclosure agreement, or NDA as it was known in the geek brotherhood.

The project was code-named WHIP, a typically heroic acronym for the decidedly less exciting "Wireless, High-density Internet Protocol." The name came as no surprise to Paul. Dominic was well-known in the industry for his relentless hard-charging, as well as his ability to motivate his employees. Consequently, TeraMemory had something of a reputation as a burn-out shop.

WHIP was a classic Silicon-Valley-style scheme to pre-emptively dominate a market that did not yet exist. Lots of pundits and futurists had declared that it should exist, that in the future it would exist, and that all thinking people assumed its eventuality inevitable. Articles appeared in places like *Wired* magazine and *Red Herring* about how it would change everything from entertainment to the simplest consumer rituals.

But the sober fact was that—in the here and now, at least—

the market demand was very nearly, if not actually exactly, zilch. But not to worry; WHIP—as a realized technology—was also entirely hypothetical. This created an exciting symmetry: WHIP was vaporware for a market of hot air.

If it ever made it out of the lab, WHIP would enable computers of all kinds to talk to each other without benefit of cabling. But the WHIP was more than a product. It was a protocol—the holy grail of infotech leverage.

The beauty of WHIP was that it would embrace a potentially huge number of lucrative opportunities. WHIP-driven devices would undoubtedly be popular with the people who presently spent their days threading miles of cable throughout the nether regions and interstices of the corporate landscape; TeraMemory would describe WHIP as a "revolutionary infrastructure efficiency enhancement," but the wire-heads of the world would be thinking more mundane thoughts like "No more crawling around on the floor or perching precariously on stepladders. Cool." WHIP would also reach into the fast-growing world of nomadic computing; laptops, pagers, routers, and cellular phones would fuse together into a market of WHIP-compliant, universal roving information appliances.

And every time somebody sold a slice of WHIPped silicon, TeraMemory would get a piece of the action.

The gods of high tech are a perverse and unreliable bunch, and any number of competing innovations might thwart WHIP's ambitions. But the Valley's biggest fortunes were founded extensively on uncertainties, and WHIP was Barry Dominic's very own pet maybe. Every mover and shaker, it seemed, had to have one.

As with every Silicon Valley company, once a potentially lucrative new market had been identified, everything needed to be done yesterday. Management at Tera had decided that this window of market opportunity was only a few months wide, and had staffed up furiously for the effort. They hit up every body shop—Valley-ese for contract recruitment agency—in a fifty mile radius. The recruiter had made Paul a lucrative offer only five hours after the first phone interview.

Tera had hired Paul to wrangle some tricky network code. Contractors were expected to hit the ground running, and his PM had encouraged him to come up to speed by subscribing to an internal mailing list for the WHIP Internal Team: whip-it. He'd jumped into the action quickly.

From: parmstrong@teramemory.com
To: whip-it@teramemory.com
Subject: Re: Driver specs

The designers should remember that the world of broad-spectrum radiation is much less predictable than the tidy, well-controlled domain of cables and voltage swings to which they're accustomed.

Depending on the operating environment, the WHIP drivers might potentially be dealing with much higher rates of incipient transmission errors. If it were my decision, I'd proactively be spending much more effort on routines for bandwidth diagnostics and dynamic optimization.

This had pleased his project manager:

From: jsacerdoti@teramemory.com
To: parmstrong@teramemory.com
Subject: Re: Driver specs

Damn. Good strategic analysis. Nicely worded, too.

But his posting had also instigated a competition for his cycles. A marketing VP had been eavesdropping on whip-it, and decided that Paul should be re-deployed on a new task:

From: csawyer@teramemory.com
To: parmstrong@teramemory.com
Subject: Re: Driver specs

Great posting. You seem to have an excellent understanding of key WHIP challenges. The project directors have an urgent need for someone with the technical background to write a series of strategic white papers for a venture capital audience. Mr. Dominic would very much like to see you redeployed as that resource.

Any problems with that?

Paul had been taken aback by this. He'd come to Tera to write code, not strategic technology documents. On the other

hand, it was still a lot more exciting than his last contract.
Maybe this was the adventure he'd been dreaming about.

Paul tapped his PM for direction, but he wasn't much help:

From: jsacerdoti@teramemory.com
To: parmstrong@teramemory.com
Subject: Re: reassignment

>I'm feeling ambivalent about being redeployed
>so suddenly.

Don't ask me, son—I wanted to keep you around, too.
I've been trumped by the big dogs on 21. Looks like
you're working directly for the boss now.

You've been poached, boy.

LIZ DESCENDS TO THE ENGINEER'S LEVEL

EVEN AFTER A few weeks as Barry's assistant, Liz couldn't shake an obscure feeling of discomfort. She had little tangible justification, only a nagging intuition. But there was no denying his avuncular manner would occasionally slip into something a little too familiar. He didn't seem to recognize professional boundaries, either, and asked her about her age, her personal life, her dating history. And sometimes his smile seemed to converge with a leer.

She had given him the benefit of the doubt so far. Most of the time it was a nonissue, anyway; Barry's attention was monomaniacally focused on WHIP.

Liz sat in a conference room with a dozen other "Terans," each listening attentively as Barry dispatched the items on the meeting's agenda. He stood at a whiteboard and created inscrutable diagrams with extravagant gestures: a tangled knot of sweeping arrows and bullet-points.

His attention settled on Liz. She tried not to wince. "Liz," Barry directed in his signature market-leading tenor, "you're already familiar with the WHIP effort, as I recall."

Liz blushed with the recent memory of her now-infamous email debacle. "Yes, Mr. Dominic."

"Well, we're moving into the VC recruitment phase any day now. We've drafted a number of documents—white papers—describing the technology and market opportunities for our venture capital prospects. It's critical that we communicate this opportunity in language they can understand. 'Venture capital' is a very fancy name, but they're just bankers on testosterone. Remember that.

"I want you to edit them for the first WHIP pitch. We need them by next week, Wednesday latest. Probably be good if you meet with the engineer who wrote them, in the interest of technical accuracy. I'm relying on you"—and here he smirked ever so slightly—"for your inimitable clarity and style."

Great, Liz thought. Another afternoon wrestling with some nerd over subordinate clauses and predicate nominatives. She really dreaded her trips to the lab.

Engineers generally had serious control issues, and nothing brought them out like the threat of collaboration.

Editing their work was like tiptoeing through an emotionally charged minefield of grammatical crimes. Move a prepositional phrase or break up a run-on sentence and you were likely to strike deeply at their essential maleness, namely, a need to do everything themselves. It was one of those acts that could elicit disproportionately extreme reactions of a peculiarly masculine kind, like taking away the TV remote. Multiplied by fifty.

Never mind that engineers had a palpable disdain for anyone nontechnical. Anyone without a BSEE or other heavy hacker cred was the Enemy, sent by the forces of evil to obfuscate the real issues and sap productivity. Never mind that engineers were far more advanced in eroding productivity on their own; between the web, MUDs, and the alt.humor USENET hierarchy, it was a wonder anything was ever delivered on schedule. The problem was, these time-incinerating activities were superficially indistinguishable from real work. Most managers couldn't tell the difference. But engineers liked to take credit for all good things while deflecting the responsibility for all bad things to elements outside their own sphere of influence—and that included evil, nontechnical droids, as they called people like Liz.

This disdain wasn't just reserved for nontechnical peers and managers, either. They vented their arrogance at directors and company officers, too. But such were the perks of the privileged caste: if you were any good, management was nearly infinitely indulgent, because programmers were absolutely necessary to the operation. Yes, techies were usually profoundly emotionally underdeveloped. Yes, they were prone to tantrums, outbursts, and generally antisocial behavior. But they were in short supply, as they themselves were so richly aware.

Consequently, they were completely insufferable. Nothing is worse than a child—virtual or otherwise—who knows he's indispensable; children are at their best when they know they're absolutely expendable.

But what really grated on Liz was the prevailing assumption that anyone on the technical side must automatically be a genius. Her experience had been quite to the contrary. Weeks of untangling and rewriting engineers' documents had led her to wonder how any of them had escaped college with a degree. Many, she later learned, had not; if you could master the right technical arcana, you could skip all the other steps—like reading, writing, and matriculation. Companies like TeraMemory would hire you anyway, solely on the depth and strength of your relationship to a slice of silicon and its litany of logical instructions. Critical thinking—outside of a narrow proficiency in solid state logic—wasn't high on the list of qualifications.

Liz carried this apprehension on her journey down to engineering. Her journey took her past the "glass house"— the harshly lit, window-enclosed room where the corporate servers and datacores lived. It was like an aquarium for geeks.

The raised floor made for a slightly below-ground level view, subliminally suggesting that those inside were taller—and more important—than those outside.

She made her way through a forest of cubbies in engineering. Most all were decorated in variations on a single theme: male adolescence. There were lots of toys—rubber dinosaurs, cartoon action figures, several jumbo inflatable Godzillas. Life-sized, luridly colored plastic parodies of assault rifles and grenade launchers—loaded with harmless foam projectiles—also figured prominently.

Liz pondered the semiotics of this workspace: totems of hostility. Agents of unmediated force. It was a museum of the psychology of impatience and instant gratification. If these were the leitmotifs of technical culture, she ruminated, well, that would explain a lot.

But what really took her breath away was the sartorial savagery. Ripped jeans, garish athletic shoes, heavy-metal concert T-shirts, bright blue hair, noserings, studded leather accessories—worn by men well over thirty. This, it seemed to Liz, stepped well over the boundaries of the adolescent and into the psychopathic.

The numbers on the cubicles indicated she'd nearly reached her destination. After a few brief detours, she located it. She peeked inside with apprehension.

She saw a slim, clean-cut, and—by engineering standards—unthreatening young man. Handsome, even. Younger than she was expecting. No nose ring. No punctures of any kind, in fact.

"Paul Armstrong?" she ventured.

"Yes. You must be Liz Toulouse. I've been waiting for you. Welcome to the monkey house."

WHY BARRY CARRIES A MiG STICK

WHEN BARRY wasn't in the office, he was making every minute count. Whether he was on the stick of his MiG-21 fighter jet or at the helm of his blue water racing yacht, he was always, as any well-heeled California sportsman might say, "totally going for it."

While other Silicon Valley chieftains embraced hobbies like fly fishing, hockey, wind-surfing, and white water rafting—all of which had become popular among legions of adoring engineers—Barry's pastimes were particularly expensive and elite. They also required extensive support crews, guaranteeing no copy-cat nerdlings would be following him onto his chosen playgrounds.

Avocations can betray everything. People seem to choose hobbies that allow them to work out their deepest and most profound personal issues. If there is any truth to this premise, Barry's issues were plain: Insecurity. Control. Power. Restlessness.

Take his flying habit. Whereas air travel might raise feelings of dread and insecurity in many, there was one thing Barry absolutely knew for sure: it was impossible for him to feel insecure in the cockpit of the MiG-21. When he leaned on the throttle and lit up his afterburners, there was absolutely no one—outside of the U.S. Air Force and Area 51, perhaps—who could catch him. This did things for Barry that years of therapy and hundreds of motivational seminars could not.

Then there was the rush of control. Unlike TeraMemory, the MiG had no CFO to suggest how much fuel to burn or how fast to fly. Barry hated collaboration, and delegating authority was like pulling out his own teeth. Dependency on others made him anxious. He liked doing it all himself. The jet spoke to that need.

As for power, there was something about having a plaything that was, until very recently, the supreme instrument of force of a world superpower. Never mind the raw speed and aerobatic capabilities of this aircraft; Barry had only to add his name to the former owners' to become drunk with his own power and importance: Brezhnev. Gorbachev. Dominic. And since the end of the Cold War, his own company's market cap actually exceeded the national economies of what was left of the Soviet Union.

A restlessness like Barry's can only be abated by an

infinity of choices. Mach 2 is crack cocaine to the restless; a change of heart and a wiggle of the stick, and you could be dining in Telluride instead of Las Vegas.

Yet the cyber-billionaire cannot live by afterburners alone. What the jet did for obliteration of geographic barriers, the boat did for social ones. Yacht racing is a rich man's sport, and winning is reserved for the egregiously wealthy. But it's also the quickest shortcut across class barriers available to a relentlessly ambitious, cyber-industrialist *arriviste* like Barry. Even the Yalies in their club ties grudgingly afforded a measure of respect when Mr. Dominic—and the very elite, very expensive crew aboard the *Singularity*—jibed victorious through another San Francisco regatta.

It felt good to be on top—in and out of the office. But the gratification never lasted very long for Barry. His ascent had presented him with a persistently insoluble problem: no matter how often he stepped up in the world, he was immediately treated to a view one step above that. And to a certain kind of personality, a fundamentally insecure personality like Barry's, being one step down from anywhere—or in this case, anyone—was an unacceptable breach of the natural order.

And who, in particular, did Barry see on the next step, catalyzing his insecurity? Undoubtedly it was Seattle Bill, the mightiest information-age magnate of all. The specter of Bill and his billions hung over Barry like a cloud, its shadow arousing such feelings of envy and inadequacy as to drive him wild.

And drive him it did, this stolen limelight. He thought of little else but the chariot that must sooner or later present itself, shining and ready, hitched to the twin steeds of technology and capital, ready to propel him to the promised land of unexploited market share.

He would WHIP the horses.

MANAGING FOR TOTAL CHAOS

DESPITE HER apprehension, Liz was disarmed by Paul's easy manner and sympathetic personality. Editing his white papers had also proved to be surprisingly without hazard; he had a firm grasp of the written word and good instincts for creating organized, coherent documents. They hadn't required much work at all, which was a welcome change.

His professional demeanor was out of the ordinary, as well. Though he brought the same pride and attention to detail as did other engineers, he didn't seem as highly invested in being an expert, or in being right all the time. In particular, he seemed to be aware of—and to actually welcome—Liz's point of view. Finding such cooperation in an engineer was a minor miracle in itself.

And he seemed to care about words. His mechanics were

solid—he actually diagrammed one of his sentences for clarification—and he gave an unusual degree of consideration to
tone. He was a chimera: a literate techie.

Which was why Liz was not unhappy to find both she and
Paul had arrived a few minutes early for Barry's weekly
WHIP status meeting. They took chairs across from each
other at the conference room's long table, and Liz took the
opportunity to express her gratitude for Paul's work:

"I can't tell you how much of a pleasure it was to edit
your writing," she commented. "It was all pretty clear and
balanced. Well thought-out, and really gets the WHIP vision
across without getting overly wrapped up in detail. Moved
nicely, too."

"Thanks, but don't let it get around," he said with a grin.
"It'll hurt my credibility with the guys in the lab."

"Don't worry," Liz assured him with a smile. "Your
secret's safe with me. You *do* seem a little out of place,
though."

"Well, I wasn't always a nerd. I started out as a liberal-
arts type in college—though I've aggressively concealed this
on my résumé. Hiring managers don't like it. Nontechnical
outside interests. Bad sign."

Liz's curiosity was provoked. "What did you study?"

"Journalism, mostly. Dalliances with English lit, creative
writing, philosophy. It was all a cover for my naïve dream of
becoming a novelist and winning a National Book award.
Silly me."

"Not silly. I'm impressed."

Paul seemed to become a little self-conscious about this inadvertent self-exposition. "But enough about me . . . ," he deflected. Then, continuing with a theatrically self-important grin, "What do *you* think of me?"

"Oscar Wilde. I love that line."

"Me too. I wish I'd said it."

"Oh, you will, Paul, you will."

He blushed a little, and twinkled.

Liz twinkled back. And, despite her weeks of adverse conditioning to engineers, she found herself feeling ever-so-slightly intrigued.

The usual crowd began to gather in the conference room. Paul and Liz retreated from their conversation and concentrated on meeting points and Filofaxes.

Barry was the last to enter, carrying a laser pointer in one hand and a palm computer in the other. Usually he sat down for a minute or two and traded a few shots with his lieutenants, but on this particular morning he burned with righteous fire. He jumped up to the head of the room and began scribbling on the whiteboard: WHIP MANAGEMENT OBJECTIVES, in red, double underlined.

"Good morning," Barry intoned, with a gravity Liz found immediately suspect. "I've been doing some strategic planning for our project directives, with the benefit of some outside perspectives." He dropped the name of a well-

known, flamboyant management guru who was currently
inhabiting a slot on *The New York Times* business bestseller
list.

The room's attention sharpened. Barry paused dramatically, and embarked on a rambling diatribe about the "New
Economy" and WHIP's role in its vanguard.

"I expect the WHIP project team to embody the qualities
of the New Organization: provide value, embrace the
radical technology edge, exist in a state of continuous innovation, and manage for historical change. Tera is a market
leader, and we're changing the paradigm for the New
Economy. We're a matrix organization, and the matrix
organization is results-oriented. It depends on trust, communications, teamwork—there's no 'I' in 'Team'—and
giving one hundred and ten percent."

It was clear Barry had made a recent trip to the well of corporate inspiration, as he did from time to time. Barry's pleasure
in bingeing on the latest management hype was exceeded only
by the pleasure he took in disgorging it upon the troops. Amazingly, Liz noted, everyone seemed to enjoy it.

Everyone but her. The tortured language, trendy catch-
phrases and pointless neologisms always made her cringe. But
today Barry was filled with the Holy Spirit; sitting through
this meeting was going to be torture.

Barry wrote the phrase THRIVING ON CHAOS on the
whiteboard—this time in blue, circled several times—and

turned back to his enraptured audience. Liz braced for another fusillade.

"Our spontaneous organic coordination will allow us to create cross-functional teams to implement our vertical integration with the leading edge of cross-networked, knowledge-based enterprise. Thriving on competence is our core quality—we're managing for total chaos."

Barry beamed triumphantly, unaware of the slip. Liz felt like screaming. She bit her lip as a precaution.

Then, from across the table, came a barely audible sigh. Searching for its source, she found Paul Armstrong, elbow on the table, chin on palm.

She passed him a tentative, furtive glance. Discreetly he looked back, and momentarily crossed his eyes, a covert expression of exasperation.

Liz experienced a sudden sensation of relief; she wasn't alone. At least one other person was choking on the smoke. Paul had vindicated her with a single breath.

She was starting to like him.

PROGRAMMING IN VAMPIRE MODE

THE HACK WAS on. Steve had been deep into it for most of three days. A pile of pizza boxes and two cases worth of empty cola cans bore silent witness. He'd disconnected the phone and ignored the messages as they noiselessly accrued on the answering machine.

Psychrist had furnished him with a specimen of the hardware that would drive some of the "actors" in his "installation." Steve recognized it as an old 80386 motherboard—practically free these days—grafted to a small radio transceiver.

Steve was not privy to the specific details of his upcoming installation, but Psychrist suggested the performance would involve a number of roving, autonomous agents in wireless contact with a master computer host. Each agent would have a unique address and would receive instructions from the master: forward, back, left, and right.

The master host, presumably, coordinated the agents' movements on a higher level. But Steve wasn't supposed to know about that; his task was to create a wireless communications program and burn it into the boot PROMs on the motherboard.

His curiosity was killing him. Psychrist's performances were something of a legend in the Bay Area. Aside from being artistically significant and loaded with a sort of cyber-bohemian technical angst, something always got spectacularly burned, blown up, shredded, or crushed beneath impossibly heavy objects. Steve hoped that if he finished his piece quickly, Psychrist would confide in him how the whole thing was going to work.

He briefly considered adapting some old network code he had hanging around, but thought better of it. This one was for art's sake; he would do it from scratch. He put Mingus on the stereo.

Conventional wisdom dictated that before you wrote a single line, you needed a design. Tie-wearing, pocket-protected systems analysts in respected industrial computing shops insisted on it. They had all sorts of officially sanctioned, right-headed methods to facilitate the process: flow charts, dataflow diagrams, Nasi-Schneiderman diagrams, pseudocode, a thousand different ways to create a picture of what you intended to build.

The true hacker thumbed his nose at each and every one of them. And like a true hacker, Steve had started by thumping down the cursor in the editor and riffing. It was all jazz to him. He could feel the machine sing through his fingers. He could hear the megahertz whine of the chips turning over. He could see the stack in his mind, hundreds of instructions deep. Pictures were for weenies. Homey don't need no map.

The first day he built a rudimentary device-driver; it was kind of like a backbeat. Day two he built some routines for data storage and abstraction; that was the bass line. Today he had rounded out the rhythm section with a compact, packet-based communication protocol handler. Now he was finishing up with the cool, wailing harmonies of the top-level control loops.

Programming was a little like dreaming; you conjured up an imaginary machine, piece by piece, and fit the pieces together. Some of them were familiar—similar to things you'd built before, with common themes that seemed to pop up in any project—and some of them were unique to the beast at hand. But you teased them up out of nothing, like a dream.

Loops that revolved. *Ifs* and *elses* that forked and cascaded. Imaginary Rolodexes filled with numbers, or tiny words, or addresses of other Rolodexes. Traps, exception handlers, streams of data. Signals and semaphores, one function hailing another across the void. Those were the things you called out of the darkness to fabricate the intricate workings of the finite state machine.

A computer program exists in a nether region between real and imaginary. On one hand, it absolutely obeys the laws of cause-and-effect; build it carelessly, or make a stupid mistake, and the gears will grind together and it will fail, dying in its tracks. On the other hand, it is something you'll never be able to see or touch. You might observe its side effects on a monitor or in some other output device. You might infer its motion from its uncompiled source code. You might track its position with a debugger. But when it runs, its wheels turn in another dimension, a world apart, a separate reality etched in invisibly tiny pathways on fused silicates. It conducts an intensely private life of its own in some abstract parallel universe. You have to have faith it is real.

Sometimes you get lost in the details. You obsess over every moving part. You develop paranoid fantasies about all the ways that failure could emerge from the interlocking pieces. You become suspicious of yourself. You become hard on yourself. Your good intentions are insufficient to success. Nothing short of absolute rigor and perfect vigilance will suffice. The machine is unforgiving; you cannot forgive yourself.

You take many opportunities to check your assumptions. You write scaffolding functions—which you will later discard—to check your control loops and the state of your data. You consult them regularly to make sure your creation hasn't strayed from the spec.

Sometimes it seems anything that can go wrong does go wrong; reversals abound. At other times you seem invincible—you write a dozen hairy functions, you hold your breath and brace for trouble, but they compile without errors and run bug-free. Those are the times it's hardest to believe. It's enough to make you superstitious. A plastic action figure—Blue Power Ranger—was Steve's lucky charm. He'd never admit it, though.

He was nearly done. Little by little he'd tugged his brainchild out of the mist, and now it had a life of its own—a personality, almost, with its own strengths, weaknesses, quirks.

And nobody would ever know it as well as Steve did. Ever. The program was his in a way very few things could ever be, like a drawing from his own hand. There wasn't an in-line comment in sight, but it had a mark on it. It howled his name in the void.

The project had cycled Steve into vampire mode; the sun was coming up—time to sleep.

WHERE ELITE GEEKS MEET
TO EAT—AND RUN

HIGH NOON at Bistro Élan, and the burghers of the Silicon Valley were lunching to win. The bistro was more than just a restaurant; it was a bona fide strategic dining opportunity. They dined with the same high-stakes, pressurized intensity of the opening hours of an IPO. Executives, managers, and eccentric-looking technical brahmins talked in urgent staccato acronyms while wolfing down radicchio and foie gras. Cell phones and Palm Pilots were everywhere.

The bistro was arranged like many au courant California eateries: open kitchen, dining at the counter—for those who wanted a front-row seat on the culinary action—and a surrounding room of tables arranged in quirky and asymmetric fashion. The décor was stylishly understated, but the action in the kitchen was furious. Three chefs juggled their prepara-

tions without speaking, their intense concentration unbroken
by the clamor of the activity in the dining room. Flames periodically erupted from the grill, fiery homages to Escoffier.
Oversized plates, brimming with the latest in California
cuisine's savory thrills, floated from the kitchen on waiters'
trays, tantalizing smells tracing their passage.

In one corner, a well-known industry chieftain—fresh
from the wrong side of a corporate merger, but trailing a
golden parachute—gave dictation to a posse of infotech
journalists. In another, a project team from Sun Mi-
crosystems celebrated this week's once-in-a-lifetime techno-
logical achievement with the canonical victory lunch.
Judging by the wreckage of tableware and the empty wine
bottles, Sun was picking up the tab. The team's project
manager had hoisted himself halfway out of his chair, delivering an undoubtedly inspirational paean to excellence,
teamwork, and synergy, but most of his smartly dressed,
perfectly coifed crew couldn't hear him through the ambient
din of the bistro. They smiled and nodded intensely nevertheless; it was important to project that quality of super-
focused enthusiasm, even when the signal-to-noise ratio approached zero.

Laurel stood in her smartly starched white apron and
attempted to recite the plats du jour to a table of frantically
gesturing technology zealots. They could barely contain their
techie tent-revival long enough for her to finish.

"Today we have jumbo Day Boat scallops in a ginger-chive cream. Also we have the confit of duck with garlic-mashed navy beans, chanterelles, and a pomegranate reduction. Very delicious, I recommend it. Last but not least, California mussels in a chive saffron broth with *pommes frites*."

"Great, great," the most animated of them hurried her along, "I'd like the mussels. But can I substitute french fries for the *whadayacallit?*"

Laurel didn't miss a beat. "Absolutely, sir," she assured him.

"And could you see that we get our food in a hurry? We've got a meeting in Cupertino at one."

"I'll do my best."

They were all like that, Laurel reflected, these hyperkinetic infotech types—food culture was largely wasted on them. In one of the world's most fertile culinary regions, only a micro-climate away from the Napa Valley and the homeland of nou-velle cuisine's patron saint Alice Waters, the digerati couldn't be bothered to spend an extra twenty minutes to savor the ex-perience. After all, in the land of rapid and relentless inno-vation, a leisurely lunch might mean the difference between profitability and Chapter Eleven.

When the doors had closed for the afternoon, Laurel sat at the counter folding napkins with Veronique, her comrade-in-arms throughout the lunch rush. Vero was French. Mid-twenties, seized by wanderlust, she had come to California to see San Francisco and exercise her formidable cooking talents. She had loved the Golden Gate, but waiting tables at the bistro was as close as she might come to a commercial kitchen, at least without a work visa. But the owner was willing to risk Vero's tenure on the wait staff; she was—in the lexicon of legions of young Frenchmen migrating to the Silicon Valley gold rush—*une grosse nana.* "A total babe," roughly translated. Whatever the relative proportions of young, male French software entrepreneurs in the Valley, Vero guaranteed they would be over-represented in the bistro's clientele.

Laurel shared her observations on the futility of serving fine food to time-starved careerists. Vero leaped to validate in her accented English. "Oh, yes! Every-sing is always rush, rush, rush—there is no time for enjoying. *Quel dommage.* A waste. If only they can stop to—? . . . Smell these roses. But what can you do? They have money, but no time to enjoy."

"I am thinking," she said, giving Laurel a sidelong, conspiratorial look, "to start a little business where I make the food and bring it to these kind of people. They can have the good food without spending the time to go out. Maybe at home, maybe at work. I can create a . . . mobile cuisine. Maybe they can take time to enjoy it more."

"Great idea," Laurel replied. Then, bouncing up in her seat with enthusiasm, "You could call it 'Guerrilla Gourmet.'"

"Yes, yes," Vero piped, green eyes flashing. "'Guerrilla Gourmet—*prêt à manger'!* It will be wonderful! You should come and help me. You are too good for the bistro. This will be much more fun."

Laurel didn't think of herself as someone with entrepreneurial inclinations, but she found the idea strangely appealing. "Oh, let's do it," she agreed. "It'll be fun. We'll finish folding these and then go out and conquer the world with our moveable feast!" Funny thing was, she actually believed herself.

She found herself smiling a big smile. Self-determination always cheered her up.

LOOKING FOR A GAL WHO'S QUICK
WITH A VAPORIZER

IT WAS LUNCHTIME at TeraMemory headquarters, and a swarm of harried hirelings gathered for a compressed lunch hour. Twenty minutes was the standard allowance for dining-related nonproductivity, though some might take longer if they brought along a laptop, or multiplexed a project meeting at one of the larger, expensively Swedish-looking tables in the cafeteria.

Paul sat down at a table with some other guys from the lab. Collectively, their trays suggested a United Nations summit meeting. Each engineer had chosen a different entrée from some far-flung corner of the globe, thanks to the hyper-aggressive diversity of the TeraMemory corporate kitchen.

A number of short-order stations offered a dizzying variety of exotic foods. There was a Chinese section, woks a-flaming, serving chow fun and dim sum. There was a Japanese counter with teriyakis and sushi. There was food from Latin America—tacos, empanadas, and overstuffed, football-sized burritos. The Indian subcontinent landed some punches with a selection of curries, nan, and vindaloos. An American-style grill served burgers and fries mostly to the sales force, who tended toward the straight-and-narrow; they were used to dining on the road while making sales calls in Denver and Peoria. Engineer-fare, in all its wild ethnic gyration, tended to induce a sort of gustatory vertigo in the suit-wearing road-warriors.

Yet, there was something joyless about this luncheon extravaganza. It was not staged for the enjoyment of Tera's employees, exactly. There was an unmistakable whiff of corporate conniving: *Iron Chef* meets human resources, a not-so-subtle ruse to keep engineering talent onsite. The surrounding environs—Mountain View and Palo Alto especially—were also rich with dining options in every imaginable regional variation. Ordinary cafeteria fare simply couldn't compete. In the interest of luring engineers to TeraMemory—and keeping them within walking distance of their cubicles—a sort of culinary arms race had developed.

Paul munched on a potsticker and sparred with his fellow engineers. For once, their lunchroom conversation wasn't technical, nor did it revolve around the web, newsgroups, or get-rich-quick e-commerce schemes. Roger—a release engineer who worked in the cubicle next to Paul—had made himself the focus of interest by unwisely mentioning he had recently been out on a date.

Among the predominantly heterosexual male practitioners of software engineering, dating was followed with keen interest and curiosity. It was—like being hit by a meteorite or taking a vacation—a mostly hypothetical activity for the technical lions of the Silicon Valley. Unlike the cafeteria, the dating scene was not a cornucopia.

It certainly wasn't going well for Roger. The others pressed him for details in that casual, covertly urgent way that fishermen talk about bait.

"I took her to Gordon Biersch," Roger recounted dryly, contemplating a stray sprig of cilantro. "There was a salsa band. She wanted to dance."

The others laughed as they might at a comical misfortune. Nipaul, the optimization specialist from Delhi, couldn't resist a jab. "Don't tell me you actually cut a rug on the first date?"

Embarrassed, Roger began to clam up. Mitch, the C++ programmer from MIT, tried to sustain the inquisition's momentum with a more discreet approach: "Where did you meet her? How did you get her number?"

Another shot from Nipaul: "Yeah . . . I can't imagine you actually calling somebody up."

Mitch kicked him under the table.

"Well . . . I didn't," Roger confessed. "I'd been admiring her from afar for months . . . she's the receptionist at my dentist's office. When she called to remind me about my last appointment, well . . . You *know* how hard it is to meet somebody outside your vertical, so I just winged it and asked her out on the phone. Figured I could just change dentists if she turned me down. Surprised the hell out of me when she said yes."

"Oh, you're so smooth," Nipaul mocked. "You waited for *her* to call *you*. You're a complete failure as a pick-up artist, you know."

"Yeah, well, it didn't really work out so well. She was into Rolfing and macrobiotic food and past lives and other random stuff like that. I could tell that was going to be a problem. And when I ordered carpaccio, she looked at me like I'd killed somebody.

"It was all over by the third course. I told her she should loosen up, but it had quite the opposite effect."

Roger wanted to wrap up his unfortunate exposition, and looked for a way out of the spotlight. He directed it toward Aaron, the extravagantly pierced systems administrator from Austin. "So, Double-A-man, when was the last time you had a date?"

"Last year, I think," he speculated, fingering the silver rings through his eyebrow. "Gal from 24-hour Nautilus. She was divorced, but her ex kept stalking her. Once he appeared out of nowhere and sat down with us at the movies. It was like *Friday the 13th.* I couldn't handle it, so I bailed."

Richard the database consultant was the next to speak up.

"Oh, man, meeting women is such a hassle." He began a litany of grievances, counting them off on his fingers. "Number one, they're impossible to meet. Number two, even when the laws of probability are temporarily suspended and you *do* get somebody's number, finding the time is impossible. Three, if you actually get something going with somebody, your life becomes way more complicated. It takes way too many cycles away from your vertical; you can't even *think* about pulling an all-nighter on a deadline. And four, women make you completely nuts. Completely nonlinear. Small stuff just sets 'em off, like forgetting Valentine's Day. Totally nondeterministic. Nipaul, how about if your family adopts me? Arranged marriage is looking better and better."

Nipaul shot back. "Oh, I think you *would* look sexy in a sari . . ."

When the laughter tailed off, Mitch offered his variation of the lament. "I have no idea how I'd go about finding a date. I mean, even if I could meet a woman in a bar, I couldn't find the time to pursue it. I was in the stocks past nine most days last week. And rocket scientist here"—he poked at Paul—"has been pulling weekend cubicle duty, I hear."

Paul covered his eyes in a gesture of shame. "Yeah, it's true. All for the greater glory of TeraMemory." He wasn't about to jump into this conversation. His last date had been in the Pleistocene.

"So that leaves work," Mitch continued. "And I don't know about you, but I haven't noticed any women in our group. And I *would* notice. And I'm not going to resort to those personals ads in the San José *Metro*," he shuddered. "Way too creepy. 'SWF Stanford grad triathlete seeks SWM with lower body fat than hers. Must drive Range Rover . . .'"

"So, what are you looking for in a woman?" Aaron asked Mitch, a noodle dangling from the corner of his mouth.

"Well . . . cute, twenty-five years old, not too needy, no baggage, has a career of her own . . ."

". . . nice enclosure, boots quickly, no performance bottle-necks, no 'issues' that can't be resolved by power-cycling the unit . . . ," Nipaul interjected.

Randall, the long-haired, introverted Perl-hacker who was always a step behind any nontechnical conversation, perked up. "Oh, I get it . . . You're describing your work-station, dude . . . or that cyber-chick heroine in *Tomb Raider.*"

Mitch brightened, familiar with the improbably busty, computer-generated star of the popular and violent CD-ROM adventure game. "Hey, you're right: loves adventure, does gymnastic back-flips at the first sign of trouble, quick on the draw with a vaporizer . . . yep, she's the one for me."

They all laughed in a hearty way that suggested more dis-tance from the topic than there actually was. Loneliness did that to you.

But unlike Mitch's, Paul's idea of the perfect partner had, of late, been poignantly closer to the attainable. He had resolved to figure out a way to spend some non-work-related time with Liz Toulouse. While he was still young.

WIZARDS WITH HARVARD
DEGREES AND $4,000 SUITS

HE MIGHT HAVE been the official poster-boy for free enterprise if the exaggerated cleft in his chin hadn't so strongly suggested a plush, country-club version of Popeye. Andrew Lucre projected his best blue-eyed Harvard Business School potency across the vast expanse of Barry's desk. Barry turned the pages of a glossy, spiral-bound folio, admiring the colorful pie charts and caressing his chin with intent.

"Of course, you could finance the technology offering yourself," the nattily dressed management consultant intoned, "but Barry, you and I both know there's a certain cachet to venture capital these days. Venture money creates buzz. Venture partners tend to generate attention for a technology undertaking. And that's good—you want to have a certain number of sharks in the water. It lets the other fish know there's meat.

"And despite its enormous size, TeraMemory is still a growing business. Growing businesses need cash flow. Bringing in outside money will leave you free to grow Tera as fast as you want—without having to worry about feeding the new baby. A guy like you doesn't need those kinds of limits."

Andrew had been talking, of course, about WHIP. The prototypes were nearly complete. The official rollout demo was scheduled for Comdex, a scant five weeks away. This would be followed, if everything went as planned, by the spin-off of WHIP Technologies and a splashy IPO.

Ever since the Silicon Valley had established itself as the main destination of the global capitalist, the various and sundry Masters of the Universe had rushed in, hoping to establish beachheads on the shores of digital commerce. Harvard Business School had flung a chunk of its campus twenty-five hundred miles from the banks of the Charles River to the shores of the San Francisco Bay. This brazen poaching so far from their ancestral territory did not strike them as hubris—or out-of-the-ordinary, even. Wherever money was being made hand-over-fist, they claimed home ground.

It was this kind of arrogance that caused them to be despised in certain quarters, especially throughout Silicon

Valley, where many savvy technology players considered them to be far outside their depth. But the HBS reputation of yesteryear still persisted in some uninformed pockets of the collective business mind, and earned them an undeservedly high esteem.

This was especially true among newly minted technical moguls like Barry. Many nerds, with their signature lack of academic pedigree, old-boy connections, and self esteem, were vulnerable to stroking by Ivy League MBAs in Wall Street drag. Never mind that MBAs from Stanford or MIT—schools with engineering intellectual capital Harvard could only dream of—were far better adapted to the slippery world of high technology. When the anxious captains of Silicon Valley industry piloted their companies through treacherous waters, they often retained a pinstriped consultant to mop their fevered brows. In this capacity, Harvard graduates still projected the best front.

The problem was, their clients' ships seemed to run aground as often as anybody else's. Though companies arrived almost daily in the promised land of IPO, the route was ever-changing. The gods of digital commerce were infinitely perverse. Their revelries guaranteed that even the most rigorous of business plans could be blindsided by unanticipated industry gyrations. They took special pains to ensure the naïve and the clueless regularly found themselves in fortune's path, becoming moguls overnight. Today's hot new computer was tomorrow's boat anchor. Not just companies, but whole industries could arise overnight, or sink noiselessly in a moment. Who could even remember those disappeared darlings of yesterday? Push technology. Artificial intelligence. Virtual reality. Vanished.

Silicon Valley wasn't just a jungle; at least the jungle had rules. There were no discernible rules here. It was a fast-forward speedball of blindfolded corporate knife-fighting and high-stakes roulette. The carnage was tremendous, but newcomers were not discouraged; the many successes formed a comforting patina on the compost heap of ruined and gutted companies rotting in the high noon of the Valley boomtown.

In an industry where observable cause-and-effect was in chronically short supply, HBS grads practiced a kind of sympathetic magic. On the surface they looked and talked and smelled like profit, wearing four-thousand-dollar suits and tossing out terms like "incremental innovation" and "added value." But a closer inspection suggested that any alleged connection to their client's success was difficult to distinguish from a chance association. If there was a genius to it, it was that these manicured management consultants were nimble enough to move on well before their clients cratered.

But Barry's mind was unoccupied by such misgivings. He concentrated on the multicolored revenue projections of the consultant's folio. Pretty colors. Pretty money. Pretty WHIP.

Still, something troubled him. He ventured to raise a control issue, though it might ruin the mood.

"I've heard the stories, Andy. Sooner or later the venture guys always want to get their hands into things. And I'm not about to let any bean counter tell me how to run my technology."

Andrew showed a row of perfectly aligned teeth. "In thinly financed IPOs there's always a concern about venture money stepping in and taking over, but you don't have to worry about it. Collateralized against your Tera stock, we can structure the deal so you'll never lose your majority interest. As long as Tera's share price holds out, you'll be on top—and you and I both know Tera's got a long way to run. The sky's the limit, as far as I can see.

"You're the king of the world, Barry. You're going to have this Valley sewn up. Who knows where you'll go from there. No boundaries."

"No boundaries," Barry repeated. He liked the sound of that.

THE WOMEN'S LOCKER ROOM GAME—DECATHLON OF THE FLESH

"GOD, YOU'RE dating Barry D.? Wow, I dated him like ten years ago—when did the first Saab turbo come out? It was right around the time I got my first convertible on lease."

Candy listened keenly, slipping on her neon-green running tights as her companion—Leslie, a marketing executive from a nonrival tech firm—peeled off her own Victoria's Secret battle gear and continued her kiss-and-tell.

"He was in sales for Amdahl then. But then he went to AMD, and then that start-up that flamed out. The rest is history—TeraMemory has just been a rocket.

"I even interviewed at TeraMemory right after they started up, but I ended up at Cadence instead. Better stock options, or so I thought. Boy, if I had only known what I know now. A Tera recruiter hit me up last year, but I figured it's too late in the game for that. I missed the window—they don't bonus the way they used to, and the quarterly trips to Hawaii? That went out about five quarters ago."

Their conversation was still relatively tame, given the context. The women's locker room of the Decathlon Club was every Silicon Valley career guy's nightmare: an estrogen-loaded, free-fire gossip zone, hermetically sealed from the boys' network. Fortunately, few of them had any idea of what went on in there. It would definitely keep them awake at night, knowing that their careers—and their masculinity—were regularly deconstructed by the wrecking ball of feminine scrutiny.

Nearly all Silicon Valley companies gave their management employees free—or nearly free—Decathlon memberships. This was not motivated by generosity; the corporate officers were well aware that—far from being an actual opportunity for health, recreation, and stress reduction—time spent at the Decathlon was a thinly veiled continuation of life at the office. It was yet another ploy to maximize management's productivity.

It worked. Strategic alliances were forged between adjacent StairMasters. Lucrative connections were made in the pool. Spandex-clad VPs were lured from one company to another, straining all the while on Cybex machines.

And—at least in the women's locker—the dish was dished. Candy's exchange with her associate was much more than idle chat—she was on a fishing expedition. Ever since Barry had begun launching salvos of propositions in her direction, Candy had been evaluating the strategic possibilities of such a liaison. She continued her exploration while lacing up her running shoes.

"Oh, really? I didn't know you two knew each other," she lied, feigning surprise. "I just came to TeraMemory last year—VP sales, western region."

"Oh, very nice," Leslie congratulated, then took the offensive. "Were you in a relationship with B.D. before?"

Ever conscious of the velocity of rumor, Candy effected a little spin-control. "Oh, god no. Not that there's much of a relationship now, even," she commented. "We've only been out a few times." Then, jousting back, she planted a barb: "Besides, I think he's a little old for me. And I'm determined not to be one of those chicks who does every uber-goober in sight. Like that gal in marketing over at WebTV who gets with every—and I do mean *every*—nerd of the moment. People have to follow her conquests with an org chart, like *bing-bing-bing.*"

Leslie beveled a sidelong, knowing look. "Oh, I know. I think I even know who you're talking about. There are a few women like that around—gung-ho gals who use everything in the toolbox. They call them piranha ladies, the ones who sleep with all the heavies—Ellison, Jobs, Sonsini.

"They all have accounts at Tiffany and Tom Wing—you know, over at Stanford Mall? So the geek du jour—who is, like, by definition style-challenged—can drop by and get her what she wants. Really personal and spontaneous, you know?" She adjusted her jog bra and rolled her eyes. "It's like a never-ending wedding registry, but with hard project deadlines and deliverables. By the third date, it's tennis-bracelet time or no-go."

Cautionary tales aside, Candy decided she was satisfied with her own projection of distance and control over the situation with Barry. "Well, I think I've got B.D's number, anyway," she said assuredly.

But then Leslie pulled out the rug.

"Of course, you do know he's married, right? That's the rumor, anyway. Nobody's ever met her, but the story is that he's been trying to shake her forever. I didn't find out about it until I'd been seeing him for eight months. At which point I un-speed-dialed him—home, cell, and office.

"Besides, everyone says he's gotten mean in the last few years. And really aggressive—every woman at Tera who's ever been alone with the guy has a story to tell. And they all end up getting fired." Leslie wrinkled her face into a mask of discretion, pitching her words low. "Even if they *do* go along with it. It just takes a little longer that way."

Candy tensed, and rose to her feet a little unsteadily, blood pounding in her ears. She managed to pass off her wooziness as a vanity mirror-check, then moved to withdraw from the dialogue.

"Well, I'll see you later, then. I have a date with a treadmill."

Leslie, ever the games-woman, put her stamp on things. "Let's hope it's single," she shot back with a perfect, toothy smile.

"NO BOUNDARIES"
FOR BARRY'S LIBIDO

BARRY'S BENEDICTION from the Harvard management consultant left him nearly incoherent with self-satisfaction. It coursed through him like a hormone, making his limbs taught with a muscular vainglory. Every cell in his body deeply admired and respected every other cell.

WHIP was shaping up better than he had dared to hope. He could feel the wave of market opportunity moving in from the depths, mounting with every moment until the day he rode it to victory, the day that Seattle Bill would kiss his ring, confirming Barry's historical triumph as Mogul Maximus. None could stand in his way. None would resist his advance.

It was in this state of delirious bovarism that he found Liz
in his office, depositing a stack of glossy marketing tracts on
his desk. She turned to greet him.

"I've got some first drafts of the Comdex WHIP technology packets ready for your review, when you have the
time," she said smartly.

Maybe a little too smartly at that. She didn't recognize
herself these days, she reflected. She was sounding so awfully
professional and mechanical. She softened a little, and tried
for a more human tone.

"How'd the meeting go? Did you whip those management consulting boys into shape?"

It had been three months since Liz had come up to work
for Barry, and she was finally beginning to ease up in his
presence. Though she could never tell for sure whether his
interest in her was entirely professional, lately she had been
awarding him benefit of the doubt. Scary as Barry could be,
she had been trying to treat him more humanely—as a peer
or colleague, sometimes even venturing a casual informality
or so. After all, it was difficult not to develop a little human
interest in your coworkers—even a high-strung, volatile, and
demanding coworker like Barry.

"You're witnessing the start of something big," Barry
gleamed, standing in the doorway. "Very big. I'm feeling like
celebrating."

Liz decided to float another informality; Barry's enthusiasm seemed to suggest it.

"Good for you, boss-man. You've been working really hard on this." She actually was, to her mild surprise, genuinely happy for him. After a day of corporate drudgery, it was good anyone was in such high spirits, even Barry.

Liz always tried to end her work days on a good note, and this seemed her cue. "Well, I was just about to call it a day," she said. "I've got a yoga class at seven-thirty." She turned to leave.

He spoke as she passed him in the doorway. "Have dinner with me tonight."

She froze. Liz couldn't believe she was hearing what she was hearing.

"What was that?" she said timidly.

"Dinner. You, me. Tonight. Think of it as an intimate corporate retreat." He smiled like a rottweiler.

"That would be a bad idea, I think. No, thank you. It would be unprof . . ."

Suddenly Liz found Barry's tongue rooting around in her mouth like some slick, frenetic ferret. As it reared up in preparation for an assault on her tonsils, Liz recoiled, astonished, but Barry pinned her for the moment against the jamb.

"Oh, come on—I'm King of the World. Don't tell me you don't like it."

Liz pushed him away. "No, no, Mr. Dominic. This is a professional relationship. There are certain proprieties . . ." She teetered on the edge of tears. "There are boundaries."

"No boundaries," Barry leered, then reached for Liz on the high and low.

Which left him somewhat vulnerable in the middle. Liz cocked an elbow and checked him stiffly in the mid-drift. It was the very last thing he'd been expecting; Barry's ardor quickly dissipated as he listed to one side, gasping for air.

Time for a new career, Liz thought to herself, and exited down the hallway at a dead run. She careened around the corner into her office. Standing over her desk, she leaned on her hands for a few moments, catching her breath.

Just as she had begun to feel comfortable in this job . . . She should have known. Trusting a man like Barry was stupid; she should have listened to her instincts. And now she knew where this was going, which was exactly nowhere.

Once again, she found herself packing up on the run. She dumped the remainder of the Comdex presentations from the Kinko's box and hastily filled it with her personal things: A coffee cup, a half-dozen power bars, her cat Angus in his picture frame, a mouse pad, a gel-filled wrist rest, a thesaurus.

She thought she heard Barry coming down the hallway. She threw her purse in the box, grabbed it with both arms, and made a break for the elevator.

Paul stood in the lobby waiting for the Caltrain shuttle. Bay area commuter rail—awkward and clunky as it was— beat the sixty minutes of stop-and-go it would take him to drive the twenty-two miles home.

He absentmindedly stared at the bank of elevators. Three doors, like the old *Let's Make a Deal* show. He imagined the prizes that might wait behind each: a washer-dryer combo, a new car, Turtle Wax.

He hadn't picked yet, but door number two opened anyway. It was a lovely woman, holding a box. But it wasn't Carol Merrill. It was Liz Toulouse. He smiled, glad to see her. He liked this game show. She stepped out of the elevator. He stepped forward to greet her.

Something was wrong. Liz was making a beeline for the parking lot door. She didn't seem to see him. And the box she carried resembled the classic cardboard "escape pod" of personal effects of the newly terminated. There were tears running down her cheeks. He ran after her.

He caught up with her in the parking lot.

"Liz, Liz, what's wrong? Are you all right?"

She turned and looked at him through watery eyes, red with indignation. "Yes. I'm fine. I've got to go."

Paul was suspicious. "Are you sure? You definitely don't seem like the peppy Liz Toulouse we've all come to know and love." They had worked together on and off these few months, and despite Paul's little crush on Liz, he'd tried to keep things professional. Liz was clearly in the middle of some kind of personal crisis, and he wanted to help. But he was unsure about how much he could gracefully intrude. He could only look at her a little pleadingly, and tap her elbow.

Liz managed a brief smile. "Yes. Really. It was nice

working with you." She wrinkled her eyebrows up in a heap. "Please, I need to go."

Mass transportation intervened. The shuttle pulled into the circle with its usual blast of the horn. He would need to hurry if he was to make his train. Helpless, he watched her walk away for a few moments, then ran the other way.

LIZ REGROUPS AT THE CHATEAU

LIZ AND LAUREL took their breakfast al fresco on the postage-stamp patio of their cottage on the edge of the barrio. They drank coffee and ate cereal. Nearby, Angus stalked a moth, lashing his tail righteously.

Liz reacquainted herself with the midmorning sun. She hadn't seen much of it during her brief career at TeraMemory, a career which—in the light of day following Liz's executive mauling—was most definitely finished this time. The two women rehashed the grizzly scene that had played out in Barry's office the previous day.

Laurel pressed for details. "Was there anyone else around? Did anybody see?"

"No, no one. It only lasted a minute. And it was after six. The receptionist had already gone home," Liz lamented. "It's such an outrage. I mean . . . I know I'm not really cut out for high-tech, and I wasn't going to work there forever . . ."

Laurel completed the thought, speaking around a mouthful of granola. ". . . But it would have been nice to leave on your own terms. It's not fair that you're the one who has to go because some testosterone-poisoned megalomaniac can't get it together enough to recognize obvious personal boundaries. It's *worse* than getting fired."

Liz made a cruel smile. "Oh, the irony. Remember a few months ago, when I came home, terrified he'd fire me? If *only* . . . I just wish I'd left after the exploding email incident, when my instincts told me to. God, this is such a wretched . . . comedy." She managed a halfhearted laugh in spite of herself.

"It's just the injustice of it all—in an unequal power relationship, when the guy steps over the line, it's the *woman* who has to leave. Like it's *her* fault. And now I'm unemployed." She pushed out her lower lip and made a mock-pathetic, Keane-child face.

Laurel responded with her own over-the-top gaze of tenderness and sympathy. "Oh, don't you go a-worrying, little Lizzie. A pal from the bistro and I are starting a little catering company, and we're going to need extra hands. You won't go homeless. And, anyway, we still have the chateau."

Château des Araignées—"Castle of Spiders"—was the name they had affectionately given the tiny, ancient, slightly bug-infested two-bedroom cottage they shared in Mountain View. In the age before monolithic computer companies roamed the Valley, the surrounding neighborhood had been home to miles of fruit orchards. Clusters of ramshackle micro-bungalows had been constructed to house the migrant labor that brought in the harvest. Fifty years later, these shacks were the only affordable rental alternative for people who didn't want to live in boxed-in, apartmental proximity to scores of engineers with implausibly large stereos.

Despite the bad insulation and unreliable plumbing, there was something comforting about these modest dwellings. They recalled a slower, more secure world which had been all but driven out by the progress of the information age. There were even a few derelict remnants of the orchards. Liz and Laurel nursed a struggling apricot tree that leaned out from a corner of their little yard.

Home ownership was, of course, completely out of the question. Even solidly employed techies making a hundred thousand a year couldn't pull it off. A two bedroom house on a quarter acre lot was out of reach, unless you had rich parents or won the stock-option lottery. Single, nontechnical women didn't stand much of a chance in a real estate market where, as Laurel once overheard a real estate agent at the bistro say between bites, "a million dollars buys you a tear-down."

All of this served to underscore the insecurity of Silicon Valley life. In a place where people changed jobs at a furious rate—even when they weren't being fired or sexually harassed—and the dominating technology-related industries were in constant flux, it was impossible to find a place you could personally—and financially—call your own. The result was a kind of bivouac mentality; the future was a big silicon question mark. Liz had even heard rumors that a local developer was bulldozing the fruit-picker's shacks in the name of "higher and better use." More plainly, high-density town houses.

Later that day, Liz kindled her courage and called Tera-Memory to arrange for the delivery of her final paycheck. Cassie, the VP of human resources, had apparently been primed for her call. Liz was unprepared for the gross injustice of the greeting. It took her breath away.

"Ms. Toulouse? Yes . . . Mr. Dominic informs me you've resigned. And right during the WHIP crunch. What a dirty trick," she said tartly.

STALKING THE WILD FRY'S
SALESPERSON

HIS PLASTIC NAME tag read, "Welcome to Fry's! I'm NOURZOY. How may I help you?" He eyed Steve nervously and bit his thumbnail.

"Yes, sir, a '9733b.' I'm sure we have that. Let me go check the stock room." The salesman fairly fled down the aisle in the direction of home stereo.

"Well, we won't see *him* again," Steve remarked dryly. "This guy doesn't know USB from LSD."

Steve and Paul stood in the solid state components aisle of the gigantic emporium. Fry's was still something of a mainstay of Silicon Valley life—but only barely. Once it had been the main depot for electronics and computer parts—aisle after aisle of transistors, chips, printed circuit boards, ham radio components, soldering equipment, oscilloscopes, all the provisions and necessities of hacker life. But as digital equipment

became more commonplace, so had Fry's. You still stood a reasonable chance of finding obscure electronic components, but
the stock—like the hacker ethic—was shrinking quickly. It
had been displaced by miles of audio equipment, shrink-
wrapped software, CDs, and home appliances.

A few features remained intact: a seemingly endless magazine rack with legendary concentrations on technology and
naked women, and a gauntlet of point-of-purchase impulse-
buys aimed directly at the uber-geek—highly caffeinated soft
drinks, emergency-orange Hostess marshmallow orbs, mace
dispensers, laser-pointer key chains.

But the new era had brought some Kafkaesque entertainments. Fry's salespeople, knowing themselves to be woefully
less well-informed about the merchandise than any customer,
aggressively evaded contact. The result was a game of cat-and-
mouse played out in the undergrowth of this dense retail
jungle, customers stalking salespeople.

In the unlikely event they were caught, they behaved like
prisoners of war, meeting customer's interrogations with elaborate obfuscation, misdirection, hedging, or outright lies. But
by far the most common response was "Sorry, this is my first
day."

Which was plausible, actually; Fry's was one of the
bottom rungs on the Silicon Valley employment ladder. It was
easy to grab, but nobody seemed to linger for long.

Steve got down on his knees, rooting through boxes of chip sets as Paul stood glumly in the aisle, hands in his pockets.

"Okay . . . here's a 68030 . . . here's a 21064 . . . here's a 6502—jeez, and it hasn't fossilized yet—ah! Here it is. *Ta-dahhh!*" He held up his find triumphantly. Paul smiled half-heartedly.

Steve registered his friend's general lack of enthusiasm. "What is it with you tonight? I thought the Thai food would cheer you up. It always worked before. Why have you gone off your feed?"

"Oh, nothing. Just thinking about somebody at work. Until recently, anyway. Worked, I mean . . . ," Paul's voice trailed off.

"You know, it's ugly to see you having problems with rudimentary sentence construction," Steve quipped. Then, with a dawning awareness, "Uh, this somebody wouldn't just happen to have an XX chromosome set, would they?"

Paul was staring off into space. Then, snapping back, mumbled, "Sorry . . . what was that?"

"Ah, the invincible Paul Armstrong with his superpowers in remission . . . all because of some mortal female. How the mighty have fallen."

Paul quickly changed the subject. "So, what are you working on these days that requires all this funky hardware?"

Steve gave him a surreptitious look. Then, in his best

Navy Seal briefing impersonation, "Classified. Black project. I could tell you, but then I'd have to *kee-yull* you."

"And here I was thinking you loved me."

"It's for an art project, sort of."

"What, *Rhapsody in solder? Fantasia in hexadecimal?*"

Steve decided to hint at his project. "Ever heard of a performance artist named Psychrist?"

Paul cocked his head. "Um, wasn't he in *Mondo 2000* a while back? Something about a remote-controlled, industrial welding robot grafted to a flamethrower? Didn't it go rogue and burn down some derelict warehouse in Amsterdam?"

Steve grinned. "Yeah. It was totally cool."

"Oh, man, you've fallen in with the black-clothes-and-pointy-shoes set, haven't you. What's on the menu of destruction this time?"

"That'd spoil the surprise. Why don't you come along and see? It'll be fun. I get to bring a guest, but Isabella Rosellini is out of town that weekend. You can be my date instead."

Paul sighed. "Thanks, but a high-tech demolition derby sounds a little too much like the evening commute on 101. I'll think I'll stay home."

NOURZOY never did come back.

Liz and Natasha lounged in the upholstered loge of the massive wooden sleigh, taking tea and eating Toll House cookies. The horses pulled through the windswept snow on 101, harness bells jangling. The road was empty but for them. On the horizon, the TeraMemory tower burned luridly against the evening sky, a pillar of smoke arching eastward. To the west, a smothering slab of dense Pacific fog spilled into the Valley like meringue.

"I am seeing Pierre in a new way," Natasha confided, leaning closer to Liz. "He is not so old as I thought. He might make a good husband."

Liz was awakened by the sound of Laurel's key in the front door. Her friend bounded in, a bag of groceries under her arm.

"Aw, it's so nice having someone to come home to. I brought dinner, sleepyhead."

"Thanks, hon." Liz stretched and rubbed her eyes. "You saved me from the strangest dream ever." She recounted the scene in the sleigh.

"It all sounds pretty reasonable, except for the part about 101 being deserted. That's definitely delusional," Laurel chided as she stocked the refrigerator. "You need to get out more. Two straight weeks of baking and Tolstoy are starting to get to you."

"But I'm enjoying myself. Leisure suits me, don't you think?" Liz tilted her head glamorously. Unemployment was inglorious, but she was trying to make the best of it.

"No rest for the wicked. You remember that little catering scheme I was cooking up with my pal from the bistro?"

"Oh, yeah—you and your French friend were going to become tactical gourmets. How's that coming along?"

"Well, we're happening, babe," Laurel said half proudly, half apprehensively. "We just got our first job." She fell to her knees in a parody of supplication. ". . . and we could *really* use a hand," she petitioned.

"Where?" said Liz, interested.

"It's a performance art event in the city. Some artist who's famous for setting things on fire, so they can't do it in a gallery, obviously. They're holding it under one of those freeway overpasses they closed after the Loma Prieta earthquake. A week from Friday. We're doing all the food ahead of time, box lunches with attitude. Wanna come and help?"

"Sure," Liz agreed. "Sounds like a step up from my last position."

BARRY ANNOUNCES THE DEATH
OF THE NERD MAVERICK

STEVE'S SUNDAY NIGHT ritual was the most regular part of his life: take-out pizza from Pontillo's (great pie, no tables), and the *X-Files.* Sometimes his puerile curiosity got the better of him, and he switched on the TV a half hour early to catch KTEH's *Silicon Valley Business Report.* He wanted to know what The Man was thinking this week.

This week's *SVBR* was a predictable pastiche of infotisements about popular Web sites, implausibly exciting tech trends, and vaporware hype. Nothing of much interest. His attention drifted as he picked pepperoni from the lid of the pizza box and turned the pages of *IEEE Spectrum.*

An interview piece caught his attention. It was Barry Dominic, one of infotech's golden boys of the moment. Steve curled his lip in distaste. Jeanne Hammer, *SVBR's* principal talking head, floated pandering, cream-puff questions.

"How do you respond to critics who say that Tera-Memory has gotten too big for its own good, that a large organization can't be nimble enough to chase the cutting edge?"

Barry pursed his lips into a mediagenic pout and held up a finger. "I know there's this prevailing idea that only twenty-something hacker eggheads in small companies, toiling away like mad scientists, can stay on the leading edge. That has a lot to do with people's ideas about computer people."

"The stereotypical nerd maverick, you mean . . . ," she paraphrased.

"Exactly. But it's out of date, behind the times. The age of the wild-eyed, independent hacker is over. Computing is a business now. The Wild West has been won. Now that computing is a mainstream commercial activity, there's no more room for the eccentrics. It's a serious business now, and we can't trust business to hobbyists and mad scientists. Not rigorous enough."

"Gee, Dad, I wanna be just like you when I grow up," Steve mocked the TV in an adolescent voice.

Jeanne furrowed her brow, a bargain-basement Diane Sawyer. "So, being big isn't a liability?"

"Individual efforts don't count for much these days. You've got to have a big, well-funded organization that's well

integrated into the industry to make a contribution. A couple
of pimply teenagers tinkering in their parents' garage just
won't cut it anymore. There's too much at stake now. Business
is serious."

"Oh, bite me so hard," Steve snarled, growing annoyed.

"Software engineering is a science now, with well-known
principles and clear pathways to success. CASE tools, code
validators, automatic programming, and the like."

"So you can *fully automate* your artless mediocrity." Steve
shifted into high dander. "Give it up, lemming."

Barry did not relent. "The real art is no longer in crafting
programs, it's in having the vision to identify the opportunities
and cultivate the business relationships necessary to bring technology to market. This industry is mature enough that the real
innovators are no longer hunched in front of a terminal."

Steve narrowed his eyes. "What a loser. Go away. Oh,
wait a sec . . . you haven't given us the product plug yet.
Bring it on, monkey-boy. Come to Jesus . . ."

Barry complied. "We all know how Microsoft missed the
boat on the Internet, how they're frantically swimming to
catch up. TeraMemory has been onboard from the very
beginning, and we're determined to push the state of the art
in networking technology. Over the next few weeks we'll be
announcing some revolutionary advancements in that area."

Steve hoisted his arms in field-goal position and spoofed
the sound of a roaring crowd. The interview segued into
closing questions.

"How do you feel about being in the center of such a competitive industry?"

"Well, Jeanne, I have complete faith in free enterprise. The market rewards innovation, and the best man"—Barry hesitated, then cleared his throat—"or woman usually wins. It's a level playing field, for the most part. I believe that character is destiny. Not everybody survives. That's life in the most competitive business on earth."

"Speaking of competition, Barry, I understand you're the man to beat these days in the world of yacht racing." Jeanne twinkled with the insider's self-satisfaction.

"We play to win. The crew and I are going down to Australia this winter. We've got a good boat, and I think we'll do well."

The program cut to a long shot of Barry and Jeanne as credits scrolled up the screen. Steve scowled at the television. Barry was just the kind of short-sighted, unenlightened, profiteering philistine he despised. He didn't want to live in a world where such a creature could rise to the top of the heap, he told himself.

But there was more to it than that. The specter of Barry, in all his market-capitalized grandeur, plucked at his own doubts about his path in life. Nobody cared about hackers anymore. They cared about market share.

"Somebody needs to keelhaul The Man," Steve said darkly.

ZEN CATS, DRAGON'S EYES AND THE VALLEY'S GERTRUDE STEIN

TWO MINUTES of down-dog was remarkably difficult.

But not without its rewards. As the class followed the lithe, muscular instructor through a final sequence of stretches, Liz glowed with invigorated calm.

In the beginning she had come to yoga class as an antidote to the frenetic stresses of corporate life. Though TeraMemory was now well behind her, she had become hooked along the way. She didn't need a justification anymore.

The class met at the Mountain View Zen center—a modest, California ranch house redecorated in Japanese style. No shoes allowed. After class, students drifted out to the back garden to reclaim their footwear.

Liz took a bench seat next to a statuesque, sympathetic-looking woman she recognized as a class regular. As Liz slipped on her shoes, something behind her tugged lightly at her hair, which she had pulled back into a ponytail.

She turned to see one of the center's cats, a fat Siamese, perched between rosemary bushes in an elevated planter box. Clearly, he had been making sport of Liz's hairdo. He gazed at her through half-closed, slightly crossed eyes.

The woman spoke. "It looks like you've got a four-legged admirer," she volunteered playfully.

Liz reached over and scratched the Siamese behind the ears. The rotund pet pushed back appreciatively. "Oh, I've got one at home. This one can probably sense I'm a pushover. They seem to have a way of knowing."

The woman smiled. "My husband used to love cats."

"Not anymore?"

"He discovered computers," she said with a cryptic half-smile that hinted regret.

"Oh, I understand. Men and their machines," Liz replied, half sarcastically. "Appeals to the masculine bias toward action. Much more predictable than cats." She went to work on the Siamese's back. He stuck his tail in the air and purred.

Liz's comment seemed to pique the woman's interest. "What's your name?" she asked.

"I'm Liz." Liz brushed away the feline fuzz and held out her hand.

"I'm Kiki," she said, shaking it. "It's good to meet you. Do you live nearby?"

"At the end of Dana Street. Only a few blocks."

"I'm way out in Woodside. I usually go down the street for a cup of tea around now, and wait for traffic to thin out a little before heading back. Would you care to join me?"

Liz hesitated for a moment, then chastised herself; spontaneous overtures of non-work-related friendship were rare these days. Besides, the woman's persona—at once open-hearted and mysterious—had aroused her own curiosity. And amidst the Valley's info-corporate conformity, she was a vision of exotica, a hothouse flower: six feet tall, a serene, high-cheekboned, Asian-looking face, olive complexion, thick, black tresses of curls. She often wore flowing, earth-toned clothes suggesting a sort of up-market Summer of Love. Come to think of it, Liz remarked to herself, that would have been about the right vintage.

"Yes. That'd be nice. Lucy's?" Liz referred to a charming, back-alley tea room not far from the Zen Center.

"Oh, you know. Yes. Lucy's."

They sat in high-backed bamboo chairs, drinking Dragon's Eyes and Forget-Me-Not, exploring topics safe enough for first acquaintance. It wasn't long before Liz found herself explicating her delicate relationship to the working world.

"I'm between jobs. I used to work in technology, but it didn't work out very well. High tech's not my cup of tea." Liz raised her cup and smiled.

"You didn't strike me as the infotech type. When I first saw you I said to myself, 'what's a nice girl like that doing in the valley of the nerds?'"

"Well, for now I'm just doing some catering while I put together my plan B," Liz fibbed lightly. "And you?"

"I'm mostly a housewife these days. I used to help out with my husband's business, but that was a while ago. Before that I was an artist. That's how I met my husband. He was crazy for my raku." She sipped her tea. "He was crazy for me, too," she said a little more quietly.

There's that wistfulness again, Liz thought to herself. There was obviously some kind of relationship issue, but she'd known Kiki less than an hour. "Raku?" Liz asked, avoiding the subject for the moment.

"Traditional Japanese pottery—ancient, low-tech wood firing method. Every piece is different, and that's the point," Kiki explained.

Liz couldn't resist the apparent riddle of Kiki's exotic ancestry. She'd never met a swarthy, six foot tall Japanese woman before; she was pretty sure there was an interesting story. "Your family was Japanese . . . ?"

"Only my father. My mother was a Cherokee Indian."

"What an interesting childhood you must have had," Liz commented, eyebrows aloft.

"Well, there was certainly a lot of . . . dynamic tension. Especially since we lived in Japan until I was twelve. I was Keiko then. When we came to America, my round-eye pals called me Kiki. It stuck—it became my occidental name. It followed me wherever I went."

Liz, perhaps against her better judgment, now felt emboldened to round out the rest of the picture. "How about your husband?" she asked between sips. "Does he ever come with you to the Zen center?"

"Oh, we're separated," Kiki blurted in a singsong voice, almost apologetically. "As I said, he's in technology. It's a jealous mistress."

A brief awkwardness hung in the air. Liz fumbled for an avenue of conversational retreat, but Kiki sensed her unease and led the way out.

"What kind of catering do you do?"

"Fun, innovative, mobile cuisine. No kitchen required. It's called 'Guerrilla Gourmet.'"

"What fun! Do you have a card? I throw a little party once a month. I could hire you to bring the food sometime."

"What kind of party?" Liz asked.

"Oh, it's kind of a salon. I'm trying to keep alive the art of nontechnical conversation. A loose circle of friends. It's kind of a cultural support group."

"Wow. You're the Gertrude Stein of the Silicon Valley. I bet it's a lot more challenging than Paris."

"My dear," she said, raising an eyebrow à la Marlene Dietrich, "sometimes it feels positively *underground.*"

THE GURU GIVES A PEP TALK

IT WAS THE Guru's job to be smarter than all the other technical people on staff. Every Silicon Valley technology company had one. The official designation might vary from company to company—chief technologist, VP of R&D, head wizard. When Ted Nelson, the cyber-svengali and patron saint of hypertext, held court at Autodesk, his business card had read DISTINGUISHED FELLOW. But the metaname was always the same: Guru.

As a young technical lion ascended the career ladder, his path moved him inexorably away from the cool hacks and interesting problems, toward that most dreaded of stations: manager. Managers were finished, technically speaking. They experienced the technology second-and third-hand. They might make more money, but they were out of the game in all the ways that really mattered to a nerd.

Not the Guru. Though his journey's path was narrow and fraught with hazard, it did not pass through the Valley of Management, where technical prowess laid down and died. His road led to the high plains and rare air of the uber-hacker. He gave the nerds a position to aspire to.

The Guru always maintained an unusually intense presence. He was brutally pragmatic, terrorizing his underlings with an understated but devastating intellectual brute force. He could slice you to ribbons with Occam's razor. His language was excruciatingly precise—when he wasn't indulging in analogies, metaphors, parables, or other pedagogical forms he so relished. He often took refuge in high concept: "meta-issues," "semantic architectures," "paradigms." He tended to use the word *orthogonal* whenever he got the chance.

Some record of intellectual heroism was necessary to separate him from the lower technical life-forms. Every Guru had done a few years at some big-time think tank, like PARC—Xerox's Palo Alto Research Center, one of the cradles of high tech—or BBN or the Rand Corporation. He almost always came blessed with a Ph.D. from a high-powered university, except in rare cases where maverick, out-of-the-box genius had earned him a Nobel or MacArthur prize.

The Guru's background tended to be eclectic; cognitive linguistics, theoretical mathematics, and obscure branches of physics were popular. Every now and then you might encounter a kink like romance philology or nonlinear studies.

The common denominator was a kind of wild, pie-in-the-sky, head-in-the-clouds intellect unknown in fields like chemistry or economics. It was especially helpful to the Guru's image to have spent a segment of his career tilted in some perplexingly oblique angle of study—anthropological field research into Indonesian cargo cults, or the application of chaos mathematics to Marx Brothers film dialogue.

Of course, he had to maintain some sort of outrageous hobby in his spare time, just to further underscore how very different he was from the rest of the engineering crew. It was important to induce a general mystification of the technical staff, something to make them scratch their heads and say, "man, he is *out there* . . ."

There were a few universal particulars: Gurus all possessed a preternatural youthfulness, in spite of their graying hair and crow's feet. And they all loved bad puns and Indian food.

The Guru's superior experience, intellect, and vision enabled him—presumably—to call the turns in the technology wars. An air of matter-of-fact dispassion supported this projection of omniscience so crucial to his credibility. He never, ever lost his cool. He was surrounded by an invisible force field of theoretical distance.

As WHIP neared its ship date, all available technical resources were brought to bear. Management had declared that anyone who knew their way around a compiler be put on the case, so Paul had been brought back into the engineering effort as the ship deadline approached.

Paul was happy to rejoin the battle. The vagaries of spinning corporate rhetoric had begun to make him question his own worth. The value of his nontechnical efforts was not particularly demonstrable. Back in the lab, at least he had some running code to justify his existence.

The last few weeks had been hot and heavy; the mounting anticipation of WHIP's completion had quickened and intensified the focus of the technical staff. The engineers were on a mission.

They were driven by their stock options, to be sure. But there was also that other quintessential Silicon Valley motivator in play, that I'm-going-to-make-a-difference-and-change-the-world vibe, too. They were true believers.

As D day approached, it became painfully clear that meeting the final project deadline was going to be more than tough. The true believers gathered in TeraMemory's main conference room for an emergency all-tech staff meeting with TeraMemory's own Guru, Rick Roth-Parker, Ph.D.

Rick fit nicely into the Guru meta-schema: MIT, Rand, author of several important papers on signal processing, holder of three important patents, personal friend of Marvin Minsky. Avid collector of nineteenth-century typesetting machinery and prehistoric Meso-American surgical tools.

Paul hunkered down in the back row; he knew better

than to take up a conspicuous position in the room. It was best for contractors to keep a low profile. Besides being resented for their higher rate of compensation, they were also objects of suspicion. They were not employees in the conventional sense—they did not participate in company benefits, they had forsworn stock options, and thus were not "on the boat." And at times like this—times when bold affirmations of company vision and mission statement were likely—the contractor presented a specter of skepticism. Nonbelief. A virtual wet blanket. A cold shower to the technical ardor.

Of course, Paul's manager came around every few weeks and impressed upon him the benefits of becoming an employee, of coming onto the boat with both feet. And of course, Paul's resolve never to be betrayed again dictated he politely but firmly decline. It was a common dance in the Valley.

When the conference room had filled with engineers, with everyone assuming their characteristically aloof slumps and their thoughtful chin-rubbing in earnest, the Guru solicited reports from each section manager on the parallel lines of the WHIP project's progress.

One group had stalled out developing some proprietary algorithms associated with hardware-based encryption. "It's a nightmare," the project lead had whined. "A lot of the literature on sixty-four bit encryption is way spongier than we thought. Some of it's just flat wrong. And we've coded some of the screwups into our stuff."

Another was falling behind on the development of a low-level protocol handler. "Look, if we don't have a working stack, everything else is irrelevant. And it's a total hairball at this point."

One particularly haggard-looking hacker had discovered some problems with an elaborate, superefficient checksum mechanism which might set him back by weeks. "Look, man, there's no way I can guarantee data integrity at this point— WHIP's going to have blinding point-to-point transfers, except it's all going to be garbage on the far end, and I'm pretty sure most people are going to notice." At least this got a laugh or two.

Across the board, concerns were running high. The precious ship date was in jeopardy. There was an ugly undercurrent of panic.

The Guru set to work orchestrating an array of remedies. He made recommendations about technical resources, theoretical approaches, and redistributions of labor to address the most serious obstacles on the critical path. He drew many pictures on multiple whiteboards.

The challenges were great, time was running short, and the group was tottering on the edge of a toxic, paralyzing hopelessness. The Guru sensed this might be a good time for a sermon to the faithful.

He was quiet for a minute, and his audience mirrored his solemnity. He walked to the center of the stage, wiped clean the center whiteboard and wrote two words: INFLECTION POINTS. He turned to his flock.

"The history of human artifice is filled with inflection points—points at which innovation creates a quantum leap forward in our ability to apply leverage over the challenges of human life." He counted them off on his fingers: "Stone tools. Iron. Steel. Internal combustion. The telegraph. The telephone. Microelectronics."

A silent rapture filled the room. The Guru was giving them what they had really come for: inspiration.

"Take a look down El Camino Real," Dr. Rick commanded—rhetorically, as he was standing in a windowless theater. No matter. "What do you see? Some people might see an old, broken road that once stretched all the way to Mexico City, the capital of a long-fallen empire.

"I see our future. El Camino Real was once the connective tissue of the frontier. It linked all the Spanish missions, the first outposts of emerging organization in the west. It was the first network. Bandwidth of five mules a day. But it was the principal vector of the explosion of progress that is now California—the sixth largest economy in the world." He paused, narrowed his mouth significantly, and waved his arm with a sudden, sweeping jerk.

"This is the next wave. You're building the infrastructure of what will be no less of an expansion: ubiquitous, wireless digital communication. Every man and machine in constant, secure, transparent, real-time communication. It's going to impact everything. Everything. You people are changing the world."

One engineer broke the hush, exhaling a heartfelt agreement, a fervent, "Yeah. Right on."

The Guru continued. "We get this thing working and out of the lab, and we'll write our names in the sky."

The congregation began to testify: *"Yeah. Alright. Cool,"* came the exclamations as their courage stiffened.

"Do you believe?" the Guru asked. "Because you *must* believe. It—is—*inevitable.*"

The room erupted with enthusiasm. And as skeptical as he was, Paul found himself caught up in the spirit. It was almost enough to make him believe, too.

His status as a conscientious objector would not ultimately permit it. But at times like these, he could feel his resolve weaken.

THE DOOM SERVER ATOP THE
THRONE OF INFINITE LOGIC

AS THE DARKNESS deepened, the abandoned overpass loomed like a concrete basilica over the setting for Psychrist's cybernetic passion play.

It was a forebodingly apocalyptic scene. A bizarre arrangement of monoliths suggested a venue for some abstractly grave final judgment.

A roughly circular perimeter of waist-high concrete barriers—appropriated by some of Caltrans' highway construction crew confederates—enclosed a circular arena of cryptically placed, vertical concrete cylinder segments.

In the center of the circle was an ominous-looking pit. From this rude breach in the earth rose a more massive pillar with a capstone, a twentieth-century industrial facsimile of a Roman column.

Atop the column was a computer: beige minitower sans monitor or keyboard, its stark enclosure sculpturally complementary. Ten feet directly above that, a shockingly large rock hovered in the air, suspended by a cable from the steel substructure of the derelict overpass.

In each quadrant of this grim theater, each appearing cheerfully surreal in juxtaposition to the oppressive surroundings, stood a small, fuzzy stuffed animal.

A German video crew documented the event. Nearby, the director—shaved head and tiny, tortoise-shell glasses—interviewed Psychrist while a cameraman swooped and tilted his camera for an arty, video-vérité effect.

"It's a kinetic metaparable about technology and life on earth," Psychrist explicated. "The four silicon 'bots represent the hazards of the information age: passivity, detachment, alienation, and hubris. All electrically powered, computer-controlled, wirelessly networked. They're just kid's toys, really—those remote-controlled monster trucks—that we've upgraded with motherboards, packet radio, and a spring-loaded claw in the front.

"They receive their instructions from the Doom Server sitting atop the Throne of Infinite Logic." He pointed to the minitower mounted dramatically in the center of the arena. "The transmissions are all radio frequency, but we're also doubling the 'bot transponders through hopped-up red diodes on their backs. Makes it more visually interesting. Especially with the flames."

"There will be fire?" the director asked in his best post-modern Alsatian deadpan.

"Oh, yeah. We call the moat around the throne 'the Abyss.' It'll be full of flaming fuel oil during the performance.

"The vehicle here will be carbon-guided." Psychrist pointed to a menacing device that looked like an off-road lawn mower bristling with armaments. "In front, you got your high-speed, rotating tungsten saw. Flamethrowers out either side." He tugged on a long, springy metal antenna arching from the top of the vehicle. "There's also the Chip Whip—constantly rotates, three hundred and sixty degrees. Ultra high voltage contact on the end. Just right for frying semiconductors." Psychrist slapped the mechanical beast's flank. "But it's all consistent with its nature: carbon-guided, fossil-fuel-powered, all analog. No digital machinery of any kind."

Faux Herzog gave Psychrist a quizzical look. "Carbon-guided?"

"A rat."

"Rat. Is this some sort of new technology?" the German queried earnestly.

"It's a very old technology, if you want to think of it that way. It's a resilient, massively parallel, fault-tolerant, hairy little critter with four legs and a tail. A marvel of engineering. More than that. Art. They're all around this neighborhood. You should check 'em out sometime."

The videographer gaped. Psychrist recognized that a clarification was in order.

"The control mechanism is an actual rat, inside one of those transparent plastic hamster balls. The little guy has spent a couple of weeks in a Skinner box. We've been auto-shaping the rat to roll the ball toward flashing lights—which ought to come in handy, since all the 'bots will be strobing their LEDs as they transmit packets to the Doom Server. As long as they're strobing, rat'll be tracking 'em, the Carbon Buggy will hunt 'em down, and hopefully one of the weapons'll sort 'em out."

The German scribbled in a notebook, then accepted an offering of Evian from a production assistant. "Where did you get this rat?" he asked in a low voice.

"Local boy," Psychrist cheerfully volunteered. "We trapped him in a Dumpster only a few hundred meters from here. He's got the home field advantage."

The director was clearly starting to lose his grip on the translation. "Home field?" he asked meekly.

Psychrist kicked himself into semiotic high gear. "The area surrounding the throne is conceptualized as the Field of Cultural Production. It's divided into four quadrants, each representing a domain of carbon-based virtue: Self-determination. Beauty. Affect. Perversity. Each virtue is itself represented by an animal token—in this case, a little stuffed animal. Bear, pig, frog, unicorn," Psychrist counted out on the remaining fingers of his right hand. "The 'bots receive directives from the Doom Server to search them out and deliver them to the flames of the Abyss. We put in a bunch of randomly placed concrete pylons just to make things more challenging for the transit logic.

"The 'bots are blind, but the master can locate them within the field with a grid of sensors. The 'bots troll until they grab something, then the server guides them into the Abyss."

"I see," asserted the director, though he didn't.

Psychrist pointed to the massive boulder hanging over the minitower. "This guy we call 'Heisenberg's Pebble'—it represents the uncertainty of the outcome. The suspending hardware is rigged with special explosives. They blow as soon as all of the 'bots fail to check in within a five hundred millisecond interval." He smirked a little sadistically. "Snaps the cabling hardware. About three tons, straight down."

The director gripped the Evian bottle, flexing it in his hands. "And what will be this outcome?"

"Carbon Rat's got five minutes of fuel to stop the silicon 'bots from robbing the field of every human virtue." Psychrist shrugged. "Your guess is as good as mine."

The traffic on 101 crawled at an excruciating pace. To add insult to injury, a lone bicyclist pedaled along a parallel frontage road, easily outpacing the autos on the jammed freeway. Agitated commuters leaned on their horns. Some expressed their frustration by frantically changing lanes in the irrational belief that one lane might move more freely than another. These benighted drivers were unable to grasp that one hundred thousand other motorists pursuing identical strategies would ensure a perfectly distributed congestion.

Steve and Paul crept along in the #3 lane, morosely resigned to inhaling the hydrocarbons and watching the brake lights in the darkness.

Paul downshifted for the five hundredth time. "Thirty-five miles in eighty-five minutes. Ow. Can you remind me why automobiles are a significant improvement over oxen?"

Steve tried to put a happy face on the situation. "You're suffering for art, baby. Just you wait. It'll all be worth it. You'll be thanking me by the end of the night."

"I'll be happy if I escape with second degree burns. I hear this Psychrist guy is a real maniac."

"Oh, you don't know the half of it," Steve grinned at his friend. "I'm really glad you decided to come along. Thanks, man."

THE SYSADMIN VS. THE WORLD

THE SYSTEMS administrator looked darkly upon the queue of trouble-ticket headers on his screen. "Need app uprev," demanded one. "Printer problems," declared another. "What did you do with my files?!?!?" still another accused.

In the technical hierarchy of any software powerhouse, the systems administrator—contracted with typical techie economy to "sysadmin"—was the virtual janitor. In the halls and chambers of the corporate datacores, the sysadmin swabbed the disks, plumbed the network lines, and generally kept things free of any otherwise unsavory digital encrustations.

Aaron continued his glowering, trying to remember why he ever liked this job in the first place. He slurped his double latte and gently clicked his silver tongue-stud against his front teeth.

There actually were a few compensations, now that he thought about it. For, alongside the unsavory labors of online hygiene, the sysadmin also held the delicious office of gatekeeper—controlling access, granting resources, and otherwise implementing the vagaries of MIS policy. And just like any other janitor, the sysadmin had keys to everything.

Certainly Aaron loved all the power. It felt good to have all those virtual keys jangling from his virtual belt loop, and to know that no corner of the filesystem was outside his reach.

Another advantage: systems administrators never had to wear anything nicer or more binding than jeans and a T-shirt. Any day might find them burrowing like a rodent under a dropped floor, or contorting themselves, yogi-like, in some impossible position to pull a circuit board from the backplane of some topologically inconvenient host. A measured slovenliness was part of the job description. And since there was zero client contact, Aaron's enthusiasm for body-piercing fashions had been largely tolerated or ignored by his coworkers. Only one colleague gave him any ongoing grief, calling him, "Ace—because you've got a whole hardware store hanging from your face."

It was a great career for hardware fans, now that he came to think of it—the kind of people who could enthusiastically recite the specs of any server, modem or router months before its appearance on the market. And there was always an enter-taining, Trivial-Pursuits-for-nerds angle, too: you got paid to cultivate an encyclopedic knowledge of every revision, patch, and CERT advisory pertinent to your computing envi-ronment. There was a certain amount of camaraderie, even, as you developed first-name relationships with the entire product support staff of each and every one of your vendors.

The paramilitary gear was cool, too. Though the sysadmin carried most of the necessary tools in his head, he was never without a Leatherman—an extremely strong, compact tool that contained, origami-like, a pliers, wirecutters, a set of screwdrivers, and a half dozen other critically useful weapons packed into an enclosure four inches by one inch by one half inch. It was the bastard child of a Swiss Army knife and the Terminator. An experienced admin could tear a million dollar server down to its component parts with nothing more—though reassembly might also require a little duct tape.

Aaron furrowed his oh-so-hiply perforated brow. Unfor-tunately, his office didn't stop at binary spit-and-polish. The job embraced formidable human challenges as well. It was his responsibility to support users. Hold hands. Dispense clues to the clueless.

No admin could ever muster much enthusiasm for this role of digital den mother. In a job already overburdened by technical minutiae, it put the admin in a chronic state of, "everybody wants something from me now."

Aaron felt this pressure keenly, being constantly pulled in

many directions at once. This led to the sullen, passive-aggressive, victimized mentality that generally characterized his species.

Yet in spite of the weight and variety of these highly complicated and technical demands, sysadmins were invariably treated like shop clerks or errand boys, a distinctly lower caste of functionary. Programmers and developers regarded systems administration groups as dumping grounds for downscale technical talent. Marketeers and executives treated sysadmins as their personal servants for even the most simple and trivial computer operations. And nearly everyone in the company held them responsible for the various entertainments of corporate life; when the staff found they no longer had access to www.pinkbikini.com or alt.erotica.binaries.wombats, they landed hard on the systems administrators.

In this culture, it took a sysadmin a very short time to develop a potent disdain for all users. Because, with very few exceptions, users insisted on torturing sysadmins with their computational witlessness and pointed reluctance to educate themselves. Yet their every whim must be granted, each and every act of ignorance must be tolerated, every refusal to learn must be overlooked.

Aaron pulled the least offensive-looking report off the queue. This in itself was significant. When you picked up a trouble-ticket, you became part of the ticket log. You owned it. At that point, getting rid of it was tricky.

The trouble-ticket window snapped open on the display.

"Description: Printer Problems. Contact: Jerry Murton, x2536." Uh-oh. The extension suggested a member of the rapidly growing sales division.

He punched out the extension on his telephone.

"Hello?"

"Ah, this is Aaron from system support, responding to your trouble-ticket."

He heard muffled voices on the other end as Jerry wrapped up another exchange, hand over the receiver. Multitasking was a way of life.

"Yeah, yeah. My printer doesn't work."

Aaron began his diagnosis. "Okay, what's the platform?"

Jerry hesitated. "Um, it's right here on my desk."

Here we go, Aaron thought to himself. "I mean, what kind of computer is it hooked to?"

"Oh, that's easy. It's a desktop computer," Jerry said confidently.

Easy, Double-A-man, stay calm, he coached himself. Try and tease out the details without betraying your complete loathing for his phylum's monocellular nervous system. He tried an oblique approach.

"Okay, is the control bar at the top or the bottom of the screen?"

"Uh, what control bar?"

Okay, maybe a direct approach. "Is the machine running under Windows?"

Jerry's response came quickly and confidently. "No, my

desk is next to the door. But that is a good point. The guy in the cubicle next to me is under a window, and his printer works fine."

Aaron could feel the blood pounding in his temples. He clenched his jaw, leaned forward, and gently thumped his head against his monitor.

AFTERGLOW OF THE
ROBOTIC INFERNO

PSYCHRIST IGNITED the Abyss with the German's cigarette.

The lights dimmed as the four 'bots began a slow lap of the circular arena, LEDs twittering a satanic crimson with every packet from their mephitic master. Blue-tinged flames licked at the Throne of Infinite Logic, creating sinister, dancing wraiths on the monoliths and brooding underbelly of Heisenberg's Pebble.

Doom Server dispatched its four agents each to a separate quadrant, where the sinister little robot drones paused for a few moments as two of Psychrist's bedraggled technicians introduced Carbon Rat and his weaponed rover into the arena. They delicately placed the rodent—enclosed jewellike in a transparent orb—into the guidance mechanism at the front of the dangerous-looking vehicle. Pull-starting its noisy engine, they quickly backed away as the saw blade picked up speed.

The computer-controlled robot drones commenced their search-and-destroy—an awkwardly jerky but relentlessly methodical trolling routine, scouring the Field of Cultural Production for the hapless proxies of carbon-based virtue.

It was not an auspicious beginning for the carbon faction; much to the disappointment of his warm-blooded, human cousins in the audience, Rat only wandered aimless in the quadrant of Affect, nudging his bristling juggernaut pointlessly against the perimeter wall, sparks dancing as the whining blade skipped off the concrete.

The carbon virtues fell quickly into peril; the Teddy Bear of Self-Determination was the first to go. Swept up in the mechanical jaws of the Alienation drone, it was quickly delivered to the fires of the Abyss, delayed for only the few moments required for Alienation to negotiate a single pylon.

The human witnesses on the perimeter—many of them armored in hard hats and safety goggles—lowed disappointedly as the pair tipped over the edge into the inferno.

Beauty was next, captured by Detachment. Its claw closed around the fuzzy pig proxy. Registering the capture, the drone's solid-state logic oriented it toward the pit, and off it trundled toward destruction.

Finally, a little action from the carbon contestant: a shocking volume of flame erupted from the flanks of the carriage, searing the perimeter wall on one side and belching a burning tongue into the arena on the other. Rat had been rattled; his chariot lurched wildly as the startled pest pilot skittered in his control ball.

Rat Mobile came to rest felicitously aligned with Detachment and its quarry. Rat poised motionless as the LEDs strobed before him. Somewhere in the tangle of synapses of his disoriented motor cortex, he began to remember. The carriage took off purposefully after the 'bot and its captured Beauty.

They converged at the edge of the Abyss. For a moment it looked as if Detachment might be eviscerated from behind by the rotating saw, but the Chip Whip eclipsed the action at the last moment, making contact with the drone's stubby radio antenna. There was a tremendous flash, like a miniature lightning bolt.

But chance conspired against the rescue. Bereft of logic and communication, Detachment spun crazily out of control, throttle wide open. With Beauty still in its grasp, it executed a bizarre 270 degree turn—straight into the Abyss.

More groaning from the carbon faction. The chariot twitched as Rat floundered.

A second conflagration from Rat's flamethrowers turned the tide: as Passivity—having located its frog hostage—negotiated a concrete pillar, it was broadsided by a blast of fire. Amazingly, it continued for a short while, but quickly bogged down in the slag of its burning tires. The LEDs went silent after the flames engulfed its ethernet card. The fluffy frog, still gripped in the pincers, smiled a cheerfully toasted grin.

Rat intercepted Hubris and Perversity on the edge of the Abyss. Rat's rotating saw caught the drone just above the fenders, cutting into it as Rat reflexively rolled the ball toward the drone's flashing LEDs. The whine of the circular blade descended as it bisected the 'bot. A dramatic spray of chaff and sparks encouraged the humans to sound their approval.

But the blade snagged suddenly, catapulting the vehicle to the perimeter with ugly force. The 'bot caromed off the wall, smashing into pieces. The cuddly plush unicorn popped free on impact. It landed on its feet.

Four hundred and fifty milliseconds of carbon-based cheering was cut short by a blinding flash and hellacious explosion. Bits of glowing, molten steel showered down onto the arena from above.

Heisenberg's Pebble fell in that unique way that all very heavy objects seem to fall. It hung for a tiny moment, leisurely gathering momentum for its incontrovertible descent.

It was the ultimate falling curtain. In a casual gravitational gesture, the boulder compressed the minitower into two dimensions, shattered the throne into dust, and plugged the gaping maw of the Abyss. Only a few pints of flaming fuel oil, splashed from the pit by the impact, betrayed any suggestion of the scene moments prior.

There was one other casualty. Heisenberg's Pebble, in its earthward fall, clipped the Rat's chariot where it stood on the brink. The impact partially crushed it and tipped it over on one side. Mortally wounded, the vehicle's engine continued to idle roughly in protest.

Fearing a cyber-Pyrrhic victory, the attending crowd fell into a disappointed hush. Could it be that Deathmatch 3000 was only to be a negative sum game, a depressing cosmic parable of a lose/lose universe? Was carbon-based life really doomed, despite its valiant effort?

Jolted by the dying coughs of the chariot's power plant, Rat's plastic orb rolled out of the wrecked control module, bounced twice, and separated neatly into two halves, depositing Rat on the scorched pavement. The stunned rodent looked around at the smoking wreckage, gathered his wits, and fled for the nearest Dumpster. He disappeared into the darkness through a gap in the perimeter wall. The humans let out another organic hurrah.

Three fire trucks, responding to reports of general mayhem with blazing lights and wailing sirens, provided an unexpected finale.

"Unbelievable," Paul muttered, stunned as well.

"Pretty amazing, huh? Wasn't that the coolest?" Steve enthused.

"Pretty amazing nobody was *killed*," Paul clarified.

A huge portable stereo stimulated the postperformance

festivities, throbbing with techno. The crowd gravitated toward the back of an open van, where a party was in process of spontaneous organization. People were drinking from plastic cups and munching out of little white boxes—high-octane refreshments were being served, apparently. Steve noticed the boxes had been decorated with colorful Magic Marker renderings of cute little rodents and angry robots.

Paul heard a familiar voice he couldn't quite place: ". . . Muscovy duck and white bean burritos with apple salsa. Goes great with the Breton hard cider, too." He tracked its source to one of the three women serving the revelers from the back of the van.

He stared a moment, disbelieving. It was Liz Toulouse. He approached, met her eyes, and said in his best Bogart, "Of all the gin joints in all the towns in all the world, she walks into mine."

She was surprised and delighted, but she didn't miss a beat, handing him a glass of cider. "Here's looking at you, kid."

A fireman strode through the party, pointing to the still smoldering set. "Will somebody tell me exactly what the *hell* is going on here?" he demanded.

Liz handed him a glass of cider, too.

FIRE OFF THE PRESS RELEASES! SALES FORCE, START YOUR ENGINES!

FOR IMMEDIATE RELEASE

SOFTWARE LEADER UNVEILS REVOLUTIONARY NETWORK TECHNOLOGY
New protocol supersedes existing wireless, nomadic computing standards.

PALO ALTO, Calif.—Jan 29—TeraMemory, Inc., the global leader in enterprise database solutions, today announced the development of the next-generation network protocol. The proprietary technology will rapidly accelerate the pace of ubiquitous wireless networking and set new standards in communications bandwidth and privacy.

The Mountain View, Calif. database giant developed the Wireless High-density Internet Protocol, or WHIP, in response to the industry's escalating demand for cost-effective client/server and peer-to-peer internetworking solutions. Barry Dominic, President and CEO of Tera-Memory, says "WHIP will power drive the future of e-commerce by allowing degrees of interoperability and flexibility we can now only dream about. This is the dawn of a new era in connectability."

Major platform and electronic commerce vendors are rapidly embracing WHIP. The integration of Tera-Memory's WHIP protocol with major manufacturer's networking and computing hardware represents a major step forward in solving the core issues surrounding the creation of wireless computing applications for e-commerce and business-to-business interoperability.

"Today's announcement will cause the industry to stand up and take notice," said Candy Sawyer, Vice President of Sales. "We think WHIP has the potential to redefine networking, PC multimedia computing, nomadic devices, and thin client solutions, bringing a major competitive advantage to our hardware partners. This innovation should be especially attractive to power users who demand uncompromised performance for their high-end real-time networking applications."

Key WHIP proprietary firmware microprocessors will enter volume production in the second quarter of this year. System announcements are also expected in the second quarter.

Led by industry veteran Andrew Lucre, TeraMemory has secured $27 million of financing from Tohashi Cel-

lular, Venture World Capital, Woodside Associates, Ino-
vatech, and various individual investors. The spin-off of
WHIP Technologies is scheduled for the fourth quarter,
with Initial Public Offering to follow.

THE PRESS RELEASE had touched off a frenzy in the Tera-
Memory's nontechnical quarters. The sales force, in particular,
experienced a considerable quickening of pulse; they could
smell the money. They gathered en masse in cafés and conference rooms, brandishing their Mont Blanc Meisterstucks
and devising fiendish schemes on how territories and opportunities would be divided. They plotted elaborate compensation plans and tiered commission schedules. In short, they
set about their corporate conniving and preemptive back-
stabbing in that ruthless, feckless, breathtakingly ignorant
way only salespeople can.

They were, however, having more than the usual difficulty wrapping their minds around the product itself. For
days after the announcement, the digital pitchmen experienced considerable frustration grasping a simple definition—
not to mention the basic technical specifications—of
TeraMemory's new product offering.

One senior sales associate proposed that WHIPs were just
like databases, only smaller. Another was quick to debunk this
hypothesis, estimating instead that it must be the supporting
platform hardware that was smaller. Still another asserted that
WHIP ran with no hardware at all—that's what a protocol

was, stupid. This led to a serious discussion about whether WHIP might be a virtual-reality product.

Though they ultimately reached no definite conclusions, they still seized the opportunity for self-congratulation; they had satisfied the corporate requirement for a sober, hardheaded analysis of WHIP's placement within the larger industry.

After a week of such similarly rigorous discussions of WHIP's technical merits and market positioning, there emerged among the sales force one quantitative issue on which they could all agree: if WHIP lived up to the promise of its press release, they would all be driving new Porsches before the year was done. This revelation galvanized their enthusiasm in ways that bothersome technical specs did not.

There was a long-standing joke in the industry about the difference between used car salesmen and infotech salesmen: the used car salesman knows when he's lying to you. That so many of TeraMemory's sales force had once actually sold used cars might explain the enthusiasm so many of them held for their new careers at Tera: perhaps it was easier to sleep at night when your inability to understand the product left open the possibility that you'd inadvertently told some sort of truth. Maybe the intractable obscurity and sheer technical opacity acted as gentle salve on the troubled conscience of the salesman.

On the other hand, maybe not. Conscience—in this crowd, anyway—seemed an unlikely supposition.

MARKETING MUTINY AND THE
MAGIC LOVE BURRITO

CANDY SAWYER knocked back her third vente triple latte of the morning and began to devour her fresh manicure. The WHIP prototypes were late. Five days until product launch, and not so much as a single working demo from the guys in the lab. She was so frustrated she could scream.

What exactly were they doing down there? They were all supposed to be completed weeks ago, and the geeks still hadn't gotten it together. "Technical problems," a section manager had dismissively explained.

This had made her see red; she hated being straight-armed by nerds. So Candy had threatened, terrorized, and kicked butts all the way up the engineering hierarchy, only to be stalemated by Rick Roth-Parker at the apex. His main contribution to the dialogue was only to impart a slightly

more theoretical sheen to the debacle, citing "major architectural revisions," "redefinition of project timelines," and
"unanticipated shortfalls in functionality."

Bullshit. Candy was not about to let functionality get in
the way of the product launch. TeraMemory had promised the
world a revolution, and she was going to see it delivered, with
or without engineering.

In the absence of demos and product documentation, she
set to creating a presentation out of whole cloth. If those
dweebs in engineering couldn't supply her with a working
product—or even a description of a working product—she
would dictate it to them. Engineering could resolve the incon-
sistencies later, or "TBD," as they liked to say when they were
inclined to dodge their own professional commitments.

La Costeña was the final word in burritos. Perched on the
edge of the barrio, its location on Rengstorff made it a
straight shot from the clusters of high-tech hives east of 101.
It was a quick and easy drive for legions of nerds and cubicle-
dwellers when their stomachs began to growl in Spanish.

Originally it was a specialty grocery for the Mountain
View Latino community, and stepping into La Costeña was
like a mini-vacation south of the border. But lately its
backroom burrito operation had begun to rapidly overshadow
the core grocery business. And for good reason: for hordes of
burrito-crazed engineers, nothing else would do. At any time
of day a line of corporate digit-heads—bagged and tagged

with photo ID badges dangling from their denim belt loops—wound out the establishment's door.

This homogeneity had not been wasted on José, the store's owner and manager. José lived in a small house wedged in the back of the market with a wife, four children, and a brother-in-law. The front yard—a tangle of tricycles, pets, and wrecked piñatas—testified to a pleasant life of domestic pandemonium.

The contrast between his own circumstances and those of the armies of clearly unattached young male technocrats marching through his market puzzled him. So much money here in *el Norte*. So much success. Why should so many young men be without love?

His *abuela* had come to him in a dream. "José," she had sung to him in her native Mayan dialect, "as the thunder leads the rain, the stomach will lead the heart. This is the wisdom of the jungle."

José awoke with an idea: these young engineers, he had observed, were a practical bunch. He would offer them an economic efficiency, with only a small string attached. After all, it was for their own good. He hung a hand-painted banner at the burrito counter. VALENTINES SPECIAL — THIS WEEK ONLY. BUY ONE BURRITO, GET A FREE BURRITO FOR YOUR SWEET-HEART (A KISS WILL PROVE IT).

After their chance meeting Liz and Paul had agreed to meet for lunch. Nothing heavy, just casual; neither was yet prepared to admit larger romantic possibilities. Take-out burritos and Mexican sodas at a nearby park seemed to strike the right note.

But José's ruse took them by surprise. Paul took note of the special offer.

"Hey, amigo," Paul called out to the proprietor, catching his eye. Before Liz could register any objection, he quickly planted a kiss on her cheek. Liz blushed, pleasantly puzzled. She also noted the kiss was surprisingly tender for such hasty theft.

"One free burrito for the lovely lady," José called out. *"Que viva el amor!"*

As Liz and Paul walked out the door, they overheard a brief exchange between the engineers in line behind them. "I'm not going to kiss you, dude," one objected to another. "Buy your own lunch."

Paul grinned, and Liz giggled. It was a date after all.

KIKI'S SALON DES REFUSEES— NO CYBER-TALK, PLEASE!

KIKI'S HOME was a time warp, a plush vision out of some more opulent Steinbeck: generously genteel, gracefully understated in that classic Northern California way. Rambling, heavy-timbered, the Prairie School ranch house nestled with an adjoining barn on twenty acres of meadows, oaks, and eucalyptus.

It was a style that was difficult to maintain these days. In past decades such homesteads had been fairly commonplace, but as the continent tilted—rolling its misfits, second-chancers, and now digital dreamers to the West Coast—they had become increasingly subdivided. Finding this scene on the edge of the Silicon Valley in the '90s was unexpected at the very least, like coming across a druid temple in a shopping mall.

Liz, Laurel, and Vero staged the evening's gustatory excursions on the expansive marble counters of Kiki's kitchen. Kiki was the ideal catering client, happy to lend a hand and to treat the Guerrilla Gourmet gals to a Viognier from her cellar.

"It's a pathologically diverse gang of artists, writers, musicians and other oddballs," Kiki had described the evening's guests, soon to arrive. "And we have only one rule: no cyber-talk."

Liz, arranging figs on a platter, found this amusing. "No computers? No World Wide Web? No e-commerce? That's asking a lot, especially around here, isn't it?"

"You'd be surprised," Kiki replied with a conspiratorial look. "Put out the right seed, and you get a whole different kind of bird."

Vero had outdone herself: herbed gravlax on brioche, vichyssoise, ginger lobster with crabbed potatoes, endive and nasturtium salad, an enormous Paris brest for dessert, with two sauternes. It was Guerrilla Gourmet's most extravagant production to date.

The evening was like something from some other time, or another country. Kiki's guests arrived shortly after sunset, unlikely bohemian apparitions in the Valley of the Byte. They greeted Kiki and each other with kisses and elaborate declarations of fondness. They drifted onto couches, divans, and any otherwise generously upholstered surfaces of the house's rustic, cavernous interior.

The guests' easy affections were complemented by rav-
enous appetites. Starving artists, indeed, Liz thought to
herself as the canapés and champagne flew from the trays on
her fingertips. It was a startlingly diverse bunch, for the
Valley; Liz was pleasantly surprised by an even balance of men
and women, young and old, as the soiree continued to build
strength.

After a time two or three parlor entertainers established
themselves: one, a cunning draftswoman, beguiled the revelers by rendering hilarious—though often unflattering—
caricatures of the people in her orbit. Another, a
Rasputinesque sculptor with occult leanings, performed
ominous readings with a mysterious deck of cards and recited
scores of obscene limericks from memory.

The salon gathered momentum in this way for two or
three hours until Vero—in her chef's toque—announced
dinner's imminence.

Three courses and two flights of wine later, a red-bearded
dandy—and raconteur of considerable proportions—held the
table spellbound with a tipsy travelogue of a recent visit to
Budapest. The story, which involved a Hungarian antiques
dealer, a *baba au rhum,* a drunken ferret, and a false-bottomed
suitcase, was so entertainingly far-fetched that it must certainly have been true.

When dessert had finished, a willowy, elfin woman and a
stocky gentleman in a paisley vest sang songs—Schubert

lieder, a Bach aria, and a few antique advertising jingles just for fun—accompanied by another guest on Kiki's handsome piano. Liz, Laurel, and Vero listened spellbound from the kitchen door. They pronounced it sublime. The musicians insisted it was unrehearsed.

Throughout, Kiki glowed like a bulb.

A short time before midnight, a young, bedraggled and slightly singed-looking glassblower presented Kiki with one of his creations, a fantasia of slender, translucent violet pipes. On this cue the room raised their glasses to the hostess. The dandy raconteur improvised the toast: "To beloved Kiki—she who stands between us and oblivion!"

The party began to dissolve. After the last stragglers found their way to the door, Vero and Laurel set about ordering the disarray in the kitchen. Liz and Kiki gathered up the empty plates and glasses which had fled to the far-flung reaches of the house.

Liz leaned across an end table for a fugitive champagne flute, her eyes focusing on a photograph just behind, framed ornately in silver and bronze. Her Summer of Love guess had been right; it was Kiki, in full hippie regalia: headband, tie-dye, layered muslin skirt, standing in a sunlit field, her arms entwined around an earnest-looking young man. He was attired in the same idiom: poet shirt, impossibly tattered blue jeans held together by psychedelic embroidery, love beads hanging from his neck. His smiling face parted a curtain of hair.

Liz warmed at this vision of countercultural bliss. Though she hadn't been born until 1971, she felt a nostalgia for the hippie days. She could not imagine a time or place more charmingly, idealistically naïve. The Northern California she knew now bore no resemblance.

There was something about the man in the picture, Liz thought to herself, something that persisted in snaring her attention. She was sure she knew his face. Perhaps he was a famous musician, or a well-known political activist; maybe someone her parents might know.

Then she dropped the glass. It bounced once, ringing like a bell, then shattered on the floor.

She had placed the man in her memory. It was Barry Dominic.

WHAT'S AN NDA
BETWEEN FRIENDS?

THE AQUARIUS THEATER hung precariously but tenaciously to its lease. It was one of the last surviving slices of pre-Internet Palo Alto, wedged between the boutiques and trendy microbreweries choking downtown like kudzu.

The Aquarius screened pictures few other theaters would touch. Paul and Steve had just attended an edgy but highly problematic cinematic opus involving nonlinear math, stock market prediction, the Cabala, computing, and do-it-yourself brain surgery. Not your standard blockbuster fare. That's what set the Aquarius apart: it was the only downtown theater that still catered to the oddball tastes of the local intelligentsia.

Another of the theater's endearing qualities was its location directly across the street from a good Chinese restaurant. Jing-Jing was a mainstay of Stanford students, Palo Alto hackers, and art film buffs. The two friends ankled across the street for a late meal.

Though Jing-Jing's clientele leaned toward the chow-mein-and-potstickers crowd, the restaurant did serve some more obscure ethnic specialties. Paul and Steve liked the nasty stuff. They placed an order for the usual daunting array of offbeat specialties: deep-fried pork intestine, geoducks in oyster sauce, a dish involving tiny dried anchovies which looked like glazed cockroaches. They poured a pot of jasmine tea between them.

There was an unscheduled floor show. A panhandler had slipped through the restaurant door, a tattered vision of '70s mania: an enormous head of hair, paisley shirt, huge, bug-eye glasses, and a wrecked top hat. The boom box he'd slung on his shoulder barely had time to beat out eight bars of "American Woman" before the proprietress expelled him, waving a stack of menus.

"Groovy," Steve grinned. The more Palo Alto became a high-rent outdoor shopping mall, the more he rooted for the local color.

Paul sipped at his tea, then was taken by a sudden conversational urge. "You know, I've been thinking . . . ," he began.

Steve cut him off, shaking his finger archly. "Hey, what did I tell you about that? It's dangerous, it's subversive, and it leads to acne and impure desires. Knock it off."

Well familiar with his friend's spasms of impertinence, Paul continued unfazed. "I'm starting to get an idea of how much time you must have put into your little robotic performance art stunt," Paul said, referring to Steve's contribution to Psychrist's oeuvre. "That's some nontrivial territory you were exploring there."

"Yeah," Steve agreed, quickly shifting gears into techie mode. "Asynch is always hard. Collision detection and rebroadcast can be a bitch, especially when the traffic peaks. You gotta be real clever to sort out the dog-pile when all your devices start chattering at the same time."

"Tell me about it," Paul commiserated, bemusedly observing a pair of diners juggling chopsticks and cell phones.

"I'm dealing with very similar issues at my current gig. Wireless networking protocol. Works great in the lab, with a finite number of nodes. Gets real squirrelly in the real world, though. Expand the network unplanned, and things get real weird real fast. Real hard to debug. You can't possibly hope to reproduce all the race conditions and asynchronous events whenever something breaks."

"Yep, it's out on the edge for sure. I did a bunch of reading up on it. Seems like nobody does it particularly well. And the more traffic you throw at it, you get this real non-linear drop-off in efficiency. Hey, how do your monkey-boys—um, I should say your *client*—deal with the compression issue?"

Paul winced. "Badly. They rewrote it three times, and it still doesn't work. What did you do about it?"

Steve looked at the stained ceiling, searching his memory. "I think I just punted, more or less. I cut-and-pasted some Huffman routines, then hacked 'em up a little bit to make 'em fit. I put most of my effort into the protocol handler. All that tap dancing between layers can be a little hairy. I mean, I kinda reinvented TCP/IP in miniature." He smirked. "I'm sure it'll earn me a place in history," he added sarcastically.

Paul grinned. "You probably coded it in a weekend, right?"

"Well, three or four days. I'm not as quick as I used to be."

"Jeez. What with all the code validators, project meetings, and standards committees, we probably did the same job in three months. Shows what superior technical resources will do for you," Paul said wearily.

By the time the glazed cockroaches arrived, Steve was convinced his little network hack bore more than a passing similarity to the core internals of TeraMemory's WHIP engines. This satisfied more than a bit of personal curiosity. He had been wondering how he fared against The Man these days.

Further, the details that most interested Steve were, not uncoincidentally, the same ones around which TeraMemory had focused its most intense proprietary effort. Steve had a gift for homing in on the meat of any computational problem, so he couldn't help but know. But he couldn't help asking to be sure, either.

"The only angle that really vexed me," he said, trying his best to be nonchalant, "was the throughput issue. I couldn't figure out how to implement a multitasking model in a compact space. If I could crack that nut, I bet my little beast could run a hundred times faster. How did your boys attack the problem?"

Paul hesitated, then answered. "Remember 'threads'?" he asked, referring to a technique fashionable with software architects in recent years. "Well, it's kind of like that. Multiparous, re-entrant code—beefed up by symmetric multiprocessing. That was the big fix. But, I'm not entirely sure it works all that well."

Paul cracked open a fortune cookie. "You realize, of course, that I've just violated the nondisclosure agreement. I'm sure Barry Dominic's Men-in-Black will burst in and take me away any second now."

Steve gave him a sidelong look. "Oh, as if . . . You know all about me and commercial coding. I'm allergic to suits. I'd never come within five miles of anyone who'd care. Besides, does it still count if I have no intention to profit economically?"

Paul glanced at his fortune. *You have many secrets.* *23–56–4–71–66.* He tossed it across the table to his pal.

Steve read it. "Not anymore," he laughed.

KIKI'S STORY: BARRY AND THE BIG RED BONG

"SINCE SHE RAN away, Gretchen has always insisted she's an orphan. And as her mother, I've had a hard time convincing her otherwise."

Kiki's voice drifted to Liz over the smooth terra-cotta wall separating the narrow, Japanese-style bathing stalls as the two women steeped lazily in cisterns of hot water. Their baths smelled vaguely of sulfur.

"All she knows is that TeraMemory took her father away. Now she doesn't trust computers, and she doesn't trust money. She prefers to live on her own."

Liz looked out under the low roof and contemplated the whispering stream as it shouldered its moonlit way against the mossy cliffside. She felt a thousand miles from civilization, dissolving by candlelight in the volcanic spring of a

Buddhist monastery on the edge of the world. She idly sponged her back, rolled over, and reflected on the chain of events that had brought about this unlikely detour.

Kiki had followed the sound of breaking glass to find Liz gawping in surprise at Barry's picture, hand clasped over mouth. Liz had tried to cover, feigning mortification at her own clumsiness. Perhaps it was better, she thought, to be discreet, to make no mention of her connection to Barry.

But Kiki's perception was far too acute; there was something about Liz's disquiet that was distinctly familiar.

"I think I know . . ." She had pointed to the picture.

"My husband?" Kiki completed with surprise.

"I think I used to work for him."

The rest had come out in a rush: TeraMemory, the job, her backfiring email, Barry's unprofessional advances, and the derailing of a career Liz wasn't sure she ever wanted in the first place.

Kiki listened carefully, the soul of empathy. She rested her hand on Liz's arm and said, "Honey, if he treated you one tenth as badly as he treated me, you need a vacation."

As it turned out, Kiki had extended an invitation, not just an observation. Two days later she collected Liz at *Château des Araignées* and drove her the 150 miles to Tassajara Hot Springs. It was the very least she could do, Kiki had said, and besides, now they really had something in common.

They drove south to the Zen retreat in Kiki's hulking SUV, the kind Liz had always despised on grounds of sheer size and waste. The congestion of 101 gave way to the more placid Highway 1, which dissolved into rustic G14, which all but vanished into dirt and wilderness. The last twenty miles of the journey had changed Liz's mind about Kiki's vehicle; ruts, rocks and steep, gravelly grades induced a reconsidered appreciation of four wheel drive.

"So how did you meet?" Liz queried, floating. "Was he always such a . . ."

"I think the word you're looking for is *bully.* Though I'll accept *jerk.*" Kiki released a sigh. "And no, he wasn't. He wasn't even Barry."

"What do you mean?"

"We were reinventing everything else in those days, why not ourselves? We all took new names. Barry's was particularly silly, even for the sixties."

"Barry had a hippie name?" Liz asked incredulously. "Oh, you've got to tell me—what was it?"

Kiki hesitated. "It's hard for me to say it, even now. It's still precious to me, in a way. It's like his true name," she explained, her voice trailing off a little mournfully. Then, she perked up. "Let's just say that it fit him to a T; he was always the first one up in the morning. The seed of his mighty corporate success, no doubt."

Liz steered the conversation toward firmer ground. "Well,

he certainly is a hard-driving achiever, that's for sure."

"He wasn't always like that. Once upon a time, Barry was an incredibly sweet, patient guy. The kind of man who would take the time to pet a cat, or put a baby bird back in a nest. But that's the thing about success, you know? When you make a fortune, in a sense it makes you, too. It rubs off; he took on all the qualities of the technology and the free market that made his riches possible: speed; precision; efficiency; ruthlessness. Anything that doesn't show up on the bottom line doesn't exist. You know, the Barry Dominic who's celebrated in all the business magazines, like *Upside,* and *Business 2.0.*

"And now I'm the only one who can still remember, who knows that somewhere under all that armor and ambition is a tender little hippie who slept in a tree house, strummed a guitar, played with his baby daughter," Kiki laughed a little nervously, adding, "and sometimes he smoked pot out of a big red bong."

Liz could not begin to imagine what Barry must have been like stoned, but she didn't ask. She wanted to go straight to the bottom of the saga. "So, what happened?"

"Oh, we were living in a commune in Malibu, right after Gretchen was born. One day Barry fell in with the wrong crowd."

"What, like he started hanging around with accountants?" Liz quipped, wryly.

"Darned near. Aerospace guys from up the road. Hughes

Aircraft. There were lots of pockets of techies in Southern California in those days. After a while it started to take him over. One day it was Dylan, Mao and patchouli oil, and the next it was transistors and circuit boards. He started a little company.

"At first he thought it wouldn't change him—or us. We talked all about staying grounded, about raising our daughter with the right values, about sharing our good fortune with the 'community.' But the more successful he got, the further we drifted from our agreement."

Liz listened as Kiki's tale unfolded: the progress of Barry's ever-quickening electronics career, the rise of TeraMemory, the withering of the marriage, and the gradual alienation of their daughter, Gretchen. She had run away at fifteen.

"Oh, that's so sad," Liz sympathized. "It must have been awful to see somebody you love become such a different person. How could he have changed so much?"

Ordinarily, Kiki wasn't one to dwell on the past. But this recapitulation of her personal history had put her in a philosophical mind. She attempted to draw the larger figures from her life with Barry.

"When the machine asserts itself into your life, it displaces everything else. Marry that with drive and ambition, and it's a pretty bad combination. It'll blind you to anything that might save you: friends, family . . ." Her voice trailed off against the tiles. "At least it was that way with Gretchen. She may not have been an orphan, but she was Tera's forgotten stepsister.

"In some ways, technology is incompatible with human love. Computer people are already in love with control and efficiency. But those values don't translate well to relationships. Love—life—is messy. Lots of wasted effort. Drives nerds mad with frustration. They'd rather not deal with the ambiguity.

"For all these years, it's felt to me like Barry's fallen under an evil spell. It's true, he treats me like dirt. But I remember what he was like before he was hypnotized by the machine. I'm not ready to give him up for lost."

They lingered awhile in the overhanging silence. Liz watched as the moon disappeared behind the cliff, softening the melancholy.

After a perfect vegetarian dinner, they spent the night in tiny, paper-walled tatami cabins. No electricity, only hurricane lamps hanging along the path outside. Liz lay for some time on the edge of sleep, listening to crickets, and an owl. Sometime around ten, she heard a sandal-footed monk blow her lamp dark.

STEVE DRAWS A BEAD
ON THE MAN

ONCE STEVE had caught a glimmer of the similarities between WHIP and his own recent hacks, he couldn't help himself. He had to tease out the details from his friend, NDA or not. He wasn't fishing for proprietary secrets, exactly; his motivations were more obscure and less commercial than that.

True hackers take great pride in being completely unpredictable. Of the signal qualities of digital wizards, this fundamental perversity stands out most prominently. They took glee in thwarting expectation.

This unpredictability had attained epic proportions of late. As a conflux of greedy industrial programmers poured into Silicon Valley to scramble for the winnings, the business-wary hacker underground was busy subverting and reinventing the very roots of digital commerce. In particular, they had been collectivizing their efforts in loosely structured, electronically networked federations, neatly segmenting and conquering sticky computing problems.

The startling thing was not so much that it all took place completely outside of any commercial framework. Never mind the money. What made it remarkable was that in many instances the resulting products were markedly superior to commercial offerings. They simply worked better and crashed less.

But most infuriating—and threatening—to the corporate software world was the exclamation point with which the hackers had emphasized their effort: they gave it away. After all, these weren't commercial products—they were works of art, rendered by hackers for hackers. Hackers were not businessmen; they were informed by higher motives. As artists and craftsmen, they created a community on an entirely different plane. The exchanged capital was purely reputational. It didn't matter who you were in "real" life— hobbyist, callow teenage misfit, a professional with a repressed anarchist streak. Build something really cool, and you earned the undying respect of your colleagues on the net. In this crowd, that was compensation enough.

This "Free Bits" movement—as it was known in the computerdom—was a topic of rabid debate: was it online Marxism, or a welcome restructuring of intellectual capital? A breath of digital fresh air, or a threat to the American Way? Whole Web sites became clearinghouses for the rhetoric of the revolution:

There were reformers:

Posted by Commander Burrito on Tuesday March 30, @09:59AM EDT

Corporations are fundamentally stupid. Look, when you put all that time and energy into maintaining corporate secrecy, not to mention legal departments and extensive CYA, you can't help but lose lots of collective IQ points. It isn't that the Free Bit'ers are so much smarter—they just refuse to mentally handicap themselves. We concentrate on the stuff that matters: it's the code, stupid.

There were alarmists:

Posted by Anonymous Coward on Tuesday March 30, @10:07AM EDT

Make no mistake: the Free Bits gang is coming for your livelihood. In their Brave New World, we'll all have great, free OSs. And no jobs. Gimme cutthroat capitalism any day.

Some angrily hurled indictments:

Posted by Mister Pfister on Tuesday March 30, @11:14AM EDT

Free Bits has gotten this far for the same reason rich, spoiled kids like Bill Gates get so far . . . they sponge off their rich parents and don't face the same obstacles and pressures that your average company does. Who else could afford to work for free?

And many more were typically impertinent.

Posted by screw_u@biteme.flonk.flonk.flonk.org on
Tuesday March 30, @11:23AM EDT

The answer is "sudo rm -rf /*". Now, what was your
question again?

Steve had keenly followed the packet-switched polemic.
And after his last geek-out with Paul over Chinese food, he
found the possibilities of a Free Bits WHIP equivalent
increasingly tantalizing. Of course he could recruit any
number of coconspirators out in net-land; the computing
issues alone were sufficiently fascinating to lure any number
of hobbyists and hackers to such an effort.

But if he were to be honest with himself, he'd have to
admit at least one darker motive. Ever since he'd heard Barry
Dominic declaring on TV the demise of the Hacker at the
hands of Big Business, Steve's mind had brooded on a way to
prove him wrong. Others had already launched successful
assaults on infocapitalism; already a Free Bits operating
system had begun to stand the server market on its ear. Maybe
Steve's own Free Bits project would be another shot across
The Man's bow. Maybe it would demonstrate Barry Dominic's
eminence as a Class A turd-knocker.

Maybe Steve would call it "Network Encrypted Multi-
System Internet Standard"—NEMSIS for short.

He liked the sound of that.

CANDY'S COMDEX FREAKOUT

SPRINGTIME IN THE Silicon Valley, and a young man's thoughts turn to Comdex. The stampede was on. Hundreds of thousands of young geeks prepared to converge on the legendary computer industry trade show held—appropriately enough—in that gambler's paradise, Las Vegas.

There was always a competition among industry front-runners over what they euphemistically called the "booth." Real infotech hard-ballers demonstrated their dominance by having the flashiest, most spectacular, and—most importantly—largest booth at the show.

Once upon a time the word *booth* had made some sense, when it had been just that: a ramshackle enclosure with a few card tables of product literature, some oversized poster graphics on the back wall, maybe a few working demos or mockups. But in the old days the booth was just home base, a placeholder, a tilt-up for the technocrats and pitchmen who hovered in the aisles hustling customers and trading business cards.

What was once a relatively modest commercial enclosure was now, for most high-tech companies, more like a traveling circus, only without the animals (unless you counted the salespeople, of course). High-tech companies had become very serious about their trade-show facades. The booth was now an important totem pole of industry power and market share, so much so that in Silicon Valley, an architectural subspecialty had sprung up around booth design. Trade-show booths weren't boxes anymore; many of them made the structures of Gaudi or I.M. Pei look like grandpa's toolshed.

Many were so elaborate they required three semitrailers, a team of roadies, and two days of continuous setup effort. These portable, multistory minipalaces contained fully stocked courtesy lounges, modest auditoriums, and banks of tiny suites where sales staff could more effectively isolate and hypnotize the hapless or unwary prospect.

Of course there were the usual vertical tournaments. The largest booths invariably featured prominently towering structures from which to fly the company colors, usually in full neon. The result was an aerial advertising dogfight; the airspace above the convention's floor became a high-altitude clash of futuristically stylish, swooshing corporate logos.

The hall of the Las Vegas Convention Center—tens upon tens of indoor acres—is for most exhibitors a fury of activity right up until the moment the doors open to the first attendees. TeraMemory was no exception. Five A.M., and Paul and the rest of the WHIP demo crew hadn't slept in two days.

There was a dark cloud over the booth: three of the five prototypes had gone silent, the leased T3 line was misconfigured, and the hub was on the fritz. Plus there seemed to be some strange radio frequency anomalies the WHIP designers apparently hadn't taken into account, because the two remaining functional demo units were experiencing never-before-seen rates of transmission errors. The techs blamed it on Nevada's fabled UFO activity. This was one time they were happy to attribute control to anybody else.

By six A.M. the booth had a network, and one of the recalcitrant demo devices decided to break silence. But no sooner had the engineers eked out this modest, eleventh hour success than Candy Sawyer strode into the hall like a runway model—perfectly dressed, microscopically groomed, and expecting the world.

"Everything up and running? No problems, right?" she asserted.

Paul reflected that she must have gotten up at three to look that way. He, on the other hand, had bags under his eyes big enough to hide in. Which, at that moment, was what he felt like doing. But being the only consultant, Paul had the least to lose by delivering the bad news.

He stepped into the fire. "Um, we've encountered a couple of—ah—issues we're not going to resolve before the hall opens."

Vertical lines appeared in Candy's perfect forehead. "Issues? *Issues?* You guys were supposed to have this stuff under control, right?"

Paul opted for the avuncular approach. "Candy, you know these product launches never go perfectly the first time out of the lab. It's going to be a little touch-and-go. We'll have something to show the people, but we may have to tap-dance a little. Don't worry. It's going to be okay."

Wrong approach. Her cosmetically enhanced cheekbones lit up a stylish shade of red. "It's *not okay*," she snapped, voice rising. "I'm working off a script here, bub, and if all the demos don't work just like I scripted them, then my presentation isn't going to run fifteen minutes. And Barry says it's gotta run *fifteen minutes!*"

Paul could see that diplomacy wasn't going to get him very far. He bit his tongue and developed a sudden interest in his shoes.

Candy's temper rocketed toward the stratosphere. "Look, whatever it takes, you guys just get the whole deal working as planned, and nobody gets fired, okay? I don't want excuses, I don't want details, okay?" Then she attained escape velocity, hollering, "Just—make—it—happen!" Orbit.

Under any other circumstances, Paul might have taken Candy's performance personally. But this wasn't Paul's first product launch. He'd seen all of it before, on the very same floor, working for other clients. It was one of the few situations in which he'd developed a rock-solid faith, in fact: nothing ever went according to plan, all the machines broke down at the last minute, and the suits freaked out. Just another coming-out party in computerville.

LAST CHANCE—SQUATTERS
OFF HIGHWAY 17

LIZ AND KIKI had decided to return to Silicon Valley through the back door: Highway 17. Californians take their driving very, very seriously. In a land where the car is perhaps the most important statement of personal identity, it should come as no surprise that the very roads themselves have become bold semaphores for class and status.

Highways 101 and 280 dictated Silicon Valley revolve on a more-or-less north/south axis. Fortunately, the San Francisco Bay and Pacific coast also consented to this general alignment some millions of years ago, so the matter was settled: Silicon Valley would be framed between the two mighty transit bookends, 101 to the east, and 280 to the west.

Either would take you from San Francisco to San José. But as one Silicon Valley chieftain had already observed, the journey is the reward.

This was more than an airy, information-age aphorism; it seemed to be quite literally the case. While 101 ran straight up the commercial corridor packed with office parks, billboards, warehouses, and gritty, blue-collar industries, there were long stretches of 280 that looked like a tourist brochure: tree-covered mountains, rolling meadows, pristine lakes. Any cross section between the two roads betrayed a naked class stratification: Sunnyvale and Saratoga, Alviso and Los Altos Hills, East Palo Alto and Woodside. Geography spoke louder than words: the money preferred the western passage.

There were a number of opportunities for east/west class-jumping: 92, 84, and the newest cross-Valley express, 85. As the worker bees of the Valley commuted westward, they dreamed of real estate.

Highway 17 was more like a leap into the great beyond. This narrow, winding, famously dangerous, and chronically clogged road climbed out of Silicon Valley and down into Santa Cruz, where innovation and entrepreneurial drive dissolved in indolence, beach life, and left wing politics. Some, it was rumored, actually made the commute daily. There was wide agreement that these people were insane.

Fortunately, there weren't many opportunities for side trips along Highway 17's path. But those who did wander from the road soon found themselves in a parallel universe of survivalists, hippies, cannabis farmers, and other unconventional rustics. The dense redwood forests and secluded canyons collected them like filters.

Which was why Liz was more than a little surprised when Kiki had mysteriously suggested such an excursion. They wound upward over roads with names like Branciforte and Zayante, until finally the road markers—and the pavement—disappeared altogether. Still farther they bumped over dirt tracks flanked by giant sequoia and madrona trees, until Kiki turned onto an ominous lane marked with an off-kilter, weathered wooden board pointing the way with the words LAST CHANCE.

They parked the car and walked through the forest for a few hundred yards, their feet crunching in the pineneedles; enormous, lurid yellow slugs oozing across fallen logs. Just as Liz began formulating a gentle protest—what the hell *were* they doing all the way out here, anyway—the women came to a clearing. Bedraggled-looking counterculture apparitions seemed to be cooking over an open fire.

And there were *teepees*.

One of the firetenders, an unthreateningly muscular, bearded man—shoulder-length hair and naked to the waist—smiled and waved like a dancing bear. He called out to the tents in what seemed to Liz a German accent.

"Jah Love, Gretchen—I think your mama has come to visit."

A young woman emerged, dressed in harem pants, sandals, and a tattered wool sweater: raven-haired, beautiful, spectrally slender, except for an obviously advanced pregnancy. She cupped her swelling belly with one hand and ran to greet her mother, toe bells tinkling.

Mother and daughter fell into their own private world, with their own intimate language, suddenly absorbed by each other's company.

It was a strange interlude, and a bittersweet scene at best. Liz had stood, a little awkwardly some distance away, as they sat under a tree, holding each other and speaking tenderly. It seemed Kiki was trying to persuade Gretchen of something, but Gretchen gently but firmly resisted, speaking in ever-widening circles about love, and freedom, Babylon, and "Jah Love." Kiki attended to her daughter's words kindly and patiently, but clearly with a mother's troubled concern.

Later, the three of them joined Gretchen's feral family in toasting tofu dogs and *mochi* over the open fire, and for a time it seemed like Gretchen and Kiki teetered on the edge of some kind of conciliation.

But by the time the setting sun poked its fiery fingers through the redwoods, nothing had resolved between mother and daughter. They hugged, kissed, and parted. Liz and Kiki made their way back through the trees and the creatures, toward civilization.

"That was a real eye-opener," Liz said as Highway 17 emptied them onto the Valley floor. "I'm amazed people can live that way. "

"It's a personal choice," Kiki said matter-of-factly, changing lanes without a blinker. On the hostile, congested freeways, it was best not to signal your intention.

"How does it work? Does Gretchen's clan actually own that land up there?"

"It's government land," Kiki explained with a little reluctance. "Technically, they're squatters, but it's an open secret that they're living up there. That's why they live in teepees— they can move anytime, anywhere, if their little commune raises any local resentment. Fortunately, that doesn't happen very often; they're so far off the beaten track it's not worth anybody's time to run them off."

"Still," Liz insisted, "it must be a pretty precarious life, especially if you're expecting a child. I must confess—I'm a little worried about your daughter."

Kiki waited a long time before answering. "Yes," she agreed, wiping the corner of her eye. "It's not what I had hoped for."

COMDEX BURLESQUE—BARRY PREACHES TO THE CHOIR AS PAUL DUCT-TAPES THE DEMOS

A COMPUTER-GENERATED TeraMemory logo drifted across the expanse of the huge rear-projection screen, rebounding noiselessly from the borders. Similarly embossed foam boomerangs—a favorite with the conventioneers—whizzed festively across the conference hall. Anticipation was riding high. Barry's "Race for Cyberspace" address was shaping up to be the most attended event at Comdex. Hordes of tech enthusiasts poured into the hall.

WHIP had created an enormous amount of buzz, to be sure, more than sufficient to fill the room. But WHIP was just the icing on the cake; Barry himself was the main event, an object of cult fascination among infotech weenies. He had it all: big market cap, the best toys, and buck-naked ambition. He could draw a crowd, even in the midst of the gold rush. The faithful came to pay tribute to the personification and validation of their own private dreams of conquest and control. Barry Dominic was the proof in the pudding, the beacon lighting The Way, a bona fide infocapitalist messiah.

The lights dimmed and the screen began to broadcast a video clip: a smartly dressed executive—in conference with a dozen similarly young, dynamic, eugenically perfect personnel—tapping out a message on a sleek, paper-thin, completely hypothetical palm computer. Zoom in on the message: "Running late. Start without me." The stylus pops the SEND button.

Zoom in tighter, a fantastical plunge through the screen of the fictional PDA, into the circuitry of the device, where the message is shown decomposing into a stream of bits. Collapse the perspective tighter still, down to a single bit of information in the chain.

Then a bit's-eye view of manic electronic transit through a host of WHIPped devices: wireless packet relay, hub, LAN, WAN. Hurtling across rooms, through walls, under buildings, across cities—a wild, vicarious, hyperspeed ride through the infrastructure of the information age. The audience ooohed as the perspective whisked them through a satellite bounce, an instant trip into orbit and back.

Arriving at its destination, the bit is reunited with its kin and reassembled into the original message. Perspective pulls out, out through the skin of the device at journey's end: a futuristic home entertainment system. It springs to life, displays an acknowledgment on its console, and records the opening serve of a televised beach volleyball match. Another TeraMemory logo, underwritten by the slogan, "WHIP. It's a whole new ball game."

Wild cheering from the audience. Candy Sawyer, tracking the excitement from the edge of the stage, pumped her fist. Volleyball had been her idea.

A monster sound-system began to pound out Devo's *Whip It* as spotlights illuminated a rising podium in the foreground. Barry strode onstage, a vision of Italian tailoring, mouth bared into a feral smile which the screen amplified obscenely as he stepped into the pulpit. More cheering. More baring of ten-foot-high teeth.

"Inflection points . . . ," he began. "We're on the threshold of a time when all this . . . chaos . . . is going to start making some sense. TeraMemory is here to show the way."

Meanwhile, life on the floor of the exhibition hall continued unrepentant. As Barry's fanfare built to a crescendo in the adjoining auditorium, events in the TeraMemory booth, truth be told, offered much less cause for such raging optimism.

Not that anyone could tell the difference. In light of Candy's directive to make the demos work at any and all costs, Paul and the other engineers had resorted to a little technical sleight-of-hand: a shell script here, a little hidden hardwiring there, one or two discreetly redirected I/O cables, and one shamelessly bogus videotape loop spoofing a console interface. They had, in short, turned substantial portions of the WHIP demo into a high-tech puppet show.

It wasn't a complete lie, of course; much of it actually worked as advertised. But conference-goers were a merciless bunch. Generally they responded to any demo hiccup with derision, savage criticism, and propagation of rumor far more damagingly fictitious than any of engineering's ruses in the booth. Paul's new mission—in the absence of technology tough enough to face the public—was to effect a mildly covert saving of face.

No observer would even come close to uncovering the flim-flam; the only telling detail was the occasional, surreptitious glance passed between Paul and his engineering comrades as the TeraMemory booth bunnies performed the demo's scripted routines. After a short while it even began to feel perfectly natural to Paul. After all, this was the nature of the trade show: an increasingly uncomfortable interface between nascent, tentative technology and manic market boosterism. The two could never come together without a few modest prestidigitations.

MODEM VOODOO:
CAUSE-AND-EFFECT BREAKS
DOWN IN THE LAB

SQUEAKY WAS THE name TeraMemory's sysadmins gave the toy frog that perched on the main console in the lab.

Which was not as ridiculous as it sounded, when put in context; the lab was a discouragingly colorless place: racks of faceless machines, windowless, beige walls and a sense-numbing atmosphere of humming hard disks and climate-controlled white noise. The sysadmins had adopted the mascot as a way of perversely subverting the sterilized regimentation of their surroundings.

They had even made a game of venerating and anthropomorphizing the rubber amphibian: they had given him an email address, squeaky@teramemory.com; when one of the sysadmin crew felt the need to anonymously set the world straight—an urge which came surprisingly often for sysadmins—a message would emanate from Squeaky:

From: squeaky@teramemory.com
To: admin-all@teramemory.com
Subject: Environmental Degradation

Hey, whoever's the slob leaving half-eaten candy bars
all over the lab—KNOCK IT OFF. I eat insects, not
Snickers.

—An Angry Frog

Aaron, like any systems administrator, was forever dogged
by bandwidth shortages. As users became ever hungrier for
more and faster streams of data, the sysadmins found themselves
on the front lines of an escalating technical arms race. They
spent their days on search-and-destroy for info-structure bot-
tlenecks, which they obliterated with assaults of newer, faster
technology.

Today, Aaron's mission involved the retirement of a
modem linking the lab's router with the telephone company's
T1 line. He pulled the shiny new replacement—an NCD
TR5000, the latest generation technology—from its Sty-
rofoam packing, set it down on the bench and ogled for a
moment in absentminded admiration, toggling the rings in
his eyebrow back and forth like switches.

The new modem was supposed to be ten times faster
than the old one. Certainly its plastic enclosure suggested
speed; though the device would spend its days perched on a
stationary rack in the air-conditioned computing facility, the
product designers had endowed it with an ultra-sleek, black

casing which bore more than a passing resemblance to the
fuselage of a high-altitude spy aircraft.

At least until Aaron plugged it in and switched it on—
when a thousand twinkling LEDs and illuminated digital displays sprang to life on its beveled face. Then it seemed more like
some over-amped, exhibitionist UFO from planet Fabulon.

As much of a gadget-head as he was, this particular new
toy filled Aaron with a sense of foreboding; generally he hated
modems. In all his experience, Aaron had found that modems
expressed electromechanical perversity more strongly than
any other device in the lab. Modems exhibited a remarkable
degree of individual quirk, especially for manufactured com-
modities; they were magnets for nondeterministic effects. It
was for this very reason they induced some pretty bizarre
behavior in humans, particularly nerds.

For a nerd, observable cause-and-effect is everything. Predictability is the foundation of the nerd's most basic confidence. Which is why nerds generally loved a machine; with
sufficient analysis of a machine's design—its structure, sub-
systems, moving parts (virtual or otherwise)—you could
anticipate its behavior with a high degree of certainty. Armed
with that predictive certainty, you could engineer it to do
your bidding. In short, you could assert control. And control
is the primary currency of the geek life.

But it was just this kind of control that seemed to become
so tenuous when you danced with a modem. For reasons
unknowable, modems just didn't play fair; as machines, they

were somehow invested with an infuriatingly free will.

Aaron connected all the cabling, and warily began the configuration process. He squared himself against the main console, pushed his hands over the keyboard, and dove in.

debug modem, he typed.
Modem control/process activation debugging is on, the modem responded.

```
#debug chat
Chat scripts activity debugging is on
#term mon
#clear line 1
[confirm]y
17:30:53: TTY1: Line reset
#at&fs0=1&d2&c1%c1\\n5
OK
#open tty1
```

According to the TR5000 administrator's guide, the next response from the modem was supposed to be to signal its cooperation: "Link up," followed by "Ready."

But this particular TR5000 had other ideas. It bluntly rebuffed Aaron's request.

LINK DOWN

Take it easy, Double-A-man, Aaron coached himself. He must have missed something on the first pass, he decided; it wouldn't have been the first time he fumbled a keystroke or two. He flipped back through the user's guide, power-cycled the modem, and tried again.

The modem reprised its curt reply:

LINK DOWN

A spike of annoyance modulated his mood. No matter, he asserted, this is just a temporary setback. After all, he was a pro; he wasn't about to be bested by a mere finite state machine.

Over the next hour, Aaron reread the user's guide eight more times, to no avail: "Link Down" was the modem's relentless refrain. He'd even tried to anticipate and remedy every conceivable typo and omission the guide's authors might plausibly have committed. Technical writers, he assured himself with disdain, screwed things up all the time.

And it wasn't as if the modem was experiencing an across-the-board failure; it worked in every way it should have, right up until the threshold when Aaron typed "open tty1." Certainly it must be operator error, a failure of carbon-to-silicon communication.

But time after time, the response was the same:

LINK DOWN

After another hour of struggle, Aaron briefly considered packing up the device for return to the manufacturer. He decided that was a bad idea, as it had taken a month of incessant badgering to wrest a purchase order from his manager. And Aaron also knew—from previous skirmishes not unlike this one—that each modem had a unique constellation of kinks, and sometimes the devil you knew was better than the devil you didn't. Besides, returning it would be an admission of failure. Failure of control. Bad, bad.

Though Aaron would not yet admit it to himself, the modem held him in check. He began a series of increasingly desperate moves.

He tried changing its position on the rack. Currently it hunkered between the router and an enormous file server. Who knows what sort of mysterious electromagnetic effects to which it might be susceptible? Maybe an adjacent device was broadcasting some bad voodoo.

That didn't work. Aaron began to cast around for other implausible remedies.

Perhaps it was just out of operating spec—it was in many respects a rudely solid-state device, subject to swings in ambient temperature. He'd heard wild stories from some of his wire-head colleagues about thermal effects in telecommunications equipment.

He put the modem in the kitchen freezer for half an hour, and reattached it to the router's serial umbilicus.

#open tty1
LINK UP

Aaron's heart leapt. Then, after a moment's hesitation on the console, his torment returned anew.

LINK DOWN

He repeated the freezer experiment another six times, hoping to reproduce the effect, if only fleetingly. But the modem's flicker of cooperation never returned.

His thoughts became increasingly obsessive: Okay, so it wasn't too hot, Aaron diagnosed silently. But there seemed to be positive evidence of a thermal effect. He would continue exploring this hypothesis with appropriate scientific rigor.

He hit it with a ten-minute blast from a blow-dryer in the men's locker room of the company gym. This time, the apparition reappeared, only without the brief interval of hope:

LINK UP
LINK DOWN

Of course, this decidedly compulsive quest begged a much larger question: even if his hypothesis was correct, could he really hope to operate the device in a freezer or at the barrel-point of a hair-dryer?

But if he was successful, at least he'd have recaptured his faith in cause-and-effect before he abandoned the device— along with a nasty note—to the manufacturer. This exercise wasn't about modems anymore; it had transcended that. This was a battle for pride and predictability.

He repeated the experiment.

LINK UP
LINK DOWN

He was rapidly reaching boiling point; he suddenly felt a pressing need for an extravagant expression of frustration. Fortunately, Aaron's lab enjoyed restricted access, and this afternoon Aaron was all alone. And though he felt like hurling the modem against a hard surface, he wisely opted at the last instant to launch the lab's rubber mascot, instead. He grabbed Squeaky and spiked him into the wall with an angry, "god *fucking* dammit!"

The toy amphibian uttered his signature squeak on impact, then rebounded straight back into Aaron's lap.

It hadn't helped much. Still angry, annoyed and beaten, he placed Squeaky hastily atop the uncooperative modem and slumped forward onto the bench, burying his head in his forearms.

It took Aaron a surprising length of time to regain his composure. Eventually, he picked up his head and glanced scornfully at the console monitor.

LINK UP
READY

His head exploded. Was this just a cruel hallucination? He decided to press his luck and test this mirage.

```
#&status
NCD MODEL TR5000
SELF-TEST . . . . . . PASSED
CONNECTED AT 3.2 MBIT/SEC
LINK UP
READY
```

He looked at the device mistrustfully. A few minutes ago, it didn't work. Now it did. Only one thing had changed.

He removed the frog.

```
LINK DOWN
```

He hastily replaced it, then gaped in disbelief:

```
LINK UP
READY
```

At that moment, he heard someone punch in the combination on the lab's exterior door. The lock popped, and the door swung open.

It was Guy, a network administrator, his usual upbeat self.

"Hey-ho, Double-A-man! What's up? Oh, hey, you've got one of those new hot-rod TR5000s. They're all the rage.

Oh, hey, Squeaky." He reached for the toy, still perching pertly on webbed feet atop the modem.

"Don't," Aaron snapped through clenched teeth, violently waving Guy away.

"It's okay, dude, chill. I just want to squeeze the frog," Guy pleaded defensively.

Aaron's faith in electronic cause-and-effect—as well as his self-control, at this point—still teetered dangerously on the edge. "I'm telling you, man," he said in a dark, menacing voice, dripping with sublimated rage, "don't fuck with the frog."

Guy gave Aaron a circumspect glance. "Oh . . . this place is getting to you, man. You need to get out more."

LIZ AND PAUL'S DATING GAME

EARLY IN A romance there's a delicious interval—before memory fades and habit takes its toll—when two lovers have accumulated a significant history between them, yet can still remember every detail.

Liz and Paul, both endowed with excellent powers of recollection, had sustained the spell past all previously known endurance. In fact, they had made it into an ongoing game. Walking barefoot through the sandy surf of Half Moon Bay, arms looped around each other's waists, they played yet another round.

"Okay, date number eleven: *Shop Around the Corner,* Stanford Theater," Paul recalled. "Then, tacos at Andale. I talked like Jimmy Stewart for half an hour."

The rules allowed for a single cross-examination per turn. "Chicken, or pork?" Liz was playing to win.

Paul rolled his eyes skyward and feigned a moment's confusion, just for suspense. Then, "Chicken," he declared with absolute conviction. "Your turn."

"Twelve. Picnic at Pulgas water temple. Ha."

Paul touched his forehead. "Thirteen. We rented *101 Dalmations* and watched it at my place."

"Yeah—but I think it was the special, R-rated director's cut. The one with extra canoodling," Liz said, blushing. "The one where you get to see where puppies come from . . ." Then, realizing a potential advantage, "Cruella DeVille—white hair on the right side, or left?"

"Uh, you'll forgive me if I wasn't paying much attention to the movie. I throw myself on the mercy of the court."

"The judge accepts your answer," Liz reported. "But only because she's a sucker for love. Fourteen: miniature golf. That place out by the harbor in Redwood City."

"What was your score?" Paul parried.

Liz protested with flashing blue eyes. "Oh, you're kidding! Who keeps score at miniature golf?"

Paul gave her an imperious look. "Oh, certain results-oriented, numerically meticulous, and might I add wicked-good miniature golfers who would prefer to remain unidentified at this particular time . . ."

She pursed her lips. "Fifty-one," Liz blurted.

"Oh, *you wish.* Try sixty-three. And I shot fifty-five." Paul registered Liz's exasperation. "All right . . . wait . . . the judges accept your answer, in reciprocation for your previous leniency. You may proceed."

Liz gave him a skeptical look, kicked up a volley of sea droplets, then continued. "Fifteen: we met for lunch at Tressider Union. Tuna sandwiches, strawberry smoothies. Two games of air hockey. I won both."

"Only by violating some obscure pneumatic gaming statutes put forth in the Geneva Convention. My protest is still on file. Sixteen: we went for a walk up on Windy Hill."

"Wrong!" Liz clanged, laughing. "You left out the time we rented one of those silly plastic paddleboats at Shoreline. Game, set, and match!"

Paul slumped in a parody of defeat. "I yield to your superior power," he said submissively.

"Oh, but it was well played, my lord. Your chivalry has been duly noted." She planted a kiss lightly on his chin. He smiled sheepishly, consoled.

Liz made the bittersweet observation that she and Paul wouldn't be able to play this game much longer. But she was beginning to feel confident that they'd be a couple long enough to make up new ones.

Paul's own thoughts at that moment were leaning in the other direction in time. He reflected back on the unlikely combination of odd events—the TeraMemory contract, a detour into technical writing, Barry Dominic's intemperate libido, an evening of robotic performance art—that had led

Liz and him together into the present. Now they found themselves each in the most improbable of situations: Paul successfully juggling a high-tech career and a significant other, and Liz actually dating an engineer.

Not that Paul wasn't tempting fate. He had actually left work at five o'clock on a number of occasions over the past few weeks. The recent recalibrations of his personal life had not gone unnoticed by his colleagues in the lab. He could tell that his project managers were beginning to question his commitment.

And he had only to scan his weekly contracting invoices to reckon the cost of a relationship in digit-land. Paul figured it at about $1,600 a week. Only in a place like Silicon Valley were the trade-offs between livelihood and real life so naked.

Paul didn't care; being with Liz had an odd way of putting it all into perspective. She made the prevailing fanatical devotions to technology seem positively two-dimensional.

TERAMEMORY STOCK CATCHES FIRE; PRODUCTIVITY PLUMMETS

BARRY LOVED breakfast meetings, especially on Mondays; while the rest of the world was still shaving and thinking about the weekend, he was doing deals. He gripped his knife, ripped another section from his panettone French toast, and moved in for the kill.

"So, Bob, you want to sell stand-alone bean-counting boxes the rest of your life, or do you want to come with me and conquer the world?" he asked, chewing vigorously.

Robert McConnell, president and CEO of McConnell Decision Systems, herded his oatmeal tentatively around the bowl. "Barry, I'll level with you: I'm usually pretty skeptical about unproven technology, especially something as ambitious as this WHIP scheme of yours. But my people seem to be pretty excited about your little swindle, so I'll tell you what: if you can get the components ready, along with a good technology transfer package, by Q2, I'll fold your stuff into Topaz," he said, referring to MDS's highly anticipated, midsized server technology offering. "But I want a front-row seat at the WHIP IPO. I'll need an early in to cover my development costs."

Barry lifted his chin slightly, swallowing like a lizard. "Breakfast is on me, Bobby. You got a deal."

By afternoon, the word was spreading quickly among the inhabitants of planet TeraMemory:

From: afisher@teramemory.com
To: jmurton@teramemory.com
Subject: MDS deal

Jerry:

Things are really picking up momentum. Nobody's supposed to know yet, but Barry just did a huge deal with MDS to include WHIP in the Topaz server line. This is going to be mega, man, for sure. Tera's in a position to totally dominate. You know how things go in the server market. With MDS on board, everyone else is going to fall in line behind them. I think MDS is smart. They know WHIP will come to eat their lunch if they're not on board. And you just know any hardware vendor that ignores WHIP is going to be history.

Nothing else travels with the velocity of a secret. By Tuesday morning, rumor had escaped TeraMemory at a dead run, acquiring an ever-thickening crust of apocrypha as it went:

From: rburns@teramemory.com
To: rlageman@regisquest.org
Subject: Merger/takeover. Top Secret

Just got the inside scoop: Tera is partnering with MDS
to put WHIP on Topaz. No-brainer for MDS. Duh. And
MDS could really use an edge right about now. They're
pretty desperate, with flat/negative earnings for the
last five quarters. The real story is that this is just a pre-
amble to a merger/takeover, my manager says. It's all
pretty hush-hush. You didn't hear it from me.

Hush-hush, indeed. The gossip echoed merrily across the
valley, twisting with every turn. By Wednesday, the story
had found its way to the San José *Mercury*'s "Good Morning
Silicon Valley" column, one of the juicier conduits for industry gossip:

Industry insiders report Mountain View enterprise solutions giant TeraMemory is in merger negotiations with
McConnell Decision Systems.
    MDS Vice President Sanjay Sridhar, previously a
senior exec at Indian computer major Wipro, declined to
comment when asked whether the troubled company
had plans to merge. Sridhar said MDS was looking at
various opportunities but declined to elaborate on
them. "Frankly, it's too premature to say. I'm unable to
say anything at this time," Sridhar said.
    Speaking hypothetically, he said a company could
be turning itself around and courting a merger at the

same time. "At any particular point in time, there are multiple strategies that are adopted," Sridhar said.

Needless to say, this was all the confirmation the industry needed. Of course the rumors were true; in this business, "too premature to say" translated to "most emphatically yes."

This news of yet another TeraMemory conquest quickly commanded the interest of Wall Street. An analyst for the mighty Morgan & Sacks's "Internet Aggressive Growth New Millennium Fund" brought the story to the Thursday meeting. With a few keystrokes, the portfolio managers picked up six million shares of TeraMemory by two o'clock that afternoon, New York time.

The purchase stimulated the participation of the market's "momentum players"—a sophisticated Wall Street designation for copycats—by the end of the trading day. TeraMemory made the *Nightly Business Report,* which announced a "one-day, fifty-six percent rise of TeraMemory shares based on merger/takeover plans."

By Friday, the hyperbole had come full circle. TeraMemory's cubicle productivity dropped to zero as employees monitored the web at five-minute intervals, checking the value of their stock options. As the price hit twenty-eight, the programming staff found it increasingly difficult to nest their parentheses. At forty, the call queues in product support grew ever deeper as the T-shirted, head-setted techs floated away on reveries involving Ferrari Testarosas and Atherton real estate.

Tera's rocketing share price even suspended the traditional corporate antipathies and class tensions. Engineers and marketroids, until now sworn enemies, high-fived each other in the hallways. VPs and janitors greeted each other with enormous grins and, "Hey, millionaire." There was palpable electromagnetic charge in the air, and it was stronger than any wireless WHIP transmission.

HACKERS OF THE WORLD, UNITE—GEEKS PLOT PALACE COUP

STEVE'S ONLINE recruitment of NEMSIS developers had been met with considerable enthusiasm. He had touched a big nerve on the collective digital cortex. There was, as it turned out, a burning interest in ubiquitous computing protocols out in net-land.

There were a number of reasons for this. First and foremost, the endeavor contained enough fascinating theoretical issues and technical angles to keep everyone entertained. As an added bonus, wireless networking in general was shaping up to be one of the darlings du jour in commercial circles. It was getting to be the hottest game in the industry. Everybody, it seemed, wanted to play.

Not that Steve and his merry band of bit-twiddlers had

any economic conquest in mind, but it was always gratifying to establish a technical toehold well in advance of the suits. This wouldn't have been the first time it happened; a number of Free Bits mavens had already pulled this stunt in other niches, significantly impacting the industry media along the way. Free Bits stories made great copy; the computer industry pundits covered them eagerly, and geeks loved that kind of attention. For this socially backward and otherwise over-looked minority, it was better than money.

But mostly, what motivated them was the chase: a better algorithm here, an architectural tweak there, and optimizations all around. They could stretch their technical legs and run at their most comfortable pace: a flat-out, online electronic gallop.

The collaboration provided some social stimulation, too. In a very short time the NEMSIS crew had created a mailing list—nemsis-core@bests.com—to coordinate the efforts of an ever-widening pool of contributors. This electronic brotherhood (okay, there was one woman involved in the effort so far) provided rich opportunities for spirited discussion breaks wedged between all-night coding treks.

Razi, a network scientist specializing in virtual circuits, had been sucked into the effort when the NEMSIS crowd embraced some of his switching techniques which his technically short-sighted managers had already rejected. He was happy for the validation, if only from a ragtag confederation of online misfits:

From: razi@netconcepts.com
To: nemsis-core@bests.com
Subject: Node switching

Hey all,

If you evaluate the level of circuit abstraction up-front,
You'll reduce the need for downstream evaluation, especially after dynamic extension of the node_index data
structure (i.e. N>255). In short, in most cases you'll be
really glad you have the value of realnode_id loaded in
register by the time you get to the bottom of the function.
This is something I can't convince my project leader
here, because <flame> HE'S A STUPID, POND-SCUM-
SUCKING LOSER WITH A DEEP-FRIED HAIRBALL FOR
A BRAIN!!!! AAARRRRGGGHH!!!! 8-(*) </flame>

This is the way to do it.

```
if (realnode_id != (node_id_t) -1 | |
  (enode_id != (node_id_t) -1 &&
    enode_id != old_realnode_id))
      current->snode_id = current->enode_id;
current->fsnode_id = current->enode_id;
if (current->enode_id != old_enode_id)
      current->dumpable = 0;
return 0;
```

Richard was a frustrated programmer who hadn't written
a line of code in all the months his project had been stalled
amidst a re-org. NEMSIS had provided him with a necessary
outlet:

From: rmorgan@teknowledge.com
To: nemsis-core@bests.com
Subject: Re: Node switching

Hold on a minute. With all respect, Razi, don't you
need to be able to determine the state of
current>fsnode_id no matter where you are in the
decision tree? Seems like you need one more arrow in
your quiver, like this:

```
if (realnode_id != (node_id_t) -1 | |
   (enode_id != (node_id_t) -1 &&
   enode_id != old_realnode_id &&
   current->fsnode_id != old_enode_id))
       current->snode_id = current->enode_id;
```

Gene—a precocious and pimply high school sophomore
who thought NEMSIS was more fun than Dungeons and
Dragons—had his own ideas:

From: warg32@pyramid7.net
To: nemsis-core@bests.com
Subject: Re: Node switching

hey, your both right. but you can cut out won more step
and make it more elligent. Cuz for all values of N>255,
enode_id_t == old_enode_id. Like this:

```
if (realnode_id != (node_id_t) -1 | |
   (enode_id_t != old_enode_id))
       current->snode_id = current->enode_id;
```

sea what I mean? some times less is more.

Out of the mouths of babes. That was another one of the great things about these networked, ad hoc jam sessions: sometimes breakthroughs came from the most unlikely sources.

Systems administrators are often frustrated software developers, not to mention performance freaks. Aaron was no exception. Following the NEMSIS effort from the comfort of his cubicle in the TeraMemory tower presented a ready antidote to the tedium and drudgery of his primary responsibilities. It also put him in the position to make a contribution of his own, one he just couldn't resist despite the obvious conflicts of interest.

From: doubleaman@teramemory.com
To: nemsis-core@bests.com
Subject: Benchmarking: WHIP -vs- NEMSIS

I probably shouldn't be posting this, but I thought you guys might like to know: I've been benchmarking your stuff against the WHIP kernels on the Sparc Ultra 10Ks and Erickson IR Ethernet. It's NEMSIS by a neck: 68.698 KBPS at 300 virtual circuits, versus 62.022 for WHIP. And that's when our stuff isn't flaking out and falling over.

Tell me when you start hiring. I wanna be first in line.

All of this had pleased Steve immensely. It was the validation of all his technical prowess, and his instincts, to boot: he really was smarter than The Man.

From: shall@bests.com
To: nemsis-core@bests.com
Subject: Benchmarking: WHIP -vs- NEMSIS

> It's NEMSIS by a neck: 68.698 KBPS at 300
> virtual circuits, versus 62.022 for WHIP.
> And that's when our stuff isn't flaking
> out and falling over.

Dude, this is awesome. Want to join the core team? We
can't offer you anything but immortality.
Is that enough?

KIKI'S CRYPTIC ERRAND—SHADY DEALS IN THE APRICOT ORCHARD

LAUREL SAT AT the kitchen table eating a tuna sandwich and turning over the pages of her Filofax. Angus lay sprawled across her lap, napping with his front legs stretched out and hanging into space.

"Just look at this," she complained. "We're booked solid through next week. We're doing a lunch at SGI. Then lunch at MetaExchange. Then a corporate retreat in Portola Valley. Then another lunch at Network Synergy Solutions. Then a dinner at some fat-cat cigar club at Filoli. I swear, Guerrilla Gourmet's completely on fire. If this keeps up we'll be turning away more business than we take in."

Liz, taking a break from *The New York Times* crossword, made a mock-frown and rubbed her thumb and forefinger together just below her chin. "See this?" she asked. "World's smallest violin."

Laurel petulantly launched a cookie at her just as the phone started to ring. Liz took a bite and picked up.

"Liz? It's Kiki. Do you have a minute?" Her voice sounded as if her head were packed with Jell-O. Liz heard her cover the mouthpiece and blast out a sneeze.

"Oh, hi there. You don't sound very good. You need an emergency transfusion of chicken soup?"

Despite the fact that Liz had only seen Kiki a few times in the weeks since their trip to Tassajara, they had developed a strong affection. As well as enjoying a number of common interests and an off-kilter sense of humor, they also shared a certain private esprit de corps; they had both, to greater or lesser degrees, been shaped by what they called the "Barry Experience."

"Any more chicken soup, and I'm going to lay an egg," Kiki sniffled. "But there is something else you can do for me. Actually, you're probably the only person who *could* do it for me. Can I beg a big favor?"

It was nothing like the usual kind of favor one might perform for a sick friend. The favor in question revolved around the execution of a property transaction. It was about as far from chicken soup as you could get: Kiki needed Liz to act as a courier and executor in a rather cryptic real estate deal. All Liz needed to do, Kiki explained, was to pick up some deeds and title documents, deliver them to an address in San

José for a signature, and return them to an escrow office in Palo Alto.

Kiki's odd request raised a number of questions. Though Liz didn't want to seem unhelpful, she couldn't help but ask at least a few of the more obvious ones. But Kiki's answers, vexingly, created even more mystery.

"Why me? Why all the cloak and dagger? Couldn't you just send it FedEx?" Liz had asked.

"Because it's kind of a delicate matter. And because I trust you, and I think the seller will, too. There are some tender feelings involved, and it requires a gentle touch. You're the gentlest person I know." Kiki honked like a migrating waterbird. "I'd do it myself, if I weren't a raging river of phlegm.

"The seller is a sweet old man. You'll love him. But he never leaves the place. He just isn't a FedEx-and-email kind of guy. He doesn't even have an answering machine."

Liz teetered, split between apprehension and intrigue. "Well . . . okay. As long as you're sure I won't mess things up."

"You won't," Kiki reassured. "Just be your usual kind and charming self."

"This isn't illegal or anything, is it?" Liz asked playfully.

"Oh, don't you worry. It's all for the greater good." Then, Kiki gave her last and most tantalizing instruction: ". . . and remember, all you need to tell him is this: I won't touch the trees."

The next day Liz collected the documents from a realty office on University Avenue, then drove out to an address in East San José.

The trip took her past dozens of tech companies housed in salt-box office parks rising out of asphalt parking lots shimmering in the heat. After only a few miles, Liz decided she'd uncovered the recipe for a high-tech start-up: combine *mega, cyber, tele,* or *web* with *gen, net, com,* or *sys,* add buckets of money, bake in the sun, and serve smoldering. Presto! Garnish with dot com.

Then, wedged between *Meganet* and *Cybergen,* Liz saw something she definitely hadn't anticipated: an apricot orchard on maybe a dozen acres, with a dirty mauve ranch house squatting like a shingled toad at the edge of the parkway. Liz could see it was her destination by the fading numbers on the mailbox.

The weather was hot, and this was the hottest part of the Valley, so Liz was not surprised to see the main entrance guarded so casually by a single screen door. But she dared not knock; the door, flimsy and corroded, looked like it might fall off its hinges with little provocation.

There was no doorbell in evidence. "Hello? Anybody home?" she called out tentatively.

A stout, elderly Latino gentleman appeared from the dusky interior. *"Hola,"* he said, smiling a broad smile, swinging the screen door with one antique hand and holding out the other. "I'm Señor Jorge."

Liz accepted his invitation to sit and have an iced tea. They sat across from each other at a dingy, orange-flecked Formica table, drinking from ancient fountain glasses which spoke of thrift and the passage of time; Liz recognized them as gas-station giveaways from the dawn of her memory. Señor Jorge had a sweet tooth; he loaded his with sugar.

Señor Jorge, apparently, didn't get many visitors. He began happily rambling away about the apricot business, fruit canneries, the history of his dwindling orchard, and the many big changes to his neighborhood over forty-seven years. He was happy for a sympathetic ear; maybe Kiki knew what she was doing after all.

"I love my trees. I don't want to sell them, but it's no good here for me anymore," the farmer explained. "All the other land is bought up. I couldn't expand if I wanted to. And then there are the taxes. Besides, my kids and grandkids all move away. I want to be closer to them."

He eyed her a little cautiously. "You know the buyer, young lady?"

"Yes. I think I know her pretty well."

"And she doesn't own a computer company? She won't put up a lot of offices and fences and parking lots?"

"She says she's going to leave the trees right where they are."

He turned over his spoon and pursed his weather-beaten lips. "Well, that'd help me to sleep better nights, anyway." He smiled. "I hope she likes picking 'cots."

Sensing the opportunity, Liz handed him the folder of documents. The old man spread them out on the table, took a pen into his leathery fingers, and signed where the Realtor's yellow highlighter had indicated.

Liz, always compulsively curious, glanced at the documents as Señor Jorge labored over his signatures. They listed the seller as "Jorge Diaz," as she would have anticipated. But where Liz had expected to see Kiki's name, she read only an enigmatic, "Tejinder Preservation Foundation."

She had become certain there was more to Kiki than met the eye.

IPO—WHERE'D PAUL'S
OFFICE GO?

IT WAS AN astronomical event, the birth of a new planet. Out of the swirling collective vapors of investor expectation, corporate hype, and industry buzz, WHIP Technologies Inc. had finally condensed into a solid mass. White-hot, it spun out of TeraMemory's orbit, dragging Paul in its gravity.

The announcement of the cosmic birth went out in the form of a "red herring"—a slick, crimson-lettered prospectus describing this newest heavenly body in the corporate cosmos. It also signaled to the world an open invitation to the initial public offering.

Of all the Silicon Valley acronyms, nothing quickened the pulse like IPO. On those three letters hung the hopes of every bit-slinging entrepreneur in infotech. For any high-technology mogul whom industry history (all twenty years of it, alas) would count as a success, the initial public offering would mark the biggest one-day percentage leap in personal wealth in his (or, in the very unlikely event, her) life.

If these unsentimental, ruthlessly pragmatic scions of electronic industry held reverence for any ritual, this was the one. The IPO was the rite of spring, the canonical Silicon Valley baptism: the infant corporation is lowered into the murky lagoon of the NASDAQ, the water teeming with underwriters, syndicates, investment banks, brokerage houses, and not least but definitely last, the general public, all elbowing for prime position and a piece of the new arrival.

At least that was the scenario everyone hoped for, anyway—including the christened. A successful IPO was conducted exactly like a feeding frenzy, in fact: a spiraling, escalating orgy of greed and acquisition with no conscience, brakes, or moderating influence of any kind. Buyers lined up around the block to pay ever-increasing prices for ever-scarcer stock, and to be thankful for the privilege. P.T. Barnum would have wept.

Nevertheless, a wide assortment of high-wire investors and hot-rod financiers—adrenaline junkies, all—couldn't get enough of the scene. The IPO offered much more potential stimulation than the usual day at the races; the average speed of the stock market—even the go-go NASDAQ—was sedate by comparison. A good IPO was like a whole year of racing collapsed into a few hours. If General Motors equity was the stock market equivalent of the family sedan, then Tera-Memory was a Porsche—and the WHIP Technologies IPO a nitro-burning funny car, screaming, belching fire, and laying burning stripes of molten rubber down the middle of Wall Street.

A red-hot IPO was never a given, of course; there had been a number of high-profile fizzles. Everything hinged on how much rabid enthusiasm the offering's officers could generate in the weeks leading up to the conflagration.

Much of it could be done by the book; a number of well-established tools and techniques lent themselves handily to the shaping of investor expectation: PR, innuendo, cunningly crafted press releases, outright hearsay. But at the core, the fertilization of a good IPO was black art. And as in so many other risk-laden endeavors of persuasion, it all came down to a good story. This would explain why so many pre-IPO management team leaders were also Celtic bullshit artists; the blarney stone was the wellspring of their core competence.

Barry had celebrated by throwing a Cristall-soaked, WHIP Technologies employee bash with a name-brand rock band.

Paul never even got an invitation. For him the transition

was marked primarily by the mysterious disappearance of his workplace: he arrived at work one Monday morning to find the entire lab had been ripped out by the roots—dismembered cubicles, whiteboards laying in heaps, 10BaseT cables dangling from the ceiling. He made a discreet inquiry to a workman brandishing a cordless drill in the spot where Paul's office used to stand.

The workman answered curtly, uncoupling the segments of another cubicle. "You *wheep tech* now. You move. *Ayet-teen pipty Embockaday-o,*" came his spicy explanation.

1850 Embarcadero. The location offered a number of advantages: proximity to the bay (and breezes), ready access to upscale Chinese dim sum, and—for those employees deluded enough to believe they'd ever leave work before dark—an easy walk to the Palo Alto municipal golf course. Of course, nothing came for free: the office park was wedged up next to 101. The thoroughly congealed freeway was the only avenue of drive-time access. Hello, books-on-tape.

When he finally made his way to WHIP Technologies' new digs, Paul found most of the members of his lab in a freshly painted and barren conference room, negotiating with the group manager for cubicle positions. Everyone, of course, wanted one on the outer edge of the cluster, nearest the windows. The manager declared these should be awarded by seniority.

Except in Paul's case. Though he—amazingly enough—theoretically held enough seniority to place him in a cube with a sliver of direct sunlight, his manager passed him over.

Paul was a consultant; he'd end up dead center in the pod.

BIDDING FOR A DATE WITH THE CFO ON THE EBAY OF LOVE

THE MIDDAY SUN shouted its radiation down out of a cloudless sky. A group of executives huddled for shelter under canvas umbrellas on the terra-cotta terrace of WHIP Technologies' new campus. For nearly an hour they had been dynamically discussing e-commerce while poking mistrustfully at their arugula.

"Well, I'm definitely not in Kansas anymore," the new CFO observed. "Catered, outdoor strategy lunches. Raw fish. Designer fruit salad. What's next? Corporate surf safaris?"

Candy picked over the remains of her lunch: three deconstructed pieces of California roll and half a bottle of San Pellegrino. "Hey, that's not a bad idea," she remarked. "I think you're getting the hang of it already." She smiled at him. She had better; he was the product of six weeks' executive search.

HR had to poach this one from an aircraft company in Topeka.

She continued to lay it on. "It's great to have you on board. Really. Anything I can do for you, let me know."

"Okay, I'm letting you know now. You know any nice, single women?"

So much for Midwestern restraint, Candy reflected. "You get right to the point, don't you?"

"I do when I'm on a deadline: I'm sitting on a pair of three-hundred-dollar Stones tickets for this weekend. It was part of the salary negotiation. I said Stones tickets would help me make up my mind. I was joking. They were serious."

At 1:04 P.M. Candy sent an email to Gabrielle—a PR goddess at Cisco—inquiring about available, cute females from the technical marketing department.

To: gabbyg@cisco.com
From: csawyer@teramemory.com
Subject: Recruiting talent

Gab,

WHIP Technologies has a new CFO. He just moved from somewhere in the Midwest. He's got it all: cute, nice, single, Stones tickets for the weekend. No date, though. I told him I'd try and hook him up. Any prospects on your end?

Gabrielle was on the inside of any scoop, one ear to the ground at all times. She knew one in particular—Mimi, a size-2 Vietnamese marketing exec who'd been whining for months about the shortage of cool, smart, hip, nice, well-paid, good-looking guys in the Valley—all the while dating a succession of UPS and FedEx delivery guys. Realizing the scarcity of single CFOs on the market, Gab went straight to her Pilot for Mimi's number.

In the meantime, Candy speed dialed Deanna, a junior partner at Oryx, Herringbone & Stuffitt, a Menlo Park law firm specializing in intellectual property. Deanna, as it turned out, had a colleague—Kristin, a blond, long-legged paralegal—who had been desperate and dateless for months. Deanna jotted down the CFO's specs and told Candy she'd call back.

As Candy put down the phone she noticed that her 1:00—Jenn, a thirty-something, brunette, freelance graphic designer—had walked into her office a few minutes late, overhearing the end of the conversation.

"Hey, I want a shot at the CFO, too," she declared.

At 1:12 Gabrielle called with her candidate's number.

"Hey, I just got your email. I've got a great match for Mr. Corn-fed CFO," she announced. "Her name's Mimi. Cute, sassy, petite, and highly motivated. Your guy's gonna love her."

"He just might," Candy responded. "But I've got to hear back from the other bidders first."

"Oh, you *bitch*. You're working the network, aren't you?"

"Hey, this is the Bay Area, remember? Thirty percent of the guys are gay, thirty percent are terminal geeks, and the rest are married, or never leave their offices. We've got to give all the girls a chance. Let the market do its magic."

The AT&T operator broke in.

"I have Deanna and Kristin on conference call. May I connect?"

"Go ahead, operator," Candy said. The line popped twice. "Gabby, Deanna, Kristin, I've got another player here, Jenn. We're going speakerphone." Candy punched up the external audio and gave a shotgun introduction. "Everybody, meet everybody."

"Hi, everybody," they said in unison.

Gabrielle escalated immediately. "Hey, kids. How's it going?" Gabby only sounded casual. She wasn't about to let her own candidate get squeezed out. "Give me a sec, okay? I'm going to conference in Mimi on my end." She put the group on hold for a moment, then dropped back in. "Everybody say hi to Mimi."

"Hi, Mimi," the women chanted in unison.

"Hello," came Mimi's singsong voice, a little tentative.

Deanna, accustomed to quarterbacking meetings, took point: "Okay, everybody. We're meeting today to discuss something of importance to everyone here: who gets the CFO with the Stones tickets. Let's all listen to what Candy can tell us about him."

The aggressive start caught Candy a little off guard. "Well, to be honest, I don't really know him all that well."

Everyone groaned on the line simultaneously. Candy quickly retrenched.

"Hold on, now—he seems like a really great guy. He's brand new—he's the new CFO at WHIP Technologies. We talked during a strategy lunch. Maybe during a couple of meetings, too. I mean, he seems neat—made a couple of smart comments, and he chose the vegetarian entrée at lunch."

This last detail was met favorably, judging by the babble of the conference call. Candy was a mistress of spin; interest was on the rise.

"So, is his photo online?" Kristin asked.

Mimi loosened things up with a joke: "Yeah, and do you have a PowerPoint presentation on the guy?"

The women began to probe for particulars—car, fitness level, stock options, the size of his bonus pool. Jenn—because she'd worked in the Valley awhile and knew the potential hazards better—asked about personal hygiene.

"Teeth okay? Does he have those gross hairs in his ears? Any indication of back hair? Big garlic fan?"

"Hey, he just arrived from the Midwest," Candy assured them. "He reeks of fabric softener and Ivory soap. No discernible aftershave. And no—I repeat no—body jewelry or obvious piercings.

This brought an amplified sigh of relief from Jenn, as well as the others.

"Well," said Gabrielle, moving to consolidate a position, "I think it's time to drill down to core issues. I think Mimi should get the first shot. After all, she was first in line."

This provoked protests from Jenn and Kristin, who began arguing for some kind of lottery procedure. Candy did her expenses and read email while the rest of them debated.

But at 1:16, the bottom fell out of the negotiation.

"What about his last relationship?" asked Jenn.

"Yeah, what's the catch here? Something sounds fishy," Mimi said.

"Details, Candy," Kristin demanded.

Candy was stuck. The rules required full disclosure. "I think his assistant said he's divorced and has two little girls back in the Midwest somewhere, but it's amicable, it's all good with the ex-wife."

Like accountants, Kristin and Mimi quickly ran the numbers and backed out of the deal. "Gotta go, done that, but thanks," from Kristin and "Gee, I'm really sorry, but maybe in another few months if I haven't met someone," from Mimi.

"So Jenn wins by default," said Candy, hoping to close the only remaining deal on the table.

"Cool," said Jenn. "I love the Stones, and *I* don't care if it doesn't work out. I'm just coming off an abusive relationship and can't commit now anyway." She took a breath. "But he sounds like a good buffer experience."

"Okay, thanks everybody for your participation," Deanna said, capping off the meeting with her corporate stamp.

The women all hung up in a volley.

It was 1:17.

LEFT HAND TURN: THE LOWLY SYSADMIN MOVES ONE STEP CLOSER TO BARRY

IT HAD STARTED innocently enough. As Aaron turned onto Embarcadero from WHIP Technologies' parking lot, he saw that the 101 on-ramp was completely wedged, packed solid. He couldn't face it, not today; he'd wait out the jam back in his office. He cranked the wheel unto a hard U-turn, just in front of an advancing wave of traffic spilling out under the opposing green light.

His van had other ideas. The broad turning radius wasn't going to allow for a timely change of direction. The cars were coming on too fast. Aaron calculated that a compromise would be in everyone's best interests; he ducked into a driveway conveniently in his vehicle's arc.

And so he found himself on the premises of the local

Porsche dealership, located cunningly proximate to the clusters of high-tech office parks so common in that section of Palo Alto.

A walk around the lot might be a good way to kill time, he decided. He parked, shut off the ignition, stepped out of the driver's seat, and slammed the door behind him.

Of course he gravitated to the Boxster convertible. It had been carefully designed to ensnare the attention of the information-age male. It was just curiosity, he told himself, as he nervously flipped his tongue stud across his upper lip.

He never heard the salesman approach. Out of nowhere, it seemed, came a voice resonating with strange confidence.

"So, you want to take it to the next level."

He turned to see a meticulously groomed, prematurely graying man—probably in his thirties—standing absolutely still in a starched white shirt, yellow tie, gold cuff links, and Rolex. The pleats of his tailored slacks shivered gently in the breeze.

Aaron regarded the salesman's conventional mode of dress with barely concealed disdain. He well knew where this was going. "Naw—I'm just looking," he stiffed.

"I understand. You're right to feel that way," the salesman agreed, as if Aaron's curt declaration was a subject of profound debate. "This car is powerful magic. Rest your eyes on it. Feel free."

Kind of spooky for a car salesman, Aaron reflected. He turned his eyes back to the car, and registered the conspicuous absence of a price tag. "So, what does this go for?"

"You're just looking," the salesman remarked flatly. He held up his hands and smiled.

Aaron was a little annoyed. "Okay, if I *were* looking, what would this cost me?"

"So you *are* ready for the next level."

What a weird little game. Okay, he'd play a little. "Yeah. The next level. I'm moving up these days," Aaron said with only a thin trace of sarcasm.

"I can see. What do you have there?" He kept his feet planted and twisted around for a view of the rear of Aaron's tattered van, plastered with Grateful Dead decals. "A West-phalia. Great vehicle. Excellent transportation for a college student." The salesman untwisted and looked at Aaron for two moments without blinking. "Are you a college student?"

This pricked sharply at Aaron's pride. Sure, his nose was pierced, he was wearing ripped jeans and a Phish concert T-shirt—but there was no way he was going to be intimidated by a pair of cuff links. "Uh, no," he said a little arrogantly, puffing up with Gen-X dot-com swagger. "I work for a major Internet company. I'm an engineer." Well, close enough, anyway; technically, systems administrators were classified as internal services, not engineering. But the sales guy wouldn't have any idea.

"Really? What company?"

Ha. Aaron had drawn the salesman onto his own home turf. It would be easy to dominate the conversation now. "It's a cutting-edge, start-up spinoff of TeraMemory," he said, smirking just slightly. "I don't imagine you'd know much about . . ."

"WHIP Technologies," the salesman chirped. "Www .whip.com. Oh, yeah. Sure."

"You've heard of WHIP?" Aaron asked, a little aghast.

The salesman looked a little hurt. "Enterprise network solutions. Wireless High-speed Internet. Symbol WTI, NASDAQ. IPOed at seventeen. Closed today up three and a half at ninety-eight. I've sold so many Porsches to WHIP Tech officers, I feel like an employee myself." He smiled an avuncular smile. "You're almost *family.*"

Aaron was astounded, but the salesman wasn't through. He took note of the accessory looped on Aaron's belt, looked at him a little obliquely and said, "Leatherman. I'll bet you're a sysadmin."

Now Aaron was on the ropes. "Uh, yeah," he gawped.

Aaron's conversational home-field advantage was vanishing fast. "Hey, how about those new Sparc Ultras?" the salesman asked, raising his eyebrows. "Sixty-four bit bus. Rrrrockin'," he winked.

The only way out, Aaron thought, was to keep raising the ante. "Oh, yeah, you bet. Getting three of them next week—web server, dataserver, and development. Maximum processor arrays," he bragged, sticking out his chin with a studied cyber-macho. "Symmetric multiprocessing rules."

And so salesman put the big move on. "Now, correct me if I'm wrong, but systems administration is internal services, not engineering, right?"

With that, the salesman had him over a barrel; the power to puncture Aaron's self-esteem rested in his hands—and Aaron knew it. The salesman quickly extrapolated all the remaining moves in the conversation, and concluded that the only way Aaron's pride would exit the lot intact would be in a new Boxster. Nerds weren't the only people who understood game theory. He commenced his endgame.

"One of the first hundred employees, right?"

The salesman was extending Aaron a chance to preserve his vanity. "Sixty-two," Aaron recited proudly.

The salesman's eyebrows shot up. "Yes. I could tell. Key employee. Practically a founder. Stock options, right?"

Aaron's self-image was moving steadily out of the danger zone. "Yeah," he said, a little shyly, and thumbed his eyebrow rings.

"Recently vested, right?"

"May."

"I'm not going to tell you how much this car costs," the salesman said quickly, ". . . yet. Right now I can tell you two things for sure: one, in a year you'll be able to afford five of these, and two, right now you absolutely cannot afford not to own one."

These brazen declarations jolted Aaron's credulity, if only for a moment. "How do you figure?" he parried.

"Because for a man in your position, this car attracts wealth. No, even more—it *creates* it." His speech slowed and took on gravity, putting Aaron in a mild state of hypnosis. "It induces a new state of consciousness, and that consciousness creates your circumstances."

Aaron could feel he was losing his struggle against the salesman's gravitational pull. He spent his last ounce of fight: "Oh, come on. You really expect me to believe that?"

"You tell me," the salesman challenged. "Barry Dominic has a Porsche. Several, in fact."

Aaron looked at him half excited, half confused. That's a good point, he thought to himself.

The salesman stroked the kill-shot. "Hey, even Jerry Garcia moved up to a Porsche."

With that, Aaron's sense of fiscal proportion had come unmoored. He felt somehow enchanted, or at least pleasantly disoriented. The Boxster's glinting chrome traced ghostly lines in Aaron's retina as his field of vision collapsed around the salesman's face.

"Dare," the salesman intoned. "Dare to do it."

In the end, Aaron dared. As rush hour abated, he signed the papers, traded away his trusty Westphalia, turned the key, and throttled up his new, turbo-charged ego machine. He giddily made for the on-ramp, now free of traffic.

Not without a small pang of misgiving, though. As he pulled away, he checked the rearview mirror, and saw his old van receding. He could swear he saw the steal-your-face sticker laughing at him.

LIZ WINS THE TUG-OF-WAR
BETWEEN HEART AND CUBICLE

ANYPLACE YOU went where young, heterosexual women spoke freely, it always cropped up in conversation. And ever since graduation, Liz couldn't help but overhear the conventional wisdom about men in Silicon Valley: relentlessly career-focused, narcissistic, as emotionally available as cyborgs.

Though Paul belied the stereotype in most every way, it was true that he really hadn't been spending much time away from TeraMemory recently; Liz was beginning to feel a little jealous of that other steady attachment in Paul's life. But though his work may have been an alluring and tenacious rival, Liz wasn't about to yield to a corporate inamorata.

Over the months that Liz and Paul had become a bona fide item, their relationship had happily transitioned—as

Paul had quipped with sentimental if nerdy acuity—through the entire continuum of romantic phase-changes: from airy flirtation, condensing into mushy attraction, finally solidifying into a passionate love-bond. But lately that bond was being tested by the inevitable tug-of-war between the heart and the cubicle. In the Silicon Valley, the cubicle almost always won. But Liz was a crafty and resourceful lover; she used all available means to subvert the prevailing work culture and preserve courtship's momentum.

This evening TeraMemory had imposed a particularly heavy challenge; Paul was in the midst of an epic code-push. In fact, they were always in the middle of some major effort at Tera, but this week they'd managed to convince Paul it was more of a crisis than usual.

Such were the impediments to romance in dot-com-land. But desperate times required desperate measures; Liz would find her way into Paul's heart via his workstation and Yahoo Instant Messenger.

She logged on from her laptop at the kitchen table.

"I can't believe I've been reduced to this," she mused, and tapped out a message on the keyboard.

Somewhere in the virtual belly of the beast that was TeraMemory, Paul's workstation beeped at him impertinently. **"INSTANT MESSENGER WANTS TO CONNECT. WOULD YOU LIKE TO CHAT?"** it displayed.

Argh. Paul felt a momentary wave of goal-oriented anxiety as he anticipated another potential time-sink. How the hell was he going to meet his milestones amid all the interruptions? He swatted at the Y key resentfully, and read.

> LaLiz: Hey, engineer-man. You going to come up for air any time before Y3K?

He lightened, and remembered there was something else in the world as compelling as the WHIP. Almost.

> GigaPaul: Hey, you little minx. Probably not. Can't talk long. Working on WHIP. Crazed.

She could see this was going to be harder than she'd thought. But Liz always rose to a challenge.

> LaLiz: *sigh* Have you no tender words for your coy mistress?
> GigaPaul: If we had world enough, fair rocket-babe, and time . . . but I'm majorly on deadline. If I don't get my little widgets working by the end of the week, Barry's going to be very cross with me and have me banished to Siberia. Or Gilroy.

It was clear to Liz that Paul was "wedged," as she liked to tease him—stuck in that characteristic techie tunnel vision that did not admit any consideration of the contentments outside of the machine. She had seen him like this before; whether he knew it or not, Paul was sorely in need of rescue, or at least perspective. Liz escalated to her most potent ploy.

> LaLiz: Man does not live by code alone. Besides, I've been cooking up a special surprise. You do still eat, don't you?
> GigaPaul: Ah, yeah—microwave popcorn and Jolt Cola, mostly. Must admit I am a bit peckish, tho. I've forgotten what real food looks like.

At that moment Angus exercised the universal house cat's information-age prerogative, jumping up onto the table and flouncing lightly across Liz's keyboard.

> LaLiz: /.jfdw1h
> GigaPaul: ???
> LaLiz: Special message from the cat. It's in code, I think. You two are plotting against me, aren't you?
> GigaPaul: Why do you say that? [message for Angus: kljs d0986s $^%lk] So, what's the culinary extravaganza tonight?
> LaLiz: Faceless and fickle! I thought you were on deadline!?!
> GigaPaul: Are you going to tease me all night?
> LaLiz: I hope so.
> GigaPaul: Oh, wait'll I get my hands on you . . .
> LaLiz: That's the idea.

Paul's programmer deadpan cracked into a grin. There was something about Liz's playfulness and sheer joie de vivre—it never failed to reorient him to the relative importance of things. When he heard the music in her voice—or in this case, her keystrokes—his grim, corporatized fun-house view of the world from the cubicle would fade a little, and he could remember that WHIP just might not be the most important thing in the world. He recalibrated, laughed, and continued typing.

> GigaPaul: Okay, so what's on the menu?!?
> LaLiz: Artichokes. Chicken cacciatore. Vanilla Haagen Daz and olallie berries. And a video.
> GigaPaul: What's the video?

Gotcha, Liz laughed to herself. She moved in for the clincher, typing triumphantly.

> LaLiz: 101 Dalmations.
> GigaPaul: I'm leaving now. See you in twenty minutes. Don't you dare start without me.

GEEK APOCALYPSE: FOUR DAYS TO SHIP, AND THE BUGS ARE EVERYWHERE

THERE COMES A time in every programmer's life when, after months of design, development, and debugging, he may come to discover an architectural oversight, flaw in basic reasoning, or mistaken key assumption. In a rush it dawns on him that the whole project must be scrapped and rethought. Desolation reigns.

Paul was putting WHIP through its paces. Peering into his workstation, he started up the WHIP test suite, tapping out the keystrokes on the command line. He watched as the results trickled in.

```
# whiptest -d -f /usr/eng/test/V3.6
init ==> passed
pingnode ==> passed
```

```
pushpacket ==> passed
recv_interrupt ==> passed
thrupt_50 ==> passed
 Error 920: incorrect segment length
 Error 220: missing data
 Error 6: assembly failure
thrupt_200 ==> failed
Defect(s) detected. Terminating.
Debug mode? [Y/N] n
Trace dumped to file ~/whiptrace.2157
#
```

He exhaled sharply and leaned back in his chair, testing its spring-loaded, ergonomic correctness to the very limit. Gripping his brow between thumb and forefinger, he listened to waves of despair and panic sloshing around in his skull.

This was worse than bad. This was the apocalypse. And they were supposed to be shipping in four days.

Any serious software development effort included the construction and maintenance of a "performance/regression test suite." The test suite was a sort of obstacle course for a computer program—a series of digital jumps, hoops, and contortions which defined the minimum standard of behavior for the system in question. As the programmers continued to build and refine their program, they periodically ran it against the test suite to make sure none of their recent modifications had negatively impacted their gold standard of functionality. In other words, the test suite existed to provide periodic reassurance they hadn't inadvertently broken anything while they weren't looking.

And WHIP was flunking spectacularly. It was failing the simplest tests in the suite, the easy stuff it had been breezing through for months—until now.

Of course, this was the worst possible timing for such a sobering event. WHIP Technologies' collective technical backs were to the wall, with the combined expectations of the industry pressed up against them. Not only were they supposed to deliver product shortly, but they were the darlings of the hour. All eyes were upon them.

Any of the engineers would have given their compilers for a chance to regroup and recode. But the Silicon Valley path to glory was in every way like riding a roller coaster: once the process of revolution was set in motion, there were no opportunities to pause, and getting off was suicide—and an embarrassing, highly visible one at that.

Paul reviewed the previous weeks' grim slide in his mind. How could it have come to this? WHIP was on deck to be the Next Big Thing. The technology was supposed to be bulletproof by now. What the hell had gone wrong?

Other engineers throughout the lab were caught up in similarly black ruminations. Though their project leaders projected the usual can-do attitude, there was no way to put a positive spin upon it: WHIP's technical coolness was crumbling in their hands. It was time to question sacred assumptions.

For a while, WHIP had at least appeared stable. The original design specifications had been prudently conservative: spare, modest, direct, they ensured that the early struggles with WHIP's essential complexity hadn't been too bloody.

But then came the bells, whistles, and chrome. A number of after-the-fact "requirements" and "extensions to functionality"—all conceived and commanded by factions increasingly distant from the actual engineering and programming—had tickled a number of WHIP's shortcomings and design flaws.

At first there had been vigorous warnings and dire predictions from technical quarters. Changing specs midproject was bad policy; such "creeping featurism" was always a recipe for disaster. But these qualms were overcome by a shameless appeal to engineering's vanity: WHIP was so beautiful, management had assured them, so well-designed that the very integrity of its architecture would preserve it from ruin. There was no need for worry; it was, they insisted, foolproof.

Nothing is foolproof, because fools are so ingenious. As WHIP was diddled, tweaked, dithered, and extended, the hoops in the test suite began to fall. At first this was no great cause for alarm; minor ripple effects were not uncommon, and a modest number of reversals always expected. But as weeks passed, the ripples became increasingly obscure, and remediation decreasingly effective. One set of patches would result in a whole new constellation of falling hoops in far-flung locations, and each time the explanations proved more elusive.

And so the human behavior in the lab became more buggy, too. The programmers became paranoid and defensive in their craft. A spontaneous cult of secrecy and denial developed. No one could bring themselves to face the issue squarely, even as they could feel their creation coming apart. The stakes were too high now. The revolution was in progress, and the TeraMemory spinoff was committed. Full steam ahead, damn the torpedoes, and for god's sake, everybody ignore the iceberg.

HOT WORDS AS BARRY
BARBECUES HIS BOARD

PRIDE IS A powerful narcotic. Certainly it ruled Barry; to preserve his own, he would have gladly burned his children. Fortunately, today's exercise in conceit would involve a more modest sacrifice; Barry would only be burning his bridges.

"Absolutely, positively no. We are not getting into bed with Microsoft."

Barry flexed his jaw, parked his fists on his hips, and squared off with Mission Peak through the broad span of the conference room window. Neither blinked.

This month's meeting of WHIP Technologies' board of directors was shaping up to be a tense and uncomfortable affair. It was the first real test of cooperation between Barry and his board—composed mostly of venture capital partners. All were flunking in spectacular fashion.

It was, at heart, a contest of pride and greed. While the

rest of the board recognized an opportunity to realize an immediate and handsome gain on their investment, Barry saw only a potential—nay, a certain—erosion of his power in the infotech axis.

Ed Pilphur, Venture World Capital's sixtyish president, led the drive for the greed team. "Look, Barry, everyone agrees that it would be in WHIP Technologies' best interests to license our technology to Microsoft. They've expressed a lot of interest, and they're willing to pay handsomely for the chance to partner."

Barry grimaced, eyes reddening with hate. "No way. I know how those guys work. Anything threatens their monopoly, and it's always the same: embrace and corrupt. They just want to get their hands on it so they can make their *improvements* and *extensions.*" Barry spat out the words, sneering with disgust. "But it's just divide-and-conquer, plain and simple. We play footsie with those jokers, and before you know it, WHIP won't even be a protocol anymore—it'll be a technical train wreck, and then the boys from Redmond will move into the vacuum with their own play." He turned and glared at his board. "I'm not going to walk into that trap."

To be fair, Barry's instincts were sound—though that would hardly have made a difference in any case. He wouldn't have shared his darling WHIP with Microsoft even if it made all the sense in the world. In fact, he wouldn't have done it if Bill Gates had held Grandma Dominic bound and gagged. Barry would never play into the pockets of his archrival if he could possibly help it.

The tension was unbearable, but there was too much at stake. It was clear the meeting would not adjourn until the impasse was broken. Derek Morton, Woodside Associates' wonderboy VP, unwittingly catalyzed the defining event.

"Look, Barry—we all think this'd be a good idea. It's a great opportunity for market penetration and early recovery of capital. We have a consensus here, and . . ."

"And I still have controlling interest," Barry barked. "And I don't care what you and your banker pals think. You didn't build a billion dollar company. You don't have the vision. Your opinion *doesn't count.*"

This declaration stopped the conversation dead in its tracks. Derek's color built to a crimson crescendo against the backdrop of his blond buzz cut, as the rest of the board looked on in silent horror. There it was: the venture partners had placed hundreds of millions of dollars on the table, but Barry had ruled their collective opinion invalid.

Anyone else would have realized they'd stepped over the line. Anyone but Barry, that is; he turned the heat up another notch.

"Get this through your thick skulls," he boomed. "This isn't just about money. Yeah, I know you guys have made a couple of bucks capitalizing your coffee franchises and your spit-roasted chickens, but I'm talking about the future here, and that's with a capital F. This isn't fast food. This is the fast track to world domination.

"You guys are just going to have to let me do what I do

better than anybody else. It's great to have you all along for the ride," he smirked, more than a little patronizingly, "but I'm gonna drive. And the less often I have to take my eyes off the road, the better."

If pride was a drug, today Barry was definitely DUI. But none of them was prepared for the next turn.

Barry scanned the faces at the table. "And if any of you tries to get in the way, I'll run you over. As in flat. You'll be nothing but a stain on the information highway."

Nobody spoke. A brutalized quiet filled the room, the kind that follows any swift act of dismemberment. Barry surveyed the group through a mask of terminal disdain, then stalked out of the conference room.

The board continued to sit mutely in a brutalized hush, until the spell was at last broken by Andrew Lucre's pager. He swatted at it, and glanced at the little green window.

"Yep, that's a four-two-five. Sounds like they want an answer. Shall I do the honors?"

Ed exhaled. "Hold off a while, Andy. Don't discourage our friends in Washington state quite yet."

Andrew cocked his head. "What, you think Barry's going to change his mind? You saw him. He's like a mad dog about this one."

Ed leaned back and meshed his liver-spotted fingers together. "I've seen plenty of mad dogs in my time, Andy. There's always a way to make 'em heel."

THE BAD NEWS—WHIP GETS
WHIPPED BY PUNDITS

"AW, SHIT."

Paul already knew the news was bad. His engineering group manager had been sending out emails rebutting the articles and postings that had sprung up in some of the nerdier corners of the web, but this one was different.

There was something about seeing it committed to paper. Even in the middle of the electronic age, dead trees still had an impact that HTML couldn't touch. The story sneered at Paul from the front page of *Information Weekly*. He read it and cursed.

"[WHIP] is not quite there yet," reports the director of Rand Corporation's Center for Research Informatics (CRI). "Until the technology hardens and stabilizes, it will not be a good candidate to supersede existing protocols."

Such reports appear to be dampening the electronics market's enthusiasm for the new technology. Error recovery and scalability are also emerging as serious issues. But most worrisome to the industry at large continues to be the WHIP protocol's stability. Allan Erman, an analyst at DataSearch International, summarized the concerns. "This stuff is barely out of the garage, and already they're proposing next year's extensions. Where does that leave customers who want to buy this year? People have had it up to here with instant obsolescence."

Even more worrying was that some of the industry's forward scouts had discovered NEMSIS. Already, enthusiasm for the outlaw WHIP knockoff was building. The previous week's *IW* had featured a piece on the burgeoning Free Bits movement, that band of network-roving programmers who threatened to invert the laws of electronic capitalism. Wedged in between paeans to the movement's troll-like hacker chieftains was the subheading, "WHIP Without Hype." The article had praised the NEMSIS effort for its modesty of purpose and Zenlike simplicity. Paul had ripped it out and pinned it to the outside of his cubicle, his yellow highlighting emphasizing the most relevant—and, to the engineering staff, infuriating—passage:

NEMSIS may not have all the features of WHIP, but it achieves about 80% of the functionality—at twice the speed, in a quarter the space, with near flawless runtime execution. Oh, yeah: it's free, too. With such no-nonsense appeal, we wouldn't be surprised to see a whole new crop of NEMSIS-compliant devices by early next year. Already several telecommunications giants have launched serious efforts to validate the feasibility of the NEMSIS network utility constellation.

The pundits had baldly stated what the WHIP engineers could not: on the silicon battlefield, less was more. WHIP was sinking under the weight of marketing's post-hoc ornamentation. And there was no path back to simplicity. Once you bloated, you stayed bloated.

Worst of all, Paul had the unsettling feeling he might bear some responsibility for the current state of things. After all, NEMSIS's project leader and patron saint was also his best friend. And Paul had unwittingly aided and abetted by talking around the edges of the WHIP NDA over Chinese food.

But, curiously, Paul felt no remorse, although in a perversely recursive pang of conscience, he felt guilty about not feeling guilty. After all, WHIP was already well on the path to destruction independent of Paul's intervention—ever since management had made the decision to dilute the code base with its flabby extensions to the protocol.

And when it came right down to it, the NEMSIS guys were better engineers anyway—with or without Paul's unintentional help. If WHIP was doomed, NEMSIS was merely accelerating the pace of decline. That part, at any rate, was pure Silicon Valley; everything happened a lot faster here. In this case, that would be a mercy.

"Merde, alors." Vero glared at the invoice.

Laurel paused from her goat-cheese-and-walnut constructions—creamy, nut-encrusted little pucks that sat center stage in Guerrilla Gourmet's signature salad. "Hey, honey, what's the fuss?"

"This customer—we have done many jobs for them, and they don't pay and they don't pay. And now they pay with this—" Vero waved some flimsy certificates in the air with considerable disgust. "They pay with *company stock.* 'Cash flow problems,' they say. Sixteen employees, and they say they pay all of them in stock, too. So we are supposed to be happy." She spun the papers across the table with an annoyed continental backhand. "And they are not even publicly traded. So now we own five hundred shares of—" She slapped at the pile, retrieving a certificate, and scanned the face, "'Network Synergy Solutions,'" she spat. "So, what do we do, make soup out of these?"

"Oh, let's!" Laurel enthused. "Then we'll have chicken stock, beef stock, and *stock* stock!" Vero's sour mood began to crack; the two women laughed giddily.

Laurel wiped the goat cheese from her fingers and gave Vero a mischievous look. "No, wait—I've got a better idea—we can frame them. They can be mementos of life in the Silicon Valley. In twenty years they'll give us a big laugh."

Vero's Gallic dander abated in the cheerful light of Laurel's lighthearted suggestion. She rolled her eyes, shrugging. *"Bof,"* she exclaimed with an ironic little French smirk. "Guerrilla Gourmet is now the high-tech *big shot.*"

But she couldn't resist a final shot. Narrowing her eyes, she curled her lip and muttered half-darkly, "Network-Synergy-*espèce-de-con.*"

BARRY DINES ON CANDY
AT FLEUR DE LYS

BARRY HARDLY ever dined out in the open anymore. His security guys would have a stroke.

As Darrel—his beefy director of personal security—had spelled out, "Look, Barry—you've got a former secret service agent, two hard cars, three ex-Navy Seals, and a twenty-four-seven perimeter patrol—and you want to spend two hours out in the clear, exposed to the general freakin' public? Not on my watch. Some Belgian wacko hits you in the face with a cream pie like old Bill Gates got, and I never work again. This is a competitive business, Barry, just like yours. You need to get on board." Then, cashing in on their macho camaraderie, he added, "If not for your sake, then do it for me."

Barry had relented. If he was a sucker for anything, it was for real-life action heroes pleading with him.

But Fleur de Lys had a number of private dining rooms, which had satisfied Darrel and the rest of Barry's corporate guard dogs. And this particular evening, Barry was pleased to discover an unanticipated benefit to his sequestration: it greatly facilitated his advances on the object of his affections—a position currently being filled by Candy Sawyer. He silently thanked his bodyguards as he eased his hand under the table.

"I'm so impressed with your work," Barry crooned as he caressed her shapely, muscular leg. "You're all over the strategic markets. That's one of the things I love about you, Candy—you know where to focus your efforts."

Candy swigged her Kir Royale and fixed Barry with a gaze somewhere between boudoir and boardroom. "That's nice of you to say, Barry—it's my core competence." She shifted in her seat, generating some kinetic energy under the table in the process. "You just need the right touch. You have to just feel your way into the revenue streams, and use your intuition about where you're going to find the most juice."

This statement rendered Barry uncharacteristically mute with admiration, at least for the moment. His eyes nearly crossed with delight. Candy moved into the conversational vacuum, intent on multiplying her gains.

"You've got to go straight for the big targets, and cut 'em down fast. That's the whole game, Barry," she explained, voice quickening, caressing his meaty finger. "Once you've got the strategic markets roped and tied, the regional markets just fall into line. You just sit back and watch them all come to you." She tapped her fuchsia fingernail on his knuckle for emphasis.

Seeing such hardballing ruthlessness in a member of the fairer sex inspired an almost unseemly delight in Barry. Candy was simultaneously pushing all his pleasure buttons. "Oh, you're so tough," he fawned, manhandling her knee more vigorously by the moment. "How'd a mega-babe like you learn to be such an ass-kicker?"

Candy knew an opportunity to consummate an advantage when she saw one. "Good coaching, I guess," she said with an adoring look. "And you know, Barry, you could be getting even more leverage out of me if you"—she lowered her voice just slightly—"have the desire."

"Oh, do I," came his throaty growl. "Nothing would give me more pleasure. Tell me," he commanded more than a little salaciously, "how I can get more leverage out of your core talents."

Candy was blunt. "As executive VP, Sales and Marketing."

Another suitor might have been put off by such an abrupt proposition, but Candy was demonstrating just the kind of naked ambition Barry so admired in himself. She seemed almost too good to be true; Barry was eager to find out just how firm her naked ambitions were. He decided to raise a little resistance, just to benchmark her desire.

"Now, I know you're one hell of a capable woman, Candy, and I hate to break it to you, toots, but I already have a guy in that slot. And as far as I can tell, he's doing okay."

Candy wrinkled her nose and frowned, temporarily diminishing the tenor of seduction. "Let me tell you about your guy, Barry: he's a weenie. As in www.weenie.com. This year, he's dropped the ball on at least two big opportunities."

So she wasn't afraid to step on some heads on her way up. There's that killer instinct again, Barry gloated to himself. "Oh, yeah? Tell me what you know."

"Remember that undersecretary of trade who came through town last February? That guy was ready to write checks—big ones—and your guy didn't follow through. Not important enough, he says. Then Informix swooped in for the kill—a week of skiing at Tahoe, plus the standard Reno casino junket, and they turned him. That deal should have been us."

"Hmm." Nothing roiled Barry's anxiety like the specter of missed opportunity. "Tell me more."

"Then there was that toupee-wearing spook wannabe from the NSA with the fat black budget. All we had to do was humor him by pretending to be impressed with his James Bond routine. I could have nailed that one with both hands tied behind my back. Your guy was playing footsie with some university provost over some bullshit academic discounts."

Candy downshifted before Barry's ardor could be com-

pletely eclipsed by the shadow of unclosed deals. "And there
are a few other things I have that your guy will never be able
to compete with," she asserted in a softer, breathier voice.

"Like what?"

"Like, you're holding one of them right now," she said,
launching down the dregs of her cocktail. "Nothing trumps a
great pair of legs."

Barry certainly must have found Candy's case compelling;
he tried to imagine her in a higher position on the org chart—
as well as in several more positions from the office edition of
the *Kama Sutra.*

The waiter brought their lobster salads.

By the end of the meal, Candy's play for promotion
was nearly complete. There were only a few details left to
resolve.

"It would mean that we'll have to work much more
closely in the future," Barry asserted. "We'll have to tightly
coordinate our efforts. Are you ready for a little strategic
merger?" he asked with corporate-veneered lewdness.

"I don't know, Barry—are you? There's this rumor
floating around that you've already got a silent partner. What
am I supposed to do with that?"

This wasn't the first time his zombie marriage had inter-
posed itself amidst his operations of conquest; he'd learned to
deflect it without blinking. "Oh, don't you worry about
that," he blithely dismissed, working the hem of her skirt.

"When you're king of the world, people make up all kinds of bullshit stories. Don't pay any attention. You're backed up by the full faith and credit of the Bank of Barry.

"Your proposal is intriguing," he said, returning to the deal at hand. "But I do think we should sleep on it."

"You're the boss," she said breezily.

GREEN TEA AND RED INK:
BARRY LOSES BILLIONS OVER
BREAKFAST

IT WAS THE most expensive slumber in the history of sleep. As Barry lay in his bed, he was losing millions with every passing minute. In fact, each snore was costing him roughly $84,000.

As New York trading began in the wee hours of the West Coast dawn, TeraMemory's share price plummeted. From the opening bell, it had hightailed it dead south, without so much as a pause or backward glance.

Barry would soon wake to find himself nose-to-nose with this grim reduction in personal fortune. But it wouldn't be the fiscal degradation that would torture him most—it would be the wrenching plunge in his sense of self-worth.

For the kingpins of Silicon Valley, self-esteem was largely a function of stock price. Soaring market cap was the ultimate vanity appliance: an invisible force field that attracted love and acclaim while simultaneously superseding and over-writing any contradicting sentiments: "Barry Dominic? Sure, he's an abusive, misogynist tyrant—but his company's stock is up four hundred percent in eighteen months. *You gotta love the guy.*"

Of course, there was a dark side. Aligning your personal identity with a stock market abstraction was just asking for trouble. And in the day that was just beginning, Barry would learn all about trouble.

At the heart of the slaughter was a simple guessing game, one played all over the Valley: beginning each quarter, the officers of high-tech companies concocted highly delusional fictions called "earnings estimates." The CFO of TeraMemory, for example, might declare that every $100 share of the company's stock would yield a dividend of fourteen cents by quarter's end.

It was a thrillingly inexact science, but great sport. For if, at the end of the quarter, TeraMemory yielded seventeen cents, its share price might proudly swell to $120. But if, on the other hand, it yielded only eleven cents, you could be in for a whole different kind of ride. Technology investors were a skittish bunch, and they tended to see bogeymen around the corners of the slightest downturns; the price might free-fall to $60.

TeraMemory's incipient descent seemed to be the conse-

quence of just such a narrow failure of market expectations.
But such were the intemperate rhythms of the Valley: four
times a year, fortunes were made and lost on pennies.

Which, in a broader historical context, was pretty comical.
The estimated earnings ritual was rooted in an antiquated belief
that a company's yield was a reflection of present value. In fact,
the age of NASDAQ had changed all that: in the nascent sphere
of high tech, the future approached with such speed and vio-
lence that present worth collapsed into an abstract point, while
the prospect of future value potentially expanded to infinity.
Share prices became science fiction, in essence. Infotech stocks
were no longer grounded in the world of observable financial
phenomena; they were tea leaves in the cup of the twentieth
century's strangest, strongest postindustrial brew.

Whatever dark market mechanics were in play that day,
by the time Barry had climbed out of bed, slipped on his silk
kimono and poured his first cup of green tea, TeraMemory
had seen 38% of its market capitalization evaporate into the
fiscal ether.

"Jesus," he muttered to himself, assessing the damage
reports on CNN. Barefoot and anxious he paced onto the
teak deck, speed-dialing his CFO. Barry held his breath as
the phone rang through the handset, an electronic cricket
pressed tightly against his ear. He glanced back at the TV. It
was pouring red ink. Wheeling, he peered out at the giant

koi gliding by in the glassy, black waters around the Zen compound—silent, cartoon-colored sentries ready to torpedo any bad luck that might make a run on Barry's already dodgy karma.

Only the fish didn't seem to be working today.

The CFO picked up, barely voicing a greeting before Barry began to unload.

"What the hell is up, Bob? We never figured to see this kind of downdraft on three cents. It's like the entire market has gone nuts. I never thought our investors could be such weenies."

"Easy, easy, big guy. I'm on it. We're going to break the big news. That ought to turn things around in a hurry."

"News?" Barry hissed. "What *news*?"

"You mean you don't know? I figured you already knew about it. You're telling me you really haven't heard?" Bob asked, incredulous.

"No, goddammit!" Barry fulminated. "What the hell is going on?"

"I've just been talking to Ed Pilphur over at WHIP. He's calling an emergency meeting of the board."

"What the fuck does that have to do with Tera?"

"Plenty, Ed hopes. They're going to announce the partnership deal with Microsoft," the CFO said optimistically. "Since everybody knows WHIP, Inc.'s a largely owned, de-facto subsidiary of Tera, we're golden by association. It should reverse the Tera slide within hours. Hey, all this time I was kinda thinking it was your idea, Barry. It's a brilliant move. Really brilliant,"

Barry's neck began to swell. "Absolutely no goddamn way," he howled into the phone. "Pilphur raised it last week, and I vetoed it. No grab-ass with the Redmond boys. Period." He stalked to the edge of the deck like a trapped animal. "You just remind Ed I'm still controlling shareholder—what I say goes, and I'm not changing my mind. He goes ahead with this announcement and I'll shove my lawyers so far up his ass he'll be ordering lunch in Latin."

Silence hung on the line for an uncomfortable moment. "Ahh . . . yeah. Pilphur did mention that, Barry—he says your share of WHIP Technologies is collateralized against your TeraMemory stock. After this morning, it looks like you might not be in the driver's seat anymore."

Barry's internal pressure shot up into the danger zone. "They wouldn't dare," he ranted. "TeraMemory's share price will be back by the end of next week."

Bob tried to strike a conciliatory note. "Oh, hey, absolutely, Barry. I'm with you. But we have to deal with things as they stand at the moment. And if I were you," he continued, attempting to inject a little humor, "I'd be thinking about learning to love Seattle Bill."

Of course, Bob's jest did not have the intended effect. The very invocation of Barry's rival put him off the scale. Mute with frustration, he ripped the phone from his ear and spiked it into the deck with a grunt.

With surprising resilience, the phone bounced squarely into the center of the pond, splashing discreetly amidst the scene of Oriental tranquillity. The koi were only the first to swim for cover.

THE CONTRACTOR'S
CONTRACTOR—MIGRANT LABOR
ON STEROIDS

THE ENGINEERING crisis at WHIP had precipitated a significant extension of working hours. In fact, Paul hadn't left his cubicle before ten P.M. in more than a week. The toll on his personal life was beginning to mount; this evening, he had reluctantly canceled a theater date with Liz.

She had cheerfully regrouped, inviting a girlfriend in his stead. She pretended that she wasn't hurt, but Paul knew otherwise, especially since season theater tickets had been his idea in the first place. It was the same old Silicon Valley story: as the Machine became more insistent, its human servants found it increasingly impossible to maintain any pretense of an actual life.

Paul didn't like what he was becoming these days: joyless, project-obsessed, irritable, pathologically goal-oriented. But there was something else bothering him, too: a free-floating anxiety, a submerged apprehension. He wrestled with it, but couldn't name it.

He stopped for gas on the way home from work. Oddly, it was a chance meeting—around eleven P.M., at the Exxon station on Shoreline—that precipitated the origins of his discontent.

Paul gassed his sedan and glanced over at the scruffy-looking man in the next fuel bay. Their eyes met for a moment. Paul looked hastily away; the man seemed willfully unkempt, maybe disturbed in some way. He also radiated an obscure aura of hostility. Paul didn't want to provoke him.

Too late. The man spoke anyway: "Hey, *punk*. You're up way past your bedtime."

Paul stiffened, and glanced up from the gas pump with apprehension. But the scruffy guy's grin didn't indicate any real threat. In fact, he seemed remotely familiar.

"Jim Skidmore," the man volunteered. "I taught you everything you know about tranlogs and commits, remember?" He made a dramatic, sweeping gesture with his arm. "Back in the days when Tandem boxes roamed the earth."

Paul held out his hand in greeting. Jim was right. It *had* been an age ago.

Jim was a contractor's contractor. Smart, razor-quick, superexperienced, he had been the biggest repository of technical trivia Paul had ever seen. He was an absolute engineering wonder; he cut right down to the heart of the stickiest digital puzzles with lightning speed. And he seemed to thrive on the pressure, teasing out bankable results well under deadline, on projects that management had pronounced terminally behind schedule.

He was a little ruthless, too—like many master contractors, he had a quick temper and a mean streak. He also had zero tolerance for anyone below his level. There were two kinds of people in his universe: people who knew less than he did—whom he dubbed "kooks," "idiots," and "losers"—and people who knew as much as he did. The possibility of anyone knowing more was one he did not feel compelled to entertain. He was a true mercenary, attacking requirements and obliterating milestones with a cold, bloodless efficiency. In the end, Jim always delivered. Managers loved him for that.

Paul had worked with him years ago, on a particularly hairy database engine port. Jim had been project lead; it had succeeded largely due to his expertise. His hourly rate, Paul had learned when a manager's phone conversation had escaped over the cubicle wall, was three times his own. This seemed to him fair at the very least; Jim was the sharpest knife on the team by far.

Since then, Paul had thought of him from time to time, assuming Jim had maintained this lucrative trajectory toward some far-off digital Olympus. Which was why Paul had not recognized him as he was: whiskered, bedraggled, aging quickly in the flat, jaundiced light of the sodium vapor lamps.

"Hey, long time no see. What are you up to?" Paul asked.

Jim ran his fingers through his thinning, stringy hair. "Same old, same old. You know."

"Living around here?"

"Only in the loosely bound sense of the word. Here and there," Jim reported, a little uneasily. "I split up with my girl-friend, and I've got three clients—one here, one in the East Bay, one in the city. I move around so much, I'm camping out in hotels, mostly. That way, I have no extra overhead when I go on vacation." He smiled optimistically.

There it was: he was probably the highest paid itinerant worker on the planet. Paul wondered what Jim did with all the money, but couldn't think of a discreet way to ask. He decided to let the conversation play out on the path of least resistance.

"You actually take vacations?" Paul asked with playful skepticism. "*That* sure wouldn't be in character. You ever have plans to get out of Dodge and take a break?"

"Not with my clients. They're already pissed I won't give them more time than I do." He paused, then erupted cheer-fully: "*Bah,* you know me—work, work, work. I'm a work machine. One of these days I'll figure out how to slow down and enjoy it." Then, playing his own devil's advocate, "Yeah, and maybe one day pigs'll fly, too. But hey—I'm still young."

His last comment struck Paul like a rock. Jim had been well past the prime of youth when the two had toiled shoulder to shoulder. Now the tufts of white hair were beginning to stick out of his ears, and his eyebrows were acquiring Merlin's peaks.

In Jim's tale of a life deferred in cubicles and hotel suites, Paul could hear the sound of slamming doors. The same sound, now that he came to think of it, he was beginning to hear in his own.

LAYOFF—CANDY GETS TAKEN OUT
WITH THE TRASH

Microsoft, Whip Technologies Announce Partnership

Microsoft and WHIP Technologies have signed a statement of intent for a partnership valued at $780 million based on Microsoft's closing price of 102¼ a share Wednesday.

The partnership has the potential to create a contiguous end-to-end Internet and e-commerce cross-company product spectrum combining back-end transaction platforms with front-end portals and information appliances.

Building on its new e-services mantra, Microsoft unveiled on Tuesday an e-speak technology enabling creation, deployment, and connection of e-services that will interact with each other spontaneously. In essence, the technology could serve as the universal tongue of networked communications. WHIP Technologies' Wireless

High-density Internet Protocol (WHIP) is the logical
foundation for those services, Microsoft executives
assert.

AS TERAMEMORY'S wizards of finance had predicted, the
announcement immediately halted the slide in stock price.
With just the mere proposition of this unholy conjunction,
they had managed to shore up the eroding confidence of the
investing public.

It would take a few weeks for the board to negotiate the
details of the WHIP/Microsoft partnership. They'd have to
move it along aggressively; any backtracking or second
thoughts would not be received kindly by the market.

In the meantime, Barry was going to do anything and
everything in his power to thwart the deal. He would sooner
tee up his own testicles than buddy up to Bill.

Regaining his power of veto—and his pride—would
only be possible by recapturing his controlling interest in
WHIP Technologies, Inc. And the only way to do that was
to engineer a sharp rise in TeraMemory's stock price to previous highs. To that end, everything—and everyone—was
expendable. Barry wouldn't hesitate to tread on any obstacle
in the way. His own people would be his first stepping-
stone.

None of the employees of TeraMemory, Inc. would ever
know the true motivating force behind the sudden slash and
burn. To them, it would look like any other layoff in the

Valley: bad quarterly reports, declining profit and loss statements, management's pledge to regain competitive edge, a return to profitability, blah, blah, blah.

The cycle of dissimulation began in the usual way: with management congratulating themselves on their stealth and discretion. Their plans were perfectly concealed. No employee would know, they assured themselves, until the morning the pink slips flew. Until then, industry would continue within nominal specs.

Of course, they were only fooling themselves. There is always a kind of corporate telepathy that precedes a layoff. The very moment the bean counters seized upon the idea of a reduction in staff, a mysterious tremor would radiate. People just *knew.*

The rumors would begin to circulate instantly. Lower management—project leaders, section managers, and such— would immediately clam up, communicating only with each other, and only in furtive whispers. This only accelerated the speed of hearsay. And as the higher-ups became more circumspect, so the writing on the wall became more bold.

Then would come The Fear. Nervous, hunted looks would be surreptitiously swapped at staff meetings. Productivity would decline as reams of résumés scrolled discreetly from copiers and laser printers, their owners anxiously standing at the ready to whisk them into manila folders milliseconds after the toner had set. A generalized air of panic and corporate introversion would settle in. Cryptic oaths and gallows aphorisms would appear—mysteriously unattributed—on conference room whiteboards.

As always, it was the people at the bottom of the food chain who were the least discreet; the grunts were the only ones to grumble openly. And for good reason: they had the most to lose. Though they were the least well-paid, they lived closest to the edge. And management's swift sword always seemed to cut from the bottom up. By the time the rumors had filtered down to the mailroom—and for all the hype about ubiquitous electronic communication and paperless offices, Silicon Valley info-behemoths still maintained large, healthy mailrooms—the covert anxiety had thoroughly saturated the organization. Of course it would manifest itself through the channel of least resistance.

Then the blade swung and the deadwood tumbled. A series of tearful vignettes in coffee lounges and parking lots followed, as if the newly unincorporated staff were being exiled from their own families.

This transposition of family and company was an understandable mistake; when you spent most of your waking hours with your project team, and your family—if you even had one, in the land of the unattached male—became strangers, it was easy to misplace your affections. Of course, management encouraged this confusion with its rhetoric of corporate paternity and its declaration of the kind of loyalty otherwise reserved for blood relations.

But they were all mistaken. This wasn't a family. This

was a business. Management's commitment—however sincerely pledged—never extended past the balance sheet.

That it all happened in web time didn't make it any easier. In fact, it made it kind of surreal. One moment, you were a member of a "dynamic, cutting-edge team of dedicated professionals," with milestones, meetings, project plans, and goals. The next, after a perfunctory homily from the CEO (always about sacrifice and "new beginnings") and a pat on the fanny from HR, you were a faceless nonentity with a fresh résumé and a voucher for a national career placement firm.

But, hey—this was the Silicon Valley; of course everyone would find another job, and soon. But it was the vertigo, the dissonance: If we'd really spent the last eighteen months of our careers changing the world, then why did we suddenly feel so much like a copy of last year's release, and one with a broken seal at that?

The essential people—engineering's upper crust—would never get cut, of course. The irony was, they'd leave anyway. Nothing telegraphs the impending death spiral of a business like a layoff. And in the land where the cycle from Next Big Thing to yesterday's news was ever-tightening, the engineering hot rods had become terrifyingly light on their feet. Every month a new, once-in-a-lifetime start-up opportunity rumbled through the Valley, and they weren't about to be caught flat-footed, left behind, and choking on the dust of yesterday's protocols.

They often wouldn't bother to announce their departure.

A signing bonus, double salary, and a fresh NDA would gal-
vanize an exit in a way that left no room for reflection, conscience, or good-bye. Never mind loyalty. Once the Guru's
True Believer spell was broken, loyalty became a hypothetical
construct, an irrational number. Let the grunts and marketing
'bots go down with the ship. The senior engineers were off to
chase alternate futures in parallel technical universes.

One of the terminations seemed curiously misplaced: VP
of Sales, Western region.

Candy Sawyer was strenuously wrestling a presentation
out of PageMaker when her assistant plunked the manila
interoffice memo pack on her desk. Probably reassignments
among the underlings in her region, she glossed.

Something about the way her assistant crept off gave
Candy a curious feeling. She dropped the mouse and opened
the envelope. A flash of pink complemented her cherry ver-
milion nail polish stunningly.

Today, all her hues would be leaning toward crimson.
"That bastard," she shouted, more color-coordinated by the
second. "I'm not being laid off. I'm getting *dumped.*"

DISAPPEARING BOXSTERS, MISTAKEN HOT TUBS, AND NECROPHILIA IN THE FOOTLIGHTS

LINDA TURNED her emerald eyes up into the lights, her expression a struggle of anguish and hope. "We're free and clear," she said dreamily. "We're free. We're free."

And so ended *The Death of a Salesman*. The curtain dropped, and the audience rose to its feet, cheering. Palo Alto Theaterworks was still pretty good, as community theater went. Liz looked across at Kiki. She was applauding fiercely.

Later, Willy Loman—back from the beyond—fairly tackled Kiki in the theater's espresso bar.

"I really want to thank you, Mrs. D. We couldn't have done it without you."

"The show must go on," Kiki smiled. Then, "Nice suspenders, fella," she teased, snapping the elastic against the actor's broad chest. "I want to see you stretch your character for Falstaff, okay?"

He grasped the small of her back and kissed her full on the lips. "You got it, doll. But first, there's a jar of cold cream backstage with my name on it." He glided back into the house.

Kiki batted her eyes and winked at Liz. "Oh, he's a naughty one. But great intensity. Pretty eyes, too. Much too young for me. Besides, I have a little rule about necrophilia." They both laughed.

Liz thought she was starting to figure Kiki out. It wasn't the first time this evening Kiki had been showered with unsolicited gratitude. Earlier, Liz had scanned the theater program. There, under the heading, "Many, many thanks," she had seen a familiar name, at once discreet and personal: "Kiki D."

She thought back across their friendship: The Zen Center. Her salon of quirky, artsy friends. The mysterious acquisition of the Valley's orphaned orchards. The palatial Woodside ranch house. Then there were the chance meetings with Kiki's acquaintances, all of them involved in arts organizations and preservation foundations, all of them greeting Kiki with an unspoken undercurrent of indebtedness. Liz's friend was starting to look a lot like a reticent crypto-patroness of local culture.

Her curiosity drove her to attempt a gentle clarification

of Kiki's true identity. "You know, I'm starting to get an idea about you," Liz declared coyly. "Why do I always get the feeling there's more to you than there appears?"

Kiki, keenly familiar with Liz's powers of inference, dropped the pretense without a ripple. *"Darling,"* she said in her best Zsa Zsa, "there's actually a good deal less, the truth be known." Then, in a more sober tone, "And soon there may be nothing to speak of at all, at least where charity is concerned. I'm just trying to do some good while I still can."

This ominous statement startled Liz for a moment. "What do you mean?" she asked with some urgency.

Kiki read Liz's concern and moved to reassure her. "Oh, don't worry too much about me. It's just Barry again. As you know, we haven't been together for years, but it looks like even our sham marriage may not be a thing much longer." She pushed out her lip. "Barry intends a rather drastic reduction in my circumstances—if he gets his way, I may be a charity case myself before the year is over."

Liz felt a surge of emotions: sympathy for Kiki, anger and exasperation with Barry. She narrowed her eyes. "What *is it* with that guy? Why does he torture you so? And why do you let him?"

Kiki drew a long breath. "Same old story, and I think you know most of it by now. Once upon a time, Barry made a lot of promises—to me, to himself, to the world: the 'New Florence,' enlightened markets, commerce with a soul. Somewhere along the line, he just forgot—he forgot *himself.*" She gave Liz a forlorn look. "I'm trying to remember for him. He's reaped so much, and he sows so little."

Candy had stormed up to the twenty-first floor to confront Barry over her sudden termination—as well as the unexpected downsizing of his affections.

Clearly, he'd anticipated her move; he was conveniently off-site. More like off-continent, actually; Barry had timed the *denouement* to coincide with the Sydney-to-Hobart regatta, soon to be the latest of his yachting conquests.

But he hadn't left Candy completely unattended. He had presciently arranged for her rendezvous with security in the executive suite. They collected her ID badge and card-key, and gently but firmly escorted her down to the main lobby. The blue-shirted sentries left her there with nothing but her leather folio and gym bag—a blond palm tree bent and shivering in a typhoon of rage and injustice.

She turned her angry eyes to the main receptionist, hoping for at least some expression of sympathy, but he could only look away uncomfortably. Candy flung the folio at him, slung her gym bag over her shoulder, and charged toward the main door with a shriek. Good thing it opened automatically; Candy would have otherwise walked straight through it without breaking her stride.

She made her parting gesture in the parking lot, spinning the tires of her white Porsche convertible more than a little conspicuously, finally vanishing into the pastel blue smoke of her Boxster's burning tread like some turbocharged magic act.

She turned the car north onto 101, merged across four lanes without looking. Emboldened by lighter than usual traffic, she gunned the engine recklessly.

Somewhere around Palo Alto the speedometer crept back down past ninety. She exited at University Avenue; perhaps an hour in a coffeehouse might help her to reflect and collect herself.

There was, as always, a surfeit of trendy coffee joints on University, but a famine of parking. Today she wouldn't be troubling herself with details. She dumped the car in a handicap spot, left the keys in the ignition, and walked.

Two hours, three mochas and four back issues of *Glamour* later, Candy still hadn't regained her poise. She stuffed a twenty dollar bill into her empty glass and walked in the direction of High Street, toward the last line of defense in her battle for self-composure: Watercourse Way.

She walked into the quintessentially Northern Californian bathhouse. It reeked of sandalwood and chamomile.

"Got any empty tubs?" she asked wearily.

The private bathing chambers drew their names from an innovative number/nature scheme. Today Candy would soak in Five Fishes. She pushed open the door, her thoughts twisting with preoccupation. Absentmindedly she peeled down, flinging her designer office duds in a random scatter across the room.

It wasn't until she'd reached her foundation garments that she realized she wasn't alone. Behind the etched glass divider between the dressing room and tub, she saw something move. At first, it looked a little like a bear.

She clutched a towel to herself and peered around the edge of the divider: rising Neptunelike from the roiling water, a man's tanned and muscled back, crowned by the most luxurious dreadlocks she had ever seen. On the edge of making a quick apology and a hasty retreat, she found herself reluctant to move; after months of Barry's thinning scalp, she was locked in rapt fascination.

And not just by this appealing physicality; there was an oddly compelling detail. Tattooed against the smooth, pale flesh of his scapular, a curious symbol: capital C, with a small numeral 6 hovering above, and 12.0107 subscripted below. Candy had never been one to pay much attention to quantitative details, but this one rang a faint, junior high science-class bell. Wasn't that the periodic table entry for carbon?

The man turned to face her, but looked only into her eyes. He unfolded an easy, serene smile framed by a perfect goatee.

"Come on in," he invited. "The water's fine."

CATERERS BECOME CABLE MOGULS; BARRY FLIES DOWN UNDER

IT WAS ONE of the few idle weekday mornings their high-tech catering business had allowed them in some time. Liz and Laurel reenacted their morning "rut-ual" at *Château des Araignées:* they brewed a pot of coffee and hunkered down with Angus and the morning newspaper.

Generally, Laurel wasn't the type to linger long over the business section, but this morning a story had caught her eye:

Network Synergy Solutions Surprise Buyout

PALO ALTO, CA (AP)—Cable giant Global Communications Corp. will buy privately held Network Synergy Solutions in a deal valued at about $3.6 billion including assumed debt.

> The deal, the latest in the rapidly changing cable
> TV industry, will enable Global Communications Corp.
> of St. Louis to provide customized cable modem ser-
> vices over existing infrastructure. GCC is the nation's
> fourth-largest cable company with 5.5 million sub-
> scribers.

She didn't know what any of it meant, practically
speaking. But she did know that Network Synergy Solutions
sounded an awful lot like the name of their recalcitrant customer who had paid that invoice in presumably worthless
company stock. Laurel guessed the newspaper story might
indicate a potentially lucrative turn of events. She asked Liz,
who happened to be the only person in her life even remotely
resembling a Silicon Valley insider.

"Hey, what does it mean when a little high-tech company
gets bought by a big one?"

"Usually, it means the little guys get rich," Liz explained,
rubbing the silken M on Angus's tabby brow. "Along with
their stockholders, if they have any. That's always what people
hope, anyway."

Laurel abruptly put down her coffee cup, simultaneously
dialing Vero and tossing the business section to Liz. Angus
dove under the couch.

Vero's answering machine picked up: *"Bonjour,* this is
Vero, *bienvenue, ça va.* You know what to do. *Beep."*

"Hey, Vero—Laurel. What was the name of that cheese-
ball company who stiffed us with stock? Was it Network

Synergy Solutions? Check the paper today. Business section, column three. They just got bought by some megacorporation. Maybe you should pull those certificates off the wall and see a stockbroker. Call me."

Laurel hung up the phone, turning to Liz to share her excitement over her sleuthing.

"Oh, that would be so hysterical," she exclaimed. "Guerrilla Gourmet—caterers and cable moguls."

Liz smiled wickedly. "That would be the ultimate irony, wouldn't it? I can see it now: 'Liberal arts catering babes strike it rich in technology gold rush.' As if."

But the jovial mood was quickly eclipsed as another story of more local interest caught her eye. She read, reread, and pressed her fingers to her temple.

Woman Dies in Felton Hit-and-run

A Felton woman died at Kaiser Hospital early Thursday after being struck by a vehicle on a remote section of Zayante Road Wednesday evening. Santa Cruz police report the search for the vehicle is ongoing. Bystanders identified the deceased as Gretchen Ja Love, residence unknown.

"Oh, no," Liz pleaded, softly. "This can't be. It can't be the same person."

Barry had taken the controls of the Gulfstream on the approach into Sydney. Though he didn't have the patience to ride out long, dull flights in the cockpit, he liked to jump into the saddle on landing and takeoff—during the exciting parts, in other words. Barry was the most dangerous kind of thrill seeker: an adrenaline junkie with a short attention span.

He'd even insisted on taking the stick for the refueling stop in Honolulu. His copilot—Len, a Vietnam-era fighter jock, and TeraMemory's official corporate pilot—had learned to roll with Barry's sudden fits of hands-on enthusiasm; he'd sit patiently alongside, ready to jump in if things suddenly went bad. After all, Len thought to himself, it was Barry's bucket, and he'd earned his rating. It was annoying, but a lot less upsetting than Viet Cong anti-aircraft fire.

Once in Sydney, Barry decided to skip check-in at the Four Seasons and proceed straight to the harbor. He arrived dockside to find the *Singularity* hauled out for maintenance and some small patches. The hull had picked up a few minor dings in transport; a crew member applied a restorative gloss to the ship's black, space-age keel with a spray can of marine epoxy.

There was also some serious talk about the weather. *Singularity*'s navigator had been tracking a storm system gathering in the west, out over the Indian Ocean, and it worried him more than a little.

"Not your job," Barry had admonished. "If weather's going to be a serious factor," he declared in sportsmanlike fashion, "the race officials will make the call. We need to focus on our game. We came down to win, not fret about conditions."

But in truth, Barry would have a hard time concentrating on nautical preparations; even from a hemisphere away, the mutiny of his board of directors weighed heavily upon him, preoccupying his thoughts. But with any luck, his slashing of personnel would pay off, and TeraMemory's share price would rebound by the time the blue water race was won. Then he could reassert control.

Until then, he would struggle to put the specter of the Microsoft partnership out of his mind and keep his attention on the regatta. He looked forward to his time on the ocean, at least. Out on the water there was no ambiguity; Barry could allow his competitive instincts to run wild. Hobart was seven hundred nautical miles away, and he and his crew were going to get there first.

BARRY, BEATEN: THE RICH MAN
AND THE SEA

THE GODS had finally come after him.

Barry stood at the helm of the *Singularity,* looking not so much a captain as a refugee. Though he gripped the wheel with all his strength, navigation was not much on his mind; he was hanging on for dear life, trying to stay upright as the waves washed over the cockpit.

Already he'd lost two of his crew to injuries: one with a smashed ankle, another's arm flayed by a line of broken rigging, a thin steel cable whipping in the gale's fury.

They had sailed into a churning hell on high water. The Tasman Sea had blossomed into a true monster—as angry and menacing as any of Barry's hyperaccomplished crew had ever seen, and considerably more so than Barry himself could have even imagined. Giant swells—higher than the mast—shouldered up to the boat like marauding thugs, rolling the eighty foot hull sickeningly, lashing out with quickening temper—cresting, bristling, then backhanding the deck with heavy, gelid swipes.

Yet the worst was still to come, it seemed; the heart of the storm was bearing down on them. The Australian Maritime Safety broadcasts reported it to be only a few hundred miles from the stern. With still 220 miles to Hobart, this was not encouraging news.

But as foreboding as it may have been for Barry and his battered crew, it was far worse for the rest of the competitors in the regatta. As predicted, *Singularity* had quickly seized the lead from the beginning, and had pulled away with every nautical mile. Now, the rest of the field—what remained afloat, at this point—was well behind, and being ground into bits in the storm's maw. The distress calls rang out over the radio, previews of Barry's tribulations to come.

Thus the stage had been set in the usual way: the emperor would finally face forces greater than himself—in this case, nature, death, and chance. All would play their parts with equal vigor.

It is always the same drama, more or less: Act One: Defiance; Act Two: Doubt; Act Three: Despair. And finally, a curtain call: reflection, perspective, and regret; in the theater of mortal peril the truth is always close at hand.

Far too close, in Barry's case, to admit a graceful performance. Even the gods were surprised—insofar as gods care to be surprised—by his spectacular display of rebellion. No, he fiercely insisted, no. He had not wasted his life.

But by journey's end, Barry's resistance would be lost at sea.

Never let it be said the gods don't have a wacky sense of humor. Barry would have his victory. He and his *Singularity* finally dragged each other, bleeding and maimed, into the Tasmanian harbor.

But his hero's welcome would be subdued at best. Tragedy had touched this sportsman's paradise. The devil had taken the hindmost; reports of deaths and disappearances among slower yachtsmen had been trickling in for hours.

Liz had not been mistaken. The young woman run down on Zayante Road had been the very same she had met months before, in the feral hills above Santa Cruz.

How do you console a mother for the loss of a child? Some tragedies are beyond mending, beyond consolation, beyond compensation. Liz had known Kiki only a few months, and had met her bohemian, headstrong daughter only once. How could she help her friend—so new in her life, so little shared history—manage this loss? It seemed wrong, in a way—too intimate an invasion. She felt unprepared for, and unequal to, the task.

But circumstance declared it: Liz would be midwife to a mother's grief. There would be little time for deliberation, in any case; death was, Liz would quickly learn, a busy affair:

autopsies, death certificates, arrangements for burial, obituaries, a hundred other details. She offered her assistance, and Kiki gratefully accepted.

They chartered a fishing boat out of Santa Cruz on a crystal clear day, the Pacific as limp and lazy as a summer lake. Liz had never seen the ocean so gentle, so compliant, so manifestly full of sympathy.

Kiki turned the urn out over the port bow, and the ashes spread across the motionless, mourning water, saturating, drifting into the depths like a languid, ashen rain. And for a moment, she took her grief in hand, and cobbled together a few doubtful words. Maybe it was a eulogy; if so, it was rife with question.

"Gretchen's confidence in the goodness of the world was taken early," she said, holding back the hair from her tear-streaked face. "I don't know what her life means. There's no closure—no cheerful platitude, no comforting last detail, no happy ending. Only mystery and regret. And a few certainties: she loved, she was much loved, and I'll miss her."

One detail kept revolving through her mind, a specter that had haunted her since the news of Gretchen's death, the prospect of a single consoling hope.

Gretchen had not been carrying a child when she died.

On learning this, Kiki had driven frantically up to Last Chance, to the same meadow in the high woods where Gretchen's hippie clan had pitched their teepees. But they had moved on.

PAUL FLAMES OUT—LIZ AND LAUREL CASH IN

PAUL DIDN'T sleep well that night, plagued by disturbing dreams. In one, the specter of Contractor Jim haunted him like some geeky, Silicon Valley parody of the Ghost of Christmas Yet to Be. In another, cryptic, nonsensical C programs glowed before him in the void:

```
#include <proverbs.h>
void main {
 assert(despair);
 drop(straw, camels_back);
 return NULL;
 exit;
}
```

He dragged himself stoically into work the next day, tired, bleary-eyed, and determinedly refocused on an array of slipping project deadlines. Not to be derailed, he had put the previous night's apparition out of his mind; Paul always kept his denial close at hand, a ready fallback position for those pesky ambushes by jack-in-the-box doubts.

But ordinary, run-of-the-mill denial could not stand up to Paul's new, industrial-strength misgivings. Especially not after what would happen today.

His manager had called an emergency project meeting. It seemed the new Microsoft partnership came with strings attached: they had submitted their own wish list of features to be rolled into WHIP.

At first Paul and his project team tried to play it cool, but the tenor soon rose to panic when it became clear that Microsoft's requirements would bring a new dimension of chaos to the already hellish swamp of bugs, defects, and spongy design from which they were only beginning to emerge.

Software engineering was hard enough even when the specs weren't constantly changing beneath you; coding to an ever-expanding list of requirements asymptotically approached impossible, and was an excellent recipe for complete mental breakdown to boot. It was frustrating and stupid, like trying to shoot jackrabbits with a howitzer: taking aim took a lot of energy; it was good policy to establish stationary targets.

The prospect of accommodating yet another of management's redirections filled Paul with a crashing despair. Of course he'd been in this position before; even veteran programmers are often overwhelmed by the complexities of tangled code and creeping, unmanageable designs. But it had never felt so bad and hopeless as it did now. He felt like he'd rather be anywhere else than here, in his cubicle, in the inner sanctum of WHIP Technologies, Inc.

Paul took a deep breath and recited the contractor's mantras: "Bill by the hour. Worry one day at a time. Focus on issues inside your sphere of control."

All to no avail. Today was Paul's day to plunge into the pit of terminal digital hopelessness. He hastily typed an email to his PM:

To: jsacerdoti@whip.com
From: parmstrong@whip.com
Subject: Flamed out

Boss-man,
I'm declaring myself officially fried. Because if anybody revises the spec one more time, I'm going to go completely postal. No offense, but this Microsoft thing is going to sink you, IMHO. Just remember Java. That's the Redmond way, right? Obfuscate and conquer.

So in the interest of public safety and the greater glory of WHIP Technologies, I'm terminating my contract.

Guerrilla Gourmet's client du jour, Beanietech, consisted of a number of college-aged males who had improbably succeeded in persuading some hapless investment bankers to sink millions of dollars into a network of Beanie Baby auction sites. Venture capital was really scraping the bottom of the barrel these days, apparently.

Never mind that there were already a dozen other players in the very same game. Beanietech's competitive edge—as the gangly, milk-faced founders eagerly and simultaneously explained to Vero—was that their Web site featured streaming audio. That, they gushed as the caterers transformed their conference room into a rough-and-ready bistro, would make all the difference. It would be huge, bigger than Yahoo.

After six months of Silicon Valley catering jobs, Vero had heard it all before. "You mean, these 'Beanie Babies' can talk to you?" she had asked innocently, then winked at the girls as the nerdlings earnestly launched into their marketing spiel. She had made a thorough study of the collective psyche of the young male infopreneur, and she knew how to push all the right buttons.

Later, after the brahmins of Beanietech retreated to their workstations and the women of Guerrilla Gourmet tidied up the culinary battle scene, Vero made a surprising announcement.

"I am tired of the land of *go-go,*" she said, out of the blue. "I'm thinking of going back to the Continent."

Liz, juggling one too many leftover salad accents, dropped a hefty goat-cheese morsel on the conference table. It punctuated Vero's declaration with a thump. "Really?" she asked, a little hurt. "You don't like us ugly Americans anymore?"

Laurel's reaction was both emotional and anxious. "Oh, I'm sorry to hear that, Vero. Can you give us a little lead time to find alternate employment? There's this little matter of rent . . ."

But Liz, ever the humanist, derailed the economics and went straight to the underlying motivation. "Vero, why the sudden change of heart? What's made you homesick?"

Vero gave her a curious look, midway between sad and sheepish. "I'm thinking that this place—this Silicon Valley—is too strange for me. I'm not sure I will ever get used to it."

"How is it strange to you?" Liz prodded, intrigued by this case of transcultural vertigo.

"This place is all about money," Vero began to explain, "and this give me a kind of—ennui. Back in France, we do not care so dearly about it. Other things are as important: family, culture, eating, mealtime.

"Here the money makes people blind in a way. This makes me sad, and I'm tired of always struggling against it. Like these people here—these Beanietechies," she said, rolling her eyes a little ironically, "they might even become wealthy, but for what? Because here you lose your happiness, your appreciation of life.

"Besides, sometimes life gives you a little hint, you know?" Vero gave them both a mischievous look. "A miracle, almost. A sign from above. Yesterday—I think life is telling me to go."

Liz and Laurel exchanged an agitated, hopeful glance, then Laurel turned conspiratorially to Vero. "Exactly what kind of divine intervention are we talking about here?"

"Network Synergy Solutions!" She laughed with even more than the usual music in her voice.

Laurel's eyes widened. "Oh, you're kidding!" she exclaimed. "You mean I framed those stock certificates for nothing? They're not worthless after all?"

"Well, yes—or no. Anyway, I cannot take credit. You did it. Tuesday."

"I barely got out of bed Tuesday," Laurel countered.

"Ah, but you are the one to tell me when they were swallowed up by some big company, and so maybe their worthless stock is not so worthless after all."

Liz and Laurel let out a simultaneous shriek of delight, then high-fived each other in a splatter of goat cheese.

Vero smiled in reply, but her eyes betrayed a certain confusion. "It is so strange," she mused philosophically. "I don't understand this place—big money appears out of nowhere, and then disappears into nowhere—anyway, I go downtown, to a stockbroker on University Avenue. He says yes, he will pay market price, less transaction fee."

"How much?" Liz and Laurel said simultaneously.

"At first I think it is a mistake. But, then he says no. He gives me a check for three hundred twenty thousand four hundred eighty-seven dollars." She looked at them smartly. "Oh—and sixty-six cents. *Au bon marché,* you think?"

Liz and Laurel gasped together, speechless.

"I know, I know. It's crazy, you think? Pretty good for fixing a few lunches. Two hundred times what they owed."

She gave them a winsome look. "I am thinking, this is nice. I like the money. But it does not make me so happy that I want to stay. There is more to life than the marketplace. Maybe Americans can learn that sometime." She tossed her bob, a blond Louise Brooks. "But for now, let's do the American thing, and 'get down to business.'" She produced two envelopes—one for Liz, one for Laurel, on which each of their names were written in Vero's florid continental penmanship.

They contained checks for $106,829.22—a year's pay for the average software geek, but a fortune for a humble caterer. Vero, a true European social democrat, had done the most un-Silicon-Valley thing possible: she had shared the wealth.

KIKI AND BARRY REUNITED BY IRIDIUM: SILENCE AT $40/MINUTE

KIKI HAD TRIED to contact Barry for a week after Gretchen's death. It shouldn't have been that hard; Barry had one of those Iridium superphones, the kind that worked anywhere on the planet. The real difficulty was in convincing anyone at TeraMemory that Barry even had a wife. Apparently, it was a detail he hadn't shared very widely.

She had been reduced to faxing the marriage license to TeraMemory's public relations department. That had gotten their attention, convincing them Kiki wasn't just another in a long line of jilted paramours and unhinged she-stalkers. They agreed to patch her through to the captain of the *Singularity*.

The biggest bandwidth bottleneck would be a psychological one. He answered on the sixth ring in his curt, signature baritone.

"Dominic."

"Barry? Is that you? It's Kiki."

"Why are you calling me, Kiki?" he said gruffly. "Didn't we agree it would be better to limit your contact to my attorney?"

"The lawyers can't help with this one, Barry."

She told him about Gretchen.

Barry didn't speak for a long time. The line made a steady, gentle hissing, punctuated only by the sound of hiccuping satellites.

Forty dollars a minute, and no words to say: Barry and Kiki stood on opposite sides of the earth, speechless, joined only by an evanescent strand of radio waves and electrons. They were as ghosts to each other, disembodied phantoms unable to extend any real connection across the ether of some desolate digital afterlife. It was worse than being alone. It was exactly like their marriage.

"How?" Barry finally asked, his voice higher, a thin trace of forlorn.

She told him about Last Chance, the mountainous Santa Cruz backcountry with its narrow, shoulderless roads and pitch-black nights.

"Thank you for notifying me. I appreciate your call," he responded with corporate coldness. He was walling it off the only way he knew how: by treating it as a business call.

"Barry, where are you?"

"Tasmania."

"I don't mean geographically—I mean personally. Where have you been all these years? I've missed you."

Silence. More soft hissing and geosynchronous chatter.

"I know you're back there," she continued, "somewhere behind all the anger and the ambition. Couldn't you at least come out for a moment? I'd like to talk to that man one more time. Even just to say good-bye."

His tone began to harden. "I don't know what you're talking about."

"I think you do," Kiki softly insisted. "Where is he? Where's my old 'Tejinder Coffeepot'?"

Barry spoke. "I . . . I . . ." Another long silence, then a pop and a moment of high-pitched electronic chirping.

Dial tone.

You could spot them a mile away: Silicon Valley technocrats, critically oppressed by the vagaries and uncertainties of the chase, would come to wrestle their doubts in the monastic calm of the Valley's only true ivory tower. The airy stone arches and broad lawns were a potent antidote to the relentless commercial whiplash of the Valley.

The undergrads, sheltered as they were from many of the Valley's harsher economic and vocational realities, surveyed these interlopers with some curiosity. Certainly they didn't belong on the Stanford campus; that was plain to see from their weirdly conformist "computer casual" dress and tightly wound demeanors. They were neither students nor faculty, neither fish nor fowl, entirely lacking the easy manner and unhurried rhythm of academia. They were oddities, stress refugees, indigenous tourists attempting to decompress and imagine life beyond the next round of funding or book-to-bill ratio.

Thus the two men strolling by Memorial Chapel made an unlikely pair: Steve, in his sandals, cutoff jeans, and Nine Inch Nails T-shirt, could easily have passed for a graduate student. Paul, on the other hand, had the mark of the Machine upon him: he wore the official uniform of the company town: khakis, virgin Nike cross-trainers, a crisply pressed denim button-down shirt with corporate technology logo embroidered on the breast. Gang colors for geeks.

"Let's go for a long, thoughtful walk around the quad," Steve had puckishly suggested when Paul called to explain his incipient career blowout. "That's what all the guys do when they burn out working for The Man. You can see 'em shuffling around, hands in their pockets, talking to themselves. Except for you," he had quipped. "I'll save you the embarrassment. You can talk to yourself to me."

And talk he did. More than a little. Paul talked so much he scared himself, tapping into a heretofore unknown, repressed pocket of resentment and frustration at his core.

"Oh, I dunno . . . ," Paul ruminated with a sigh, hands in pockets, as predicted. "It's getting harder and harder to see any point these days. I feel like I spend my time running a hundred miles an hour, working late every night and forsaking any semblance of a real life just for somebody else's technical pipe dream that'll probably never happen in a million years.

"I mean, the other day I took inventory: of the seven companies I've worked for in the last six years, four no longer exist. And most stuff I worked on is already obsolete. Hardly any of it ever saw an actual customer.

"And it was perfectly good code, too. But computational fashions change so fast these days. It's hard to feel like you're making any sort of significant contribution at all when all the rules are in constant flux, and history gets rewritten every six months."

Steve knew where Paul's lament was leading, but decided to play devil's advocate just for the fun of it. "Well, hey, you're a big boy—and you're getting paid by the *hour* anyway, right?"

"Yeah, but it's the futility, you know? You spend every day in the stocks, sweating and spinning a compiler, and you just know that in six months they'll cancel the project or start from scratch so they can chase the latest info-craze. After a while, not even the money can make you feel good about it. I'd rather be slinging burgers than feeling so burned-out and hopeless at the end of each day."

Steve put his hands together, prayerlike, a hacker Buddhist. "In your despair is the beginning of wisdom, grasshopper. What you do to get somewhere becomes who you are once you arrive."

He dropped the Zen pretense and laid his hands on his chest. "Look at your old friend Steve: I ain't making the big bucks. Hell, I'm barely making *any* bucks—but at least I love my work. And I don't have to worry about having my karma shafted by some wiseass, business-school dickhead with a Ferrari and a pile of venture capital.

"That's the whole hacker thing, man. It's 'Live Free or Die.' It's art for art's sake. Haven't I taught you anything? It always shakes out the same way, age after age, scene after scene: you can have the love, or you can have the money. If you ever do happen to get them both at the same time, you just gotta remember it's a temporary anomaly, a violation of cosmic law, and it can't last. That's the tragedy of the market: whenever anybody does something beautiful and pure, The Man hunts it down and kills it. Money hates beauty."

"Why?" Paul asked, dumbly.

Steve sighed and looked at his friend a moment, the lowering sun reflecting in his eyes. "Just jealous, I guess."

BARRY'S <u>SINGULARITY</u>—SHIP WITHOUT A CAPTAIN

BARRY AND HIS wounded *Singularity* had slipped away in the nautical midnight with no crew to meddle; this was a voyage strictly between him and providence. He hoisted his badass bravado, trimmed his swollen conscience, and wheeled into a fast reach.

But it wasn't the showdown he was hoping for. Though he shouted his argument to the rolling stars and pitch-black sky, no reproach would issue from that moonless night. And though the storm continued largely unabated, the sea seemed somehow more kind than the malevolent vortex of the day before. Now it extended a strange, turbulent invitation; Barry, to the end an admirer of unmitigated power, gave himself over to the muscular rocking of

Neptune's massive arms, and there took shelter from his doubts.

And like centuries of imperiled mariners before him, he turned the wheel beneath white knuckles and comforted himself by singing a little sea-chantey. Well, almost:

I skipped the light fandango
Turned cartwheels 'cross the floor

Some kind of seaman he was turning out to be. No antique, salty verses, just fragments of bygone hippie anthems.

But the old song brought a musty, long-dormant patchouli joy to his digit-encrusted heart; for the first time in months, or perhaps years, he managed a genuine smile. Not a cruel smile, or a smile born of victory or superiority, but a gentle and honest one—an unsolicited grin, arriving at no one's expense, requiring no payment or justification. It began as a tiny spark somewhere in his chest, then illuminated his insides like summer lightning.

"Note to self," he thundered ironically over the storm's din. "Stop being such an asshole."

This arc of admission effected a curious liberation in Barry. A little wistfully at first, then more broadly, then throwing back his head, he added his laughter to the tempest.

In the starboard darkness the ocean returned Barry's burgeoning mirth, rising up into a colossal, vertical smile, then erupting like laughter amidships with the voice of a million watery clowns.

The morning sky, storm-scoured to a guiltless blue, stepped out over Hobart harbor. Out to sea, a pair of helicopters crisscrossed the horizon.

The coast guard skipper landed his launch at the dock, on a mission to coordinate the day's operations with the harbor authority. He hitched it to the cleats and vaulted off the deck toward the harbormaster's office.

He ambled through the office's salt-weathered doorway. "Right, mate, we found your dingy. Bloody *kep-soized*," he reported casually in a tangy, down-under accent. "Keel up and riding pretty low," the seaman illustrated with a tilt of his forearm, "but we pulled it over and pumped it out. Towing it back now."

"Fair dinkum," the harbormaster replied jauntily from his seat at the radio. "Find any crew floating about?"

"Not bloody likely," the guardsman answered, with that oddly upbeat enthusiasm born of disaster's novelty. "Whoever was at that helm is fish food, I reckon. Won't survive out there, even with floatation. *Nah.*" He spat discreetly out the door. "All we found was a single harness line, snapped off on the end."

"Right," conferred the harbormaster. "So the rescue 'copters will hunt around for the rest of the day, burn up a ton of fuel, and then we all knock off at sunset and have a beer." He slapped his thighs and thrust out his chin. "Fine bit of sport."

"Righty-right," agreed the guardsman matter-of-factly, then gave a troubled look to the horizon. "The damnedest thing, though. There were one or two funny angles to it. Weird."

"Weird? Like how?"

"Like, here's this megapricey maxi hull out there, all the way down under from the States, and not only is it rudely inverted, but it's been *vandalized*."

This struck the harbormaster as unlikely. "Vandalized?"

"Yeah—vandalized. Like some maniac had taken a spray can to the stern—tried to black out the name—'Single-something,' from what I could see."

"No accounting for rich Yankee eccentrics. Takes all kinds, especially in the twelve meter crowd. A fair number of those blokes have more money than sense."

"Yeah, I didn't think about it much, either. Until we flipped it right. Then you could see something else had been sprayed in above it—like it had been rechristened under way, hasty, like a second thought." The guardsman shook his head. "Spooky."

This bizarre detail offered the harbormaster a rare chance to exercise his ironic sensibilities. "All right," he said impishly, "I'll bite. What did it say? 'Edmund Fitzgerald'? 'Ship of Fools'? 'Andrea Doria II'?"

"Woman's name, I think. Said, 'Gretchen'—you know, like a German bird's name."

"Well, Gretchen," said the harbormaster, lifting his gnarled coffee cup, "here's to ya, wherever you are. Must be an angel."

MIXED REACTIONS—CONFLICTING EMOTIONS IN BARRY'S WAKE

KIKI WOULD have had no idea how to go about finding marijuana these days. Fortunately, she could remain ignorant; one of her more pranksterish salon guests had left a small quantity hanging like mistletoe over the kitchen spice rack—an offering of love buds, still untouched and tied in gift ribbon.

The most challenging part had been the remedial hydrodynamics—twenty years had passed since Barry put fire to his big red bong, and Kiki had more than a little difficulty remembering the relative positions of water and herb.

After a few false starts, Kiki managed to kindle a small glow in the bowl of the ancient water pipe. She put her lips to it, clumsily pulled a little smoke through its bubbling innards and inhaled.

She coughed explosively. She hadn't smoked pot in a

decade, and her searing lungs painfully instructed her that she wouldn't be starting again. No matter; Kiki wasn't seeking the canonical cannabis euphoria. She was in mourning, jonesing for a buzz at once more elusive and sentimental.

And she had found it. For a smoky, luminous moment, she felt close to Barry.

Microsoft Founder Regrets Loss of TeraMemory Executive

San Francisco, CA—In the high-stakes, ultra-competitive struggle for Internet domination, you wouldn't expect to find any love lost between rivals.

Don't tell that to Bill Gates. After the disappearance and presumed death of TeraMemory CEO Barry Dominic in a competitive sailing mishap, Gates expressed regret.

"Used to be that every time I turned around, there he was," the founder and CEO of Microsoft remarked at the third Symposium on Internet and Government Thursday. "The guy was very intense, a great competitor, and that's how I'll remember him."

Asked if the absence of a major rival changed his thinking on the race to dominate Internet networking standards, Gates replied, "Maybe not the way you think. Barry was always one step behind, but it helped me to focus and drive my company forward. In this business, you've got to be constantly watching your back. And tomorrow when I look over my shoulder, I'm going to miss his angry face glaring back at me."

Ed Pilphur wrapped his scarred knuckles around the grip of his wildly oversized driver. "Well, I have to say, the bastard really surprised me. This is the absolute last thing I expected him to do," he commented dryly, and hacked at his tee shot.

It faded right, disappearing into Stillwater Cove. "God damned Pebble Beach wind. Mulligan." He bent over to tee up another ball. "Crazy, crazy bastard," he continued. "Went out and got himself killed. All that goddamned macho outdoorsman crap."

His second shot had similar inclinations, but stayed in the rough. "Well, at least it leaves us free to do what's best for our shareholders, now," he said, satisfied with his lie.

Andrew Lucre was still a little worried. "Yeah, I know none of us was particularly fond of the guy, but he did have vision." He paused and looked at Ed, a little sideways. "I mean, he did—didn't he?"

Ed handed the club to his jumpsuited caddy, and strode off in the general direction of his ball. "I don't even want to think in those terms, Andy. All I know is that Barry broke one of my cardinal rules."

"And what rule is that?" Andrew asked, following.

"Pilphur's law," Ed declared, turning to face his partner while continuing to amble backward down the fairway. "Never believe your own hype. Leave it to your competitors—and your investors—to do that."

They ended up on opposite sides of the fairway, Ed's slice

to Andrew's hook. "I don't know if he was a visionary, Andy," Ed called across the grass, and duffed his approach. "But I do know that he was . . ."

Ed paused while Andrew stroked his five iron. They watched the ball thump up on the green, looked across at each other, and continued the conversation.

". . . a total asshole," they both said at exactly the same time. The men doubled over, laughing. Even the caddies allowed themselves a smirk.

The truth is always an excellent tonic for concentration; they both one-putted.

Ed stamped his spikes on the cart path en route to the next tee. "That son of a bitch," he grumbled. "I'm going to miss fighting with him, anyway." He contemplated the smiling runes on his ball.

"Not a lot. Just a little."

Comparisons are odious. And, as Barry had once discovered, defining your existence in relation to someone else's can be particularly slippery business, too. Now it was Steve's turn to learn the same lesson.

Ever since the news of Barry's demise, Steve had been oddly troubled. Why fret? he had thought to himself; The Man had gotten what The Man deserved. So why did he feel so listless and bereft? He sat glumly at his idle computer, the screensaver generating herd upon herd of little, yellow-footed penguins. He pulled Blue Power Ranger down from its pedestal, and absentmindedly turned over the plastic figurine as he ruminated.

Strange circumstances had robbed Steve of his polar opposite. And it wasn't until now that he began to grasp the particular nature of the loss.

Barry had been a potent raison d'être, the principal source of the outrage that had energized Steve's life. The drama of his existence had been played, of late, against a backdrop of Dominic. Now what was he going to do?

And this *death* thing, Steve pondered warily, was on a higher plane altogether: bigger than hacking, bigger than Free Bits, bigger than The Man—and suddenly it was the one and only thing Steve and Barry would ever—eventually—have in common.

And in that realization, Steve began to feel a kernel of sympathy for his fallen foe.

Paul and Liz were walking along California Avenue when they saw the headline. They pushed some coins into the *Mercury* box, took a copy, and grabbed a table in front of Printer's Inc.

They sat and read the news, Paul lightly resting his chin on Liz's shoulder.

"Can you believe it?" Paul exclaimed. "One day, he's the biggest frog in the pond, and the next day he's toast. Or frog legs. Or frog legs on toast."

Liz slugged him gently. "Hey," she cautioned. "I'm the one he sexually harassed, and even I've got more respect for the dead."

Paul lowered his eyes in deference, but continued his irreverence. "Hey, I know he was a creep, but for some reason I thought he might be an immortal creep. Shuffling off this mortal coil was the absolute last thing I was expecting him to do. I feel so let down."

Liz finished the article, and put down the paper. "Barry was just a man who got distracted," she said.

"I don't know," Paul countered, a little doubtfully. "Distracted? By what? I mean, the guy seemed pretty focused."

"By *everything*," Liz insisted. "I mean, he had absolutely everything that could distract him—wealth, fame, status, executive toys up the ying-yang. But I can't say that I ever saw him actually happy. Excited, motivated, dynamic, enthusiastic—but never genuinely happy.

"At one point, I thought I knew him a little bit. I remember he used to talk about how great it was going to be to rule cyberspace, but I think he just wanted to hide there."

Paul had learned to trust Liz's instincts for character evaluation. "Hide from what?" he questioned.

"From the same thing all nerds hide from. From real life."

A chilly breeze—rudely un-Californian—whipped through

Liz's hair as she looked up at Paul with dewy eyes. "Promise me something?" she pleaded quietly.

"What?"

"Let's not hide from real life, okay?"

Paul let the question hang for a moment. He looked down at the paper, then at Liz, and smiled.

"Oh . . . Okaaay," he replied playfully.

LAUREL MOVES OUT, PAUL MOVES IN, AND A CEO GOES UFO

SIXTY-TWO DEGREES, high overcast, and a stiff breeze: the feeble heart of Silicon Valley's anemic winter. The apricot tree in the corner of the yard had finally, reluctantly shed most its leaves. Laurel had girded herself against the elements with a turtleneck and the addition of socks to her Birkenstocks.

"I feel so bad, leaving you here all alone with nobody but the spiders for company," she confessed to her roomate as she packed her duffel bags.

Liz was losing her friend to wanderlust. It was just as well; Laurel hadn't really been truly happy here in the Valley since graduation. And when Vero—seemingly gifted with a sixth sense for finding the zeitgeist in any decade—had declared her next destination to be somewhere in Eastern

Europe, Liz shouldn't have been surprised by Laurel's eagerness to tag along. After all, Laurel was an art history major, and places like Prague and Budapest had some of the highest culture-to-rent ratios going.

"Oh, I'll be okay, honey," Liz reassured her friend.

"Yeah, I know—but I never meant to leave you holding the lease on your own. I mean, I hope you can find another roomie who isn't a psychopath. Or a total geek."

Liz gave Laurel a look that betrayed a little too much confidence, and perhaps a small subterfuge. "Don't worry. I think I've got another roommate lined up."

Laurel was quick to take the bait. "Oh, let me guess," she said with dawning suspicion. "The second I step on the plane, that young, good-looking Armstrong boy's going to show up with a suitcase, right? Oh, you little *minx*."

Liz raised her palms in surrender, blushing a little. "Oh, I can never get anything past you. Okay, okay—guilty as charged. Living in sin—my Catholic mother will have a holy cow."

"Oh, I think you're in good hands there," Laurel said. "That Paul's a pretty darned great guy, for a nerd."

"Recovering nerd, you mean," Liz corrected. "He's had it with the programming life—he's voluntarily joining the ranks of the unemployed for a while, until he can work out a career change."

"Oh, that's so cool!" Laurel enthused. "Maybe you won't end up a digit-widow after all."

"Paul and I have been talking about living together," Liz

confessed, "and it seems like the time is right—I mean, it's like kismet central, don't you think? Like everything's been mysteriously scripted: Vero goes back to Europe—she hated it here anyway, didn't she?—you get to go along for the adventure, and Paul and I get our shot at domestic bliss—and in his case, reduced rent—it all works out for everybody. Even Angus. Paul's crazy about him. A man who loves cats—can you believe that?"

"Gee—sounds like the fast track to domestic part-nerhood," Laurel said, a little askance. "This could turn into something permanent if you're not careful."

Liz eyed her suspiciously. "Exactly how permanent were you thinking?"

"White picket fence? Cozy, home-cooked meals?"

"Well, maybe," Liz smiled. "I have to admit Paul does look great in an apron."

A few weeks later, long after Paul had unpacked his bags at the *Château des Araignées,* the phone rang.

Liz answered. Kiki's familiar voice jingled on the line.

Liz hadn't been able to reach Kiki in ages, not since Gretchen's death. "Hey, stranger," she greeted her cheerfully. "Where've you been lately? I've missed you—I called a few times. Your answering machine must have amnesia."

"I've missed you, too," Kiki said. She tried to keep it light. "The last few months have been absolutely hell on my social calendar."

"I read about Barry," Liz said a little tentatively. "I'm sorry."

"I'm sure he is, too," Kiki said in an oddly warm way, then changed the subject. "So, I've been thinking about you. Are you still catering?"

Liz recounted the recent shiftings in her immediate circle. "No, our *maîtress de cuisine* hightailed it back to Europe. She took the *sous-chef* with her, too. It's back to the classifieds for me," she lamented, "as much as I hate the corporate scene."

"I know of an opening," Kiki said in a comically optimistic voice. "There's this little charitable organization I know that's suddenly flush with a lot of grant money. They're on the lookout for a chief administrator with solid business skills, as well as that little something extra. You wouldn't just happen to be interested, would you?"

"Well, maybe," Liz said hopefully. "Who are they?"

"They is me, Liz. Me and the estate of Barry Dominic. I desperately need a smart, strong woman these days. Now that I'm a stay-at-home grandmother, the Tejinder Foundation is without a leader."

Liz paused for a moment, then erupted into gleeful, jumping surprise. She wanted to ask fifteen questions simultaneously, but all she could manage was a joyful yelp, and "Tell me—tell, tell, tell, tell!"

"A little girl. Gretchen named her Zoe."

"How did you ever find her?"

"Hey, I'm half Cherokee Indian, remember? Exactly how long do you think they could hide a bunch of teepees from me?"

TeraMemory Founder Not Dead, Abducted by Aliens Says Silicon Valley Mogul

PALO ALTO, CA—Joe Fromage, the CEO of AmeriNet who shocked shareholders last year by declaring that extraterrestrial beings have been on Earth "for about the last 2,000 years planting the seeds of the digital age," today claimed he would reveal "absolute proof that Barry Dominic did not die in a November yachting mishap as widely believed, but was recalled by alien overlords."

Fromage, the 28-year-old founder of the high-profile Internet consulting firm, insisted that Dominic's disappearance in a yachting accident off Hobart, Tasmania was "all part of a larger plan." He intends to publish "incontrovertible evidence" over the coming weeks on his Web site www.smallgrey.org.

"It's really clear that Barry [Dominic] was one of 'Them'—an extraterrestrial operative—and has completed his mission," Fromage said.

Asked if he thought any other computer industry luminaries were also aliens, Fromage replied, "Definitely. I've got my eye on the Free Bits guys in particular—Richard Stallman, Linus Torvalds, Steve Hall. Something about those boys doesn't seem quite, well, terrestrial."

AmeriNet stock declined 22% on the announcement.